The River in Winter

The River in Winter

DAVID SMALL

W·W·NORTON & COMPANY   New York London

Copyright © 1987 by David Small
All rights reserved.
Published simultaneously in Canada by Penguin Books Canada Ltd.,
2801 John Street,
Markham, Ontario L3R 1B4.
Printed in the United States of America.
The text of this book is composed in 12/14 Bembo, with
display type set in Lucian. Composition and
manufacturing by The Haddon Craftsmen, Inc.
Book design by Margaret Wagner.
First Edition

Library of Congress Cataloging-in-Publication Data
Small, David, 1937–
The river in winter.
I. Title.
PS3569.M284R58   1987   813'.54   86–12534

ISBN 0-393-02394-X

W. W. Norton & Company, Inc.
500 Fifth Avenue, New York, N. Y. 10110
W. W. Norton & Company Ltd.
37 Great Russell Street, London WC1B 3NU

1 2 3 4 5 6 7 8 9 0

*This book
is dedicated to my mother,
M A D E L Y N   D E N N I S O N,
and in memoriam
H.R.S.*

But in the deep of a green valley, father
Anchises, lost in thought, was studying
the souls of all his sons to come—though now
imprisoned, destined for the upper light.
And as it happened, he was telling over
the multitude of all his dear descendants,
his heroes' fates and fortunes, works and ways.
And when he saw Aeneas cross the meadow,
he stretched out both hands eagerly, the tears
ran down his cheeks, these words fell from his lips:

"And have you come at last, and has the pious
love that your father waited for defeated
the difficulty of the journey? Son,
can I look at your face, hear and return
familiar accents? So indeed I thought,
imagining this time to come, counting
the moments, and my longing did not cheat me.
What lands and what wide waters have you journeyed
to make this meeting possible? My son,
what dangers battered you? I feared the kingdom
of Libya might do so much harm to you."

—Anchises greeting his son Aeneas in Hades, from *The Aeneid,*
Lines 898–918, Book VI, as translated by Allen Mandelbaum,
University of California edition

The River in Winter

One

Maybe you wouldn't believe it to look at me, but my grandad was a doctor. At one time, he had big plans for me.

Henry liked to say that all time was circular. And the reason nobody could change anything was that nobody could wait around long enough to be in the same place when the same time rolled around again.

Once, in the First World War, as a young captain, he'd shot a German boy in a barn in a village in France.

"That's what did it," he said. "That's what ruined everything, when I shot that boy."

He said it had set off a series of family disasters. He claimed the bullet that killed the boy was still circling the earth like a steel-jacketed hornet, looking for its next victim. And there'd already been too many of those, all named Weatherfield.

He blamed himself for setting the deadly bullet loose. Or at least for having been the elected agent to set it free. He did what he could to reverse or cancel the calamity.

He tried to keep me out of trouble. He used to take me by

the neck and guide me down the back steps and across the lawn when we started out for a walk, edgily glancing around, prepared to push me to the ground if that bullet happened to be traveling through Dunnocks Head on that particular day.

He did other things. He made me wear a life jacket in the boat when we went fishing. He always stood behind the curtains and looked out the window before answering a knock at the door. But that was a family trait.

Henry liked to think he was a fatalist; but he wasn't really. He swam against the current. He tried to influence events. I'm just sorry he wasn't better at it.

The fact was, when things went bad, he couldn't have done anything to stop it. No more than a man can hold back a rock slide.

I never knew my grandmother. She died when Doreen was only six. Henry told me she was out in the yard trimming a rosebush one day and broke her arm. She closed the blades on a twig and her arm broke. The bone was that honeycombed with cancer. One day she was fine, out in the garden. A month later she was dead as dirt. Henry couldn't get over it.

He really went to hell after that. He drank a lot and neglected his practice. He wouldn't have anything to do with Doreen. That was when he developed insomnia, which plagued him ever afterwards.

One night he went in his dead wife's closet and buried his face in her clothes. He hung there, inhaling the faint residue of perfume and talcum powder, hiding his face in her dresses. The hangers gave way under his weight with a sound like broken harp strings. He fell to the floor. When he came to, he was buried alive in a pile of women's clothes.

During this time he actually hated Doreen. You picked the wrong one, you bastard, he whispered to God. Why didn't you take the girl instead of Lilian? Or Donald? Why didn't you take Donald? Why Lilian, God? What the hell is the matter with you? We could have had other kids. But there was only one of Lilian. That's why you did it, didn't you? Because there was only one of her. Because it would hurt more, never stop hurting. That was it, wasn't it?

He couldn't even stand to look at her. Donald was away at school at the time, so he only had one kid around to make him sick. He said the sight and sound of her made him physically ill. For two months he couldn't bring himself to say a word to her. He sat in his room and drank whiskey. He gazed out the back windows at the slow decay of the flower beds, on which his wife had lavished such care. His sister, although unwell and some twenty years his senior, had to come in and keep house for him.

"I was worthless. It wasn't the first time. It probably won't be the last. I'm goddamned ashamed of myself for it. What you need in this life is a little courage. You got to have it with you always, just like dry matches in the woods. Because you're going to need it, sooner or later. I've been caught short too many times. That time, I failed Doreen. She became what she became because I let her down."

"You worry too much. It isn't your fault. She's just no good."

"You say that about your own mother?"

Softly, like he was scared somebody might overhear us. We were sitting in the kitchen, alone in the big empty house.

"Sure," I said. "Who knows better than me?"

"You're just mad at her," he said.

"No, I'm not. She's just a bum. She always was. Always will be."

Henry looked away.

"Don't talk that way about your mother."

When he shook his head, the little driblets of loose skin under his chin trembled. His glasses flashed with the cold light pouring in the kitchen window. It was a hard, white, sunless light that picked out all the lines in his face, making him look old and bleary as he sat there in his old-fashioned ribbed undershirt, blowing the steam off his coffee. His chin was stubbled with little steel wires, and his suspenders still dangled below the waist of his trousers because he hadn't yet shaved or taken his morning crap.

I felt sorry for him. He looked so old and worried and used up. His arms were white and flabby. The fingers holding the white coffee mug were crooked and tanned with tobacco stains. He smoked all the time. The first thing he did before he got out of bed in the mornings was light up. I'd hear him in there, coughing and hacking, strangling on his morning string of sputum. I'd hear him spit copiously and endlessly into his hand-kerchief. He'd hack some more. Then it would go quiet as a sandwich on his side of the wall. And I'd know he was sitting on the edge of the bed in his underwear, having his first cigarette of the day. The consolations of tobacco, he called it.

We didn't talk much about Doreen. It upset him too much. He did tell me she'd been boy crazy. That's all he said, sighing the words and looking out the window. Boy crazy.

She was sixteen when she met McCabe. He was thirty-two, and still lived at home with his mother. He was an auto parts salesman who came through town once a month. He stocked the local garages out of the back of his truck. He stopped at repair shops in Gardiner and Richmond and other places. When he ran low, he drove back to the warehouse in Lewiston and got restocked.

People say he was a skinny good-looking devil with an eye for the ladies. Doreen never did say where she met him. But I have an idea I was put into business in the back of that truck, among the gaskets and the spark plugs.

When Doreen found out she was pregnant, she went to Lewiston after McCabe. He wasn't hard to find.

He and his mother lived at the end of a dirt road on the edge of town. Doreen knew she had the right place when she saw the silver-bodied truck parked out front.

She'd closed the perilous gap between herself and McCabe by hitchhiking the forty miles or so which separated them. Now, having found his house, she hugged her thin sweater close and shivered in the dusk, wondering what to do next. From time to time, the cold dark sky tossed a little snow in her face like a handful of confetti.

In the side yard, rigid and static black against a thin crust of gray snow, was an old Model A roadster. She had heard a lot about this car and was curious to see it close up. McCabe talked about fixing it up. He said he practically stole it for fifty dollars from some degraded moron in Waterville.

Now he was going to restore this little car to perfection, soon as he got some time and a few dollars ahead. *But when are we going to get married?* Doreen asked him. Because she was already nervous. *Soon's I get the car fixed, little girl,* McCabe told her. *Then we'll have some fun, won't we?* he grinned at her like a fox. *I guess so,* she said. *I just want to get away from Daddy, that's all. Before he drives me crazy. Don't worry, little girl,* said McCabe. *We'll have ourselves a time. Just you wait.*

She stood shivering in a thin shaving of light from the house. The wind cried faintly in the curtainless windows of the car's tattered top. A thin crescent of dirty ice lay on the driver's seat. The stuffing was coming out in two or three places. He hadn't done a damn thing to the car, except put it up on blocks and take the wheels off.

Doreen wasn't surprised. It was just a piece of junk. Just a junkyard alibi: one more lie McCabe kept telling himself, and anyone else who would listen, over and over again, till even he couldn't tell it from the truth.

Doreen mounted the steps to Mrs. McCabe's little front porch. She rapped on the storm door. Mrs. McCabe answered in her apron, a little turnip who smiled in the doorway with a warm house at her back.

"Oh my," she wiped her hands on her apron. "Who is this on such a cold night?"

"I'm Doreen. Doreen Weatherfield? Maybe Joe has mentioned me . . ."

"No, I don't think so," said Mrs. McCabe. "You really ought to wear a coat on a night like this, young lady—"

"Is Joe home?"

"Why—yes, he is."

"Would you tell him Doreen is here to see him, please?"

"He's resting," said Mrs. McCabe. "You come back. Maybe tomorrow. Tomorrow would be good."

"I can't. I came all the way from Dunnocks Head. Could you wake him up?"

McCabe's mother was a little put out by Doreen's snippety tone but told her to wait. Through the circle of the Christmas wreath on the door, Doreen watched the short elderly woman move down the hall to the back of the house. He's not taking any nap in the kitchen, Doreen thought.

She tore off the porch and around the side of the house in time to catch McCabe coming out the back door, before he could make it to the woods at the bottom of the yard. McCabe grinned embarrassedly, but his old mother went crazy, calling Doreen bad names and trying to sock her in the head with a kitchen ladle.

"Get away from here! You little jezebel!" she cried as her son held her off.

"Calm down, Ma."

Doreen said you would have thought the old woman was being murdered, the way she carried on.

"Leave my Joe alone!"

McCabe's mother broke loose and laid her kitchen spoon behind Doreen's ear.

"Keep her off me, Joe."

Doreen rubbed the knot on the side of her head.

"If she hits me again, I'll make her goddamn sorry."

"Try it," said McCabe. "See what happens to you."

But he crammed his mother, kicking and screeching like a parrot, back inside her kitchen. He braced the door against her as she pushed and shoved and shouted through the muffling glass.

"What do you want, Doreen?"

"I want you to marry me."

"I can't do that just now," he said.

"Well then I want three hundred dollars to get rid of this."

"Three hundred," he said. "Why don't you make it three million? Hell, I don't have that kind of money. Ask your old man. He's rich, ain't he?"

"He'd kill me if he ever found out. Then he'd come up here and turn you into a soprano."

McCabe thought about it some more.

"You sure you're not just a little late?"

"You think I'd be here if I wasn't sure?"

"I don't know. I don't know nothing about you. Except you can do it like a mink."

"I'm getting cold standing here, waiting for you to do something," said Doreen.

McCabe scratched his chin and eyed the distance between him and the woods. But it was too ridiculous even for him to make a break for it and have this pregnant little hellcat trying to claw him to the ground every foot of the way.

"Well, shit. I guess we'll have to get married."

She had him all along. Back then even people like McCabe, when painted into a corner, did what they called "the right thing." But if he or his old lady had had the three hundred dollars, I'd never have seen the light of day. It would have saved me a hell of a lot of trouble.

They named me Joe, after McCabe. Later, after they split up, and Doreen married Dale, they wanted me to call myself Joe Bigler. But I told them no. I hadn't been asked the first time. This time I figured I had a choice.

They said I had to, because Dale had officially adopted me. I said bullshit. I'm not a Bigler no matter what a piece of paper says.

At school the teachers tried to get me to sign my work that way. But I wouldn't. When I got my report card, there it was: Joe Bigler, typed on the front. I scratched it out and wrote in McCabe. The principal called me in and tried to make a big deal of it. I told him I had a right to my own name. He or nobody else could take it away. He didn't push it. He knew I had a bad temper. I might have been skinny at sixteen, but I was taller than he was, and a hell of a lot meaner.

I wasn't in love with the idea of being a McCabe. Hell, I don't remember much about him. What I do, doesn't make me proud. He left when I was seven. But I didn't know what else to call myself. I sure as hell didn't want to be called any Bigler.

When I went to live with Henry, we had some bad times at first. We got so mad at each other, I took off for Florida. It wasn't easy getting used to each other. But when I got back, we came to an understanding. We got along so well, I took to calling myself Joe Weatherfield, which I consider my real name.

As usual, this made for some trouble at school. I wouldn't answer to anything but Weatherfield. Henry asked me why I wanted to cause trouble.

"I don't want to cause trouble."

"Then why are you doing it then? Why have I got these damn people calling me on the phone?"

"I just thought I'd call myself Weatherfield for a while."

"Why is that? You trying to give people a rough time?"

So I told him.

"They been calling me McCabe all my life. But who's he? Then Dale comes along, and Doreen thinks I'm going to stand still for letting them call me a Bigler. But I'm no damn Bigler, I know that. I don't know any McCabe. But I know you."

His face changed.

"That's right."

"I know it's an old name in this town. Maybe you think it's too good for me."

"No, no," he said. "Go ahead, call yourself Weatherfield. That's all right with me. I should have understood what you were up to in the first place. Forgive me for being so stupid."

"Don't make a big deal of it," I said. "Just get those people off my back."

"All right. I'll see what I can do."

I could see he was pleased. It was like something he'd do himself. In some ways, we were a lot alike.

In here, they call me McCabe. I don't make trouble about it, wanting, as I do, to get the hell out of here as soon as I can. The screws tell me: it don't matter what you want. You're just a number in here anyway. But I don't care what anybody says.

You got a right to say what people call you. And I'm Weather-field, no matter what they use in here.

But I'm getting ahead of myself.

This story begins with our house in Revere Beach. It wasn't really "ours," we just rented it. But I remember it so well, it must mean something.

The yard was mostly dirt. A wire fence ran around it. Inside stood a rusty swing set and a sandbox right up against the sidewalk. I don't know how many times Doreen barked her ankles against that sandbox. It was just a damned latrine for the neighborhood cats anyway.

The house had a glassed-in porch across the front. The brown trim was peeling off, showing the mustard underneath.

I hated that house. The concrete steps were always stained with dampness. Summer and winter, the porch was hot and smelled like rubber.

Doreen stored stuff out there. Boxes of old clothes, my crib, a floor lamp with a frayed cord, mattresses, a wooden clothes dryer—all packed in, five feet high at least. A canyon-like path wove through the trash to the front door where an old wringer washer stood guard. Any stranger coming to our door could look at the junk our lives had produced. But it didn't bother Doreen a bit.

An orange chow dog lived up the street. He liked to knock the little kids down. That dog had eyes like a Jap. He was a real mean bugger.

You could stand in your yard, look up and down the street all day. You'd never see a sign of him. But step on the sidewalk and close the gate behind you. That dog would suddenly be there.

Or you'd be out playing and look up. And he'd be there, his tail coiled above his anus, his orange hair puffed out like a woolly bear caterpillar. When that dog showed up, all us little kids would break for home.

One day he sneaked up and bit me in the ass. I was just a little kid. He tore the shit out of my snowpants. But I had thirty layers of clothes on underneath, so he didn't hurt me any.

I really hated that house.

Doreen still lives there.

Two

When I was little I used to think that Doreen was beautiful. Gradually this article of faith faded.

I realized she was flashy, not beautiful. She could have been really pretty if she'd gone easy on the makeup. But her taste—and mine too—had been corrupted by the movies we went to see on Saturday afternoons, when she had change to spare. Lana Turner was Doreen's favorite. No doubt that's where we got our ideas of what made for the beautiful.

Doreen used glossy lipstick on her mouth. Sometimes she got it on her teeth. When she smiled, it looked like her gums were bleeding. Her mascara made little sticky balls in the corners of her eyes. I took these to be signs of excess, nothing to worry about. After all, Lana Turner and all the others made themselves up the same way.

Like Susan Hayward, Doreen wouldn't have been caught dead without her uplift bra. This garment, amounting to a prosthetic device, was essential equipment. Doreen offered the world her breasts whether the world wanted them or not. Men we met in the pharmacy or the grocery store often talked to them directly. Some looked ready to take a bite out of her, as if she were an apple. Doreen never noticed. She acted flattered when these nincompoops stopped to speak to her boobs.

It was more than I could figure out at age six.

Dressed in a silky green blouse and white slacks, Doreen wobbled through the stores on open-toed high heels with me, an aging midget, at her side.

Men quivered in her direction like compass needles in search of the magnetic north. Once I got so irritated with her, I told her to quit wiggling and just walk natural. She halted the grocery cart and, in a loud voice designed to embarrass me, asked me to explain just what in hell I meant by such a remark.

But she knew, all right.

When their wives weren't around men padded down the aisles after her, purring like big cats. They put their arms around her at the dairy counter. Ignoring the phenomenon of my accelerated aging, they whispered what I suspected were dirty jokes in Doreen's ear. Her dangly earrings shook with her sputtering laughter.

I was ashamed of the woman. I wanted to smash in the kneecaps of these jackasses with a can of pork and beans, and drag her home by the hair. When I finally got old enough for her to go to the stores alone, I was damned relieved.

I make a joke of it now. But back then, I wanted to kill every one of those idiots.

But that was later. At first I was crazy about her. I even regretted I had McCabe's dark coloring and single, connected eyebrow instead of her blond hair and rosy complexion, however she came by them.

I tell you how crazy I was. I used to practice falling down-stairs—to amuse Doreen, as it turned out. I was about seven years old. The stairs in our house were narrow. I discovered if

I pushed my hands and feet against the walls and scrunched my head into my shoulders I could fall downstairs with some degree of control. If I got going too fast I pressed my hands and feet against the walls to slow down. My reason for cultivating this talent was so I could become a stunt man in the movies.

I practiced when Doreen wasn't around. One night when she seemed particularly bored, and McCabe was out somewhere horsing around, I told her I wanted to be a stunt man and I'd been practicing. Would she like to see me fall downstairs?

She'd been walking around the house in her slip with what she called a highball in her hand, playing the radio loud. I guess she was so bored the idea of watching me fall downstairs offered some relief.

"You be careful, Honeyboy!" she called from the foot of the stairs.

I squatted at the head of the stairs, tucked my head, and fell forward, tumbling head over heels. I splayed my hands and feet, pressed them against the walls, and regulated my speed. Doreen squealed as if on a roller coaster as I fell down the staircase into her arms.

"Honeyboy," she breathed. The hot spots on her cheeks told me she was no longer bored.

"Just like in the movies, Mom," I said.

Doreen crushed my face against her breasts. The warm darkness and flowery perfume made me a little dizzy. Against my ear, her heart was beating like a bird in a trap.

She held my face in her hands.

"Don't ever, *ever,* do that again."

The circles around her eyes were dark.

"It's fun," I said.

I wasn't sure which was more fun—falling down stairs, or seeing her look so scared.

"It is *not* fun," she said. "I'm a bad mommy for letting you do it."

That had to be the high-water mark of my puppy-love affair with Doreen—when she pressed me to her boobs and confessed her maternal ineptitude. I guess I loved her for telling me the truth that time, whether she'd meant to or not.

On hot days McCabe, dressed in his old paisley bathrobe, sat at the dining room table and drank beer. To pass the time, he picked the labels off the bottles. The ones he got off in one piece, he pasted on the lampshade of the light over the table. One afternoon I watched him paste six labels on the shade.

A drop of sweat formed on the end of his nose as he went about his work. It enlarged like a tiny balloon, then fell with a little splat on the table. Sometimes he sat there and read the horse sheet. Other times he just studied the blurred reflection which looked back at him from the dark wood beyond the precipice of his forearm.

"What are you looking at, kid?"

"Nothing."

"Yes, you are. You're looking at me, you little shit."

"I'm not looking at you."

"Whatever you call it, cut it out."

And I'd get out of there. He had a bad temper. Likely, that's where I got mine.

I don't think he was working then. Later he got a job as a hair tonic salesman, I think it was. Something to do with selling anyway.

I really don't remember much about the man.

Once, I was playing with my trucks and cars in the flower bed alongside the house. Making roads and stuff and driving all around, growling to myself, really getting into it. Doreen and

McCabe were in the back. Drinking beer or something. I heard her cry out. Or thought I did.

I stuck my head around the corner. Doreen was lying on the sidewalk rolling from side to side holding her arm.

"Ow, ow," she was saying.

McCabe sat on the stoop sipping a beer. He must've got mad about something and pushed her off the stoop. Later we found out she broke her wrist. She wore it in a cast for six weeks. It came out all skinny and white. Really, it was so skinny when the cast came off it made me sick to my stomach.

When I saw her lying there and him just sitting there watching her like a cat, I went over to help.

"Get out of the way. Damn little kid underfoot all the time."

He helped her up.

"You okay, honey?"

"I think it's broken."

"Don't be a baby. It's not broken, for Christsakes. It takes more than that to break a bone."

"I'm not kidding, Joe. It hurts like it's broken."

"Ah shit," McCabe squinted at the sky.

She started up the walk.

McCabe followed.

"I'm sorry," he said humbly.

Doreen cradled her arm and held the screen door against her backside. She opened the kitchen door.

"It's okay. I know you didn't mean it."

"It wouldn't have happened if you'd fallen down right," said McCabe as the door shut behind them.

Things got worse.

They usually do.

He'd be gone for weeks and she wouldn't know where he was. They'd have a big fight over it when he came back.

Sometimes when he was gone, men I'd never seen before pushed through the sea of junk on the porch and came asking for Doreen. She'd tell me to go outside and play.

"Why?" I'd say.

"Go," she'd say.

I'd take my little toy trucks and cars and go play in the dirt on the shady side of the house.

One night McCabe left for good.

I heard them fighting and came out in the living room. Doreen was on the floor in her nightgown holding him by the knees, crying and carrying on. He had on his suit and his fancy pearl-gray hat with the snap brim. His old Gladstone bag was sitting by the door.

"No," Doreen sobbed. "Please, please."

"Let go," McCabe said.

"No," said Doreen.

"Let go, you bitch."

McCabe kicked at her. He yanked her by the hair. But she hung on to his knees.

When that didn't work he bent down and used his fists. It made a splat sound when he punched her in the face. Doreen began to scream. She thrashed around on the floor, kicking at him.

"You son of a bitch!"

The nightgown fell back to her hips showing her long white legs as she struck out at him. She knocked his fancy hat off with her foot. The hat had belonged to his father. McCabe went berserk, really laying it on her. Doreen stopped kicking and covered up as he punched her in the back of the head, the shoulders, the kidneys, anywhere he could.

I ran into the kitchen to get a knife. I was going to kill the son of a bitch. I grabbed the first thing I found. When he looked down and saw me trying to puncture his leg with a butter knife, it seemed to bring him back. He stopped whaling on Doreen. He took the useless knife and threw it across the room.

He picked up his hat and reblocked it with his hand.

Doreen lay face down on the carpet. McCabe put his hat on down over his eyes. I remember thinking what a good-looking son of a bitch he was.

Funny what goes through your head at a time like that.

McCabe picked up the Gladstone.

Doreen lifted her face from the carpet.

"No," she said.

I thought she was behaving badly.

McCabe opened the front door. He looked around the room like he was asking himself had he forgotten anything. He looked at me, the furniture, the woman on the floor. Satisfied, he closed the door behind him.

I heard him work his way through the junk on the porch and his rapid descent on the steps outside. On the sidewalk his footsteps suddenly stopped. He was just gone, as if he had faded on the darkness halfway to the front gate.

And that was it.

We never saw him again.

Three

A BOUT three months after McCabe left, Doreen decided we ought to visit somebody she called my "granddaddy" for a few days. He still lived in Maine in the little town where Doreen was born.

She told me we'd been to see him before, when I was three. She said Henry and McCabe got into a big fight over some silliness. She'd forgotten what exactly. Henry told her not to bother to come back again if it meant bringing along her pet idiot too. So we'd never gone back.

"Your granddaddy's the sulky type," she said. "He holds a hell of a grudge, does that man."

We put Peppy, our new dog, in a kennel and went down on the train, my first train ride. We bought sandwiches that tasted like cardboard from a vendor and ate them as we swayed back and forth on the seat.

That was the good part of the trip.

Less good was the look of the old man who met us at the train station in Bath.

"Daddy," said Doreen.

She gave him a clumsy hug. He didn't seem to like it,

standing there stiffly, while the train hissed its disapproval.

I looked at him and he looked at me. A cigarette smoldered between the bony fingers of his blue-veined hand which hung loosely by his side, the smoke snaking inside his shirtcuff. The light reflected on his round, steel-rimmed glasses making it tough for me to see his eyes. I couldn't tell what he was thinking.

His ragged mustache, not purely white in those days, twitched impatiently as Doreen felt him all over, murmuring *daddydaddy* like an idiot, as if she were fumbling for a little handle or knob that might get him to open up. But he wasn't having any, standing there stiffly, studying me, maybe even appealing to my sense of fair play, as I look back on it, an old man outraged and violated by this blond in purple slacks and high heels who claimed to be his daughter.

I had plenty of time to look him over. His upper lip was hidden by the tobacco-stained border of his mustache. He had a black dot on his lower lip big as a ladybug. I took it for a common blood blister. But it wasn't. It was the place, I found out later, where he always laid his cigarette.

"This is your grandson, Daddy. Bet you didn't even recognize him."

Doreen smiled nervously. I noticed she had lipstick on her teeth again.

Henry's expression didn't change. So far as I could tell he was still looking at me, or at least in my general direction, in mute and rigid reverie, as if he'd dived so deep within himself, it'd take a week for him to make it to the surface again.

"Say hello, Joey."

I wasn't saying hello to any wooden Indian. I wondered if maybe he had died while standing in broad daylight on the station platform.

He moved just perceptibly, the light flashing off his lenses like twin heliographs. When he spoke, I jumped, his voice sudden and cadaverous.

"He's skinny as hell."

He had a lot of room to talk. He was the skinniest old man I'd ever seen.

"He's built like his father," said Doreen.

"Let's hope he's not built too much like him."

This made Doreen red, I could tell. She lapsed into one of her explosive silences—afraid if she opened her mouth she'd blow, ending the trip before the train even pulled out of the station. From the looks of it we wouldn't be staying long anyway.

We got our bags from the stationmaster. Henry loaded them into the trunk of his old tan Dodge. We got in. He started the car with a roar like old people do sometimes, jerked it into gear, and we lurched out of the parking lot onto the highway.

We followed a gray, cold-looking river, which disappeared from time to time behind pyramids of black pines. The only sound was when Henry pushed in the dash lighter, or it popped out, and he leaned forward, his forehead almost touching the steering wheel, to ignite another in his endless string of cigarettes.

I'd never seen such a bad driver, and wouldn't again till Doreen finally got her license. I thought it had to do with his age. He wasn't yet sixty-two as I found out later. But to me at the time, he seemed a hundred.

He drove all over the road, veering toward approaching cars as if they were the other half of those sets of magnetic dogs you used to buy at the dime store. He'd break the spell and peel onto the gravel shoulder a split second before impact. The stones chunked the belly of the car as we shot back onto the road. On hills he pulled to the left. The longer the hill the more likely we'd be on the wrong side when we got to the top.

"Ma—," I said.

"Pipe down back there," he said. "Can't you see I'm trying to concentrate?"

What I could see was an early death, thanks to this old fool.

Finally we came to a little town called Dunnocks Head. We drove down Maine Street, past the stores on one side and the Commons on the other. At the head of the street before the railroad tracks we turned left and circled onto Washington Street, which ran parallel to Maine, on the other side of the Commons. We started back in the direction from which we'd come.

Opposite the band shell that looked like a little Greek temple, this old maniac took us over the sidewalk with a violent bump, bringing the car to a sudden stop in the gravel and cinder driveway of a big old house.

I had never seen anything like this man's house. Surrounded by a black wrought-iron fence, it was big and square and austere with a dark, double-leafed front door right in the center. It was painted white with green shutters, the paint chalky and blistered and peeling off in pieces big enough to roll tobacco, had it been paper instead of paint.

Halfway up the walk another brickway forked off to the right and led to a door of a converted but delapidated porch on the side of the house. On the door glowed a little wedge of brass, green with age, which said, *Henry W. Weatherfield, M.D.* But even back then he was semi-retired, opening his office to patients only a few afternoons a week.

On the roof, a little glass turret set right in the center. I was fascinated by that. Here was a man who had his own lookout tower. But I discovered it was nothing when I found my way to the attic one day. All that turret did was let in some light. It didn't even have a floor. Or any way for someone to get up in it to see what the view was like. That was a terrible disappointment for an eight-year-old.

The grass stood waist-high in the yard. The flower beds were choked with weeds. The rose bushes had gone wild, growing everywhere, overpowering the fence in places along the sidewalk out front. Still, it was an impressive place.

I sat on the backseat, staring at it out the window.

"Aren't you getting out?" Doreen asked.

We stayed a few days, just long enough for Doreen to celebrate her twenty-fifth birthday. Then we cleared out.

The place was like a mausoleum—dark woodwork and ghostly echoes in the stairwells. The bathroom didn't smell too clean. I was used to Doreen's hair in the shower drain and a ring around the toilet bowl at home. But this old man must miss sometimes and pee on the linoleum and then never clean it up. The thought disgusted me. A messy woman was one thing. But it was something else to be trapped in a house with a dirty old man.

I didn't call him Henry then. I didn't call him anything. He was just there. He didn't need a name.

I slept in a high-ceilinged room with a bay window overlooking the lush jungle of the backyard. No curtains at the windows, just green shades with crocheted pull rings. The bed was so big I got lost in it. The mattress was lumpy and damp. There weren't enough bedclothes on it to keep me warm. But I didn't feel like asking anybody any favors. Looking up at it from my pillows, the big headboard looked gloomy as a church door. I could stand up in the mahogany wardrobe even though it had drawers below the doors. The furniture in that room made me feel like a midget. Everything was big and dark and creepy.

The whole house was creepy. It was cold and musty. The sun never reached into the corners of the rooms, even though it was June.

On damp days, the house smelled of an old dog called Cicero. The dog was no fun at all. It didn't look up when I called it by name. It never wanted to go for a walk. It wouldn't even leave the back porch. It was a fat old black Labrador. Once a day, it hung its grizzled chin and, with a puzzled expression, slowly walked from room to room. Between patrols, it slept in front of the stove in the study.

I shivered all night long and woke up in knots in the morning. I had a feeling the place didn't like me. I walked around hangdog fashion so as not to excite any more of its animosity.

Henry wasn't around much. He was always out on errands or making a house call or over in his office. I think he didn't know what to do with us and so stayed away as much as he could.

I went over to his office to see what he was up to. He didn't have a nurse like a regular doctor. Just a few hard chairs in a small waiting room in the front with a coatrack in the corner and a table where he laid out envelopes of pills so people could just walk in and pick up their refills.

Behind it was a room with an examining table in the middle of the floor, and weighing scales, and an eye chart hanging on the wall opposite the table. On the other wall was an instrument cabinet and another cabinet next to it, full of bottles of stuff. Sitting on a white-enameled stand, he had what he told me later was a sterilizer, shiny as a toaster, for doing his hypodermics and other junk.

In back of this room was his office, with his desk and a skeleton hanging from a rod in the corner and his medical books and diplomas on the back wall. I remember there was a pint bottle sitting on his desk. He was alone, writing something in a file. He heard me in the doorway, I guess. I was getting ready to leave. But he looked over his glasses and caught me.

"What do you want?"

"Nothing. I was just looking around."

"Get over to the house. I don't want you poking in things here."

"Is that a real person's skeleton?"

"Get over to the house," he said. "Don't let me catch you in here again."

But that was the second day. On the first, I kept to the house and the backyard.

He didn't have much food. I peeked in what he called his "icebox." All I could see was a quart of milk and some eggs. Plus a seventy-two-year-old slab of what once might have been a piece of chocolate pie. Now it looked more like a triangular section of dry riverbed.

The first night, he went out and got us some fried chicken from the local restaurant. In the morning Doreen made us french toast which was nice, just like home, but I found it disturbing to see the old man crumble a handful of crackers in a bowl, pour milk on it, and eat the resulting mess rapidly with a tablespoon. It made me so sick I couldn't finish my fourth piece of french toast.

He brought us home some Italian hoagies the next night. I couldn't eat but half of mine for thinking this strange, only semi-clean-looking old guy had handled them, even if they were each wrapped in their own paper. The second morning he had molasses on bread for breakfast. It was even more disgusting than the crackers and milk. I couldn't see how a person could eat like that. I was either half-sick or hungry all the time we were there.

In the evenings Doreen and my "grandaddy" sat in the library in front of the little wood fire he'd build up in the Franklin stove. They stared into the fire while drinking their whiskey and water, politely avoiding conversation since it seemed to have a dangerous effect on them. He smoked all the time. A blue cloud swirled around the white nimbus of his head. He gazed into the fire, pulling on his mustache. Nobody had much to say.

The night of Doreen's birthday, though, they got into it pretty heavy, having sat there longer than usual and having drunk considerably more than usual too. They were sort of celebrating their birthdays together, since Henry's fell exactly a week after Doreen's, on the Fourth of July. But it seemed more like a wake than a celebration. Doreen was about four whiskeys in. She was having trouble getting her mouth around her words.

"There's nothing left to live for," she mumbled.

She emptied her glass, the ice cubes clinking against her teeth.

"Some hell of a birthday, huh, Daddy?"

Henry exhaled, staring into the fire. For a minute he didn't say anything.

Then he said, "You talk like a damned fool, Doreen. You always did."

"It's true, Daddy. My life is over."

"Hell, your life hasn't even begun. What are you, twenty-five today? Jesus, you talk like an idiot. I wish I was twenty-five again. You got rid of McCabe. That's a big plus. You ought to be happy to get him off your neck."

"But I love him, Daddy. I miss him awful."

"You must not have a brain in your head." He flicked his ashes on the carpet.

"You don't know how I feel. How empty everything is."

"You got that boy for one thing."

"Who? Joey? He doesn't need me, do you, Honeyboy?"

"You asking an eight-year-old whether he needs his mother? Stop feeling sorry for yourself, Doreen. Do what's in front of you. You got some responsibility—"

"Oh, responsibility."

She was slurring her words pretty good, but managing with dignity.

"That's all you know. That's all you ever knew. You sit around in this big house by yourself all the time. You pore over these old books in the evening and you're happy. You think that's all there is to life."

"Go upstairs and go to bed," he said. "Sober up and stop talking silly."

"Bullshit. I'm not a little kid anymore. You can't boss me around."

"You're a horse's ass," he muttered into the fire.

"You never gave a damn about me," she said. "You never loved anyone. Except Momma. All you ever cared about was your work and your books. How would you know how I feel?"

He looked up, wild and glassy-eyed from staring into the fire.

"I have no idea how you feel. Or what you think either. You've always been a mystery to me."

"That's right. You're damned right you don't know how I feel. You never did."

A long silence condensed in the room. The fire crackled pleasantly in the Franklin stove. They were sitting there with the lights out. The whiskey bottle on the floor between their chairs cast a long shadow on the rug. The firelight flickered on Henry's face as he looked glumly into the fire. Doreen's back was toward me, so I couldn't see her face but I imagine it was as sour. They'd forgotten I was in the room, which made it interesting. I waited to see what they'd say next.

"Sorry, Daddy. You make me so mad sometimes. You believe in all the verities. It's all such a lot of crap."

"You sure about that?"

"Damn right I'm sure. They don't exist outside of this room. Come up to Boston sometime. I'll show you the verities."

"No thanks. Your way of life doesn't interest me."

Doreen laughed.

"You don't have to tell me that. I know that."

"So there's nothing to believe in. Is that what you think?"

"I know it," she said, reaching for the bottle.

"You've had enough."

"Don't tell me. I know when I've had enough and when I haven't."

He stared angrily as she poured herself another drink. For a second I thought he might rise from his chair and hit her.

"I wasn't always without hope."

Doreen spoke slowly and deliberately with a drunk's love for melodrama.

"I believed in *love,* Daddy."

"Horseshit."

"You wouldn't understand that. It's the only thing that counts. Not your books or your hard work. Mostly you're alone. You do the important stuff alone, like worrying and hurting and dying. Alone. When you find someone who loves you, it makes all the difference. Without that, life is nothing."

"You're a fool, Doreen. You were never happy unless some boy had his hand up your skirt. That's all you think there is to life."

"Fuck you. What the hell do you know about it?"

"Don't talk like that, Doreen."

"I'll talk any way I like."

"At least remember the boy."

"The boy, the boy."

She turned in her chair, giving me a drunken smile.

"You heard worse, haven't you, baby?"

She faced Henry again, chuckling to herself.

"Yes, he's heard worse."

Then casually she passed out in her chair. Her chin hit her chest. Her glass slipped from her fingers, landing on the dog, who happened to be sleeping by her chair that night. Cicero clawed the carpet till he got his feet under him and shook the ice cubes off his back. The old dog looked shocked and indignant. He hadn't been up this late at night for years. He stood in the middle of the floor studying the walls of the room. I guess he was looking for poltergeists. Then with an unforgiving air, he waddled from the room.

Henry ran his hand through his thinning hair, sucking nervously at his cigarette. A glass ashtray, piled high with stubbed ends, sat on the floor beside his chair. The fire crackled in the grate.

Some minutes later Doreen woozily raised her head. He said in a voice so sad and gentle it surprised me, "Go to bed, child."

"Go to bed, go to bed."

She rose and walked unsteadily from the room. We heard her stumbling up the stairs in her high heels. Then we heard her door shut like the report of a rifle. Henry lighted a cigarette and poured himself another drink from the nearly empty bottle, setting it cautiously on the rug again as if it contained nitroglycerin instead of whiskey. He took a sip and studied the fire some more. After a while, he looked at me. I thought he'd forgotten I was in the room.

"See if your mother's all right."

I went upstairs and opened the door to Doreen's room. She was still in her purple slacks and high heels, passed out across the bed. I closed the door and went back downstairs.

"She's asleep."

He looked up, the smoke swirling around his head, his eyes wild and watery-looking from staring into the fire.

"Goodnight," he said.

"Goodnight."

The next day, we went home on the bus.

Four

ONE day the water pipes at school broke. So they sent us home early. When I came in, Doreen was in her slip sitting on some guy's lap in the kitchen.

"Honeyboy! What are you doing home?"

She tried to scramble to her feet but the man held her fast. I'd seen a bakery truck parked outside. Now I realized this was the driver.

"Dale, let me up."

"Hell with that," he said. "It's time the kid knew."

"Knew what?"

But I wasn't sure I wanted to know the answer.

Doreen ignored the question.

Instead she said, "Joey, this is Dale Bigler."

She didn't have to tell me that. *Dale,* said this jerk's shirt. In yellow stitching against a dark green background. *Dale* to all the world and mister to nobody.

He clutched Doreen to his knees like a ventriloquist's doll. He was grinning at me, but he wasn't smiling. His eyes said: *look out, kid.*

"Come here and shake hands."

I told him I didn't feel like it.

He put Doreen aside like a doll and stood up. Straight black hair stuck out in quills all over his head, giving him an unruly, kiddish look.

"When a man says shake, you're supposed to shake."

"Dale. Give him time."

Dale stiff-armed the air in Doreen's direction like a halfback evading a tackle.

"Bullshit, Doreenhoney. Let's get this off on the right foot."

He looked back at me. He looked pretty goddamned mad. Doreen meekly studied her hands. Under the table Peppy was growling.

"I told you to shake," he said. "Now you shake."

His blunt hand quivered on the bright air separating us. In order to take it I'd have to walk three steps forward.

"I'm not shaking. I don't shake with anybody if I don't want to."

He took a step toward me. Doreen seemed to be in some kind of trance. Peppy sounded like he was gargling under the table to keep his throat in shape. I gripped my bookbag, getting ready. If he came closer, I was going to give it to him right between the eyes.

He must have read it in my face.

"Why you little bastard."

He paused long enough for Doreen to step between us. She put her hands on Dale's big shoulders and pushed him back into his chair.

"Cut it out," she said. "Just leave him alone."

She sat down on his lap before he could get up again.

"I swear. The two of you acting just like little boys."

"He ought to learn some manners," Dale growled.

I tried to ignore the jerk. Peppy came out from under the table, wagging his stump tail, lolling out his ham-pink tongue, breathing hard, going hah-hah. He came over to me rocking like a little hobbyhorse and bumped against my legs as if to say, come on, loosen up.

"Look at that," said Doreen. "The only sensible male in the house."

Which was debatable since that spring Peppy got himself hit by a car, leaving his right front paw useless. I figured it was safe to take my eyes off Dale long enough to give the dog a pat.

"Go outside and play," said Doreen. "I'll make supper in a little while."

I had the awful feeling he was staying for supper. I couldn't stand the idea. I winged my bookbag across the room. It cleared the dirty dishes off the sink. I made my exit under cover of shattering crockery. Dale roared like a bull. Doreen held on to him like a human necklace. I suppose he would have come after me, had Doreen let go.

I stood on the front porch trying to catch my breath, so mad I couldn't breathe right. Son of a bitch, I thought. Who is that son of a bitch. My eyes rolled over the trees, the blue sky, the sagging wire fence, the sandbox full of hard gray sand and catshit.

The rusty swing set leaned to one side, balancing on three feet like a dog getting set to pee against a tree. Everything I laid my eyes on made me want to puke. In that moment my whole life seemed tainted and ruined.

I scrambled off the porch, tore open the front gate, and ran partways down the sidewalk. I was so upset I didn't even bother to keep watch for the orange chow who'd torn the seat out of my pants two winters ago.

Dale had parked his bakery truck under some shady trees

halfway down the block. Like a fool, he'd left the sliding door open a little. Any kid could go in there and help himself while he was inside peckering around with Doreen. I stood on the running board peering into the back where all the stuff was stacked on racks.

Dust motes spun like atoms in the sunlight streaming through the oval windows of the back doors. Everything was quiet and smelled like bread. I was breathing through my teeth, my lips twisted back. But coming to myself. Just standing with my head inside the warm, good-smelling truck helped calm me down. Damn that guy, I thought. He can't do this to me.

I decided to fight back with what I had at hand. I ran back to the yard, took the little rusted shovel, and dug around in the sandbox till I excavated some catshit. I ran back to Dale's truck and stuck a turd under his seat cushion. Then I took that little shovelful and flung it into the back of the truck. I heard it spatter the doughnuts, the bread, the coffee cakes.

I made tracks after that. I ran down the sidewalk as fast as I could, running hard through the green tunnel of trees, running till I couldn't breathe anymore, my side aching so bad it pulled me to the ground like a giant hand trying to tear out my insides. I slid to the gritty pavement, holding myself and panting like a dog. I breathed in the damp acrid odor of the cement.

Goddamn you, I thought. That'll fix you.

I kept out of sight behind some trees across the street. I waited for him to come out, get in his truck, and go away. It got dark. He still didn't come out. After all that, Doreen had decided to feed him. I knew it, I said to myself. Knew it all the time.

I was really mad. How could she treat him like company after what I'd gone through in the kitchen? I couldn't figure it. It just proved the woman's capacity for treachery and deceit. She acted like only Peppy and I meant anything to her. And here she had this bozo sneaking in, in the afternoons. I wanted to kill them both.

Finally, about ten o'clock, Dale came out the front door. He leaned back in to give Doreen a final smooch. She was standing on the porch hugging her bathrobe around her. When she closed the door, Dale put on his cap, adjusted the crotch of his trousers, and rapidly descended the stairs like a tap dancer.

He got in his truck and drove off. I sniggered into my hand, thinking about the catshit. I waited for a few minutes to make sure it wasn't a trick. Then I crossed the street and walked toward the light on our front porch.

Doreen was not pleased to see me. She allowed Dale had called me a bitchified brat more than once that evening. She had to admit he was right. The fact she'd discussed me with this jerk and readily agreed with his opinion made me livid. She saw that, and tried to pacify me by telling me only Dale's good sense had stopped her from calling the cops.

"You had me beside myself. Dale told me I didn't have to worry. He bet you were watching the house, waiting for him to leave."

That made me mad too. If he knew that, why didn't he leave sooner?

"You going to marry him?"

She looked away.

"Go to sleep. I swear, you tire me out."

That left me feeling hollow. With the sudden horrible insight kids sometimes have, I'd asked the right question. Doreen's answer wasn't exactly reassuring.

She got a call the next morning about the catshit. She took the fly swatter to me. That's what she used to use. She had this fly swatter hanging by the stove. When she'd get fed up with me she'd flick me a couple times with it. This time she gave me about twenty licks. She was really serious this time. I could see this bakery truck fellow meant a lot to her.

By the weekend, Dale had moved in. It happened so fast, it sort of stunned me.

"Aren't you lucky? Now you have a father like other boys."

"I don't like that son of a bitch."

"Say that again. I'll wash your mouth out with soap. Where did you learn to talk that way anyways?"

"From you. Learned everything bad from you."

"Don't let Dale hear you sassing me."

I could have killed her.

Seemed like Dale had a wife who wouldn't give him a divorce. Couple of kids too. Somebody was always coming around with a piece of paper for him. Dale was always beating it out the back door. When the phone rang or somebody knocked at the door, he always said, "See who it is."

Be goddamned if I'd answer any doors for him.

At first they got along like a pair of lovebirds you buy at the dime store. She was always sitting on his lap with her face buried in his neck. He'd give her a little goose as she was fixing breakfast at the stove.

"Dale," she'd say.

It was enough to make you puke.

When he came to live with us he brought a gun with him. A thirty-eight pistol.

I found it one day when I was poking around in their room for something to do. He had it stashed on the closet shelf in a shoe box. Wrapped in an oily rag, it was heavy with a curious dead weight. The grip felt cold and slightly oily against my palm.

I liked the faint clean machine-oil smell of the thing. I got down from the chair I'd pushed over in front of the closet so

I could reach the shelf. I walked over to the mirror on the vanity to see myself. My eyes looked smudged and dark against my pale white face. My stomach was jumpy with excitement.

The pistol, black and sinister as a snake, hung heavily by my side. I studied my face to see if that gun hanging heavy in my hand had changed it much. I expected the gun would make me look older. Instead I was surprised to see how much I looked like Doreen. I had the same eyes and mouth, so it seemed for a minute. No, I thought. I'm not ever going to turn out like her. For the first time I was glad my eyebrows ran together like McCabe's.

The pistol seemed to hypnotize me. I looked down at it, gripped it tighter. I looked in the mirror, to see how it looked. My hand looked older, like a man's hand gripping the pistol.

I stared at myself in the mirror. Slowly I raised the gun to my head. The skin at my temple tingled at the touch of the cold steel ring of the muzzle, about the size of a Lifesaver. An ice-water chill ran down my spine. I'm not afraid, I thought. I'm not scared of him or his gun.

I began to squeeze the trigger. It was a hard job to do. I watched in the mirror as the hammer began to draw back. It got back so far it looked like it was going to fall over backwards. My hand was trembling with the effort of keeping pressure on the trigger. What if it's loaded? I remember asking myself. The hammer flew forward and struck with a metal click that rang in my ears for days.

I put the gun back in the shoe box, put the box back on the shelf, replaced the chair in front of Doreen's ruffled vanity, and got out of there. I ran away from that gun. It hadn't killed me that time. I wanted to get away before it did.

In the summer, Dale liked to go to the beach. Doreen didn't like the sand. It got in her suit and made her feel dirty. She

didn't like to go in the water either, which she thought was
polluted. Once she read in the papers that a shark had been
spotted off a beach in Massachusetts. So when she went in,
which was rarely, she just went in to her ankles. The wind blew
sand in her eyes despite the sunglasses she always wore. It mussed
her hair, even though she stiffened it into neatly layered wings
with hairspray. She burned easily. She covered up with towels,
lay under a rented beach umbrella, and listened to the static on
the portable radio. Inside half an hour, she'd say, "I'm going up
to the car."

"Why?"

"The sun's giving me a headache. Give me the keys."

"You kidding? You been laying under that umbrella
wrapped up like a mummy."

"Come on. I'm getting sick to my stomach."

"Go in the water and cool off. Have a good time for a
change."

"Just give me the keys."

Or some variation each time. At first, she argued with him.
But later when he'd ask why, she'd ignore him, and start up the
beach. He'd let her go several yards before he'd holler after her.

"Hey, Doreen. Want the keys?"

She'd turn, her hair wrapped in a towel. She'd have her
sunglasses on, the ones with the big bubble lenses which made
her look like a grasshopper.

"Yes," she'd answer, pouting her lips.

Dale would toss the keys above his head, snatching them as
they fell with the air of a man catching flies.

"Well, come get them."

I guess this was the new game, since Doreen had tired of the
old one.

One time she kept walking when he pulled this. He got so

mad he threw the key ring at her, hitting her in the thigh from ten yards away.

"You bitch! You never give anything a chance."

It left a mark on her leg for a long time like a bruise in a piece of fruit.

He didn't like it when she walked off like that. Another time he ran up the beach after her and socked her in the head. She hit him with her bag. He covered up to protect himself. She put her foot into his crotch hard. He went over like a tree, landing on a fat lady's blanket. He lay there doubled-up, while the fat lady pushed at him, telling him to get off her feet.

Doreen caught the bus home that day. When Dale and I got back, a note was on the counter, saying he'd all but killed her love for him. She was going away to think for a couple of days. Where she went, I don't know. Why she left me with him, I don't know either. I have an idea she stayed with one of her girlfriends in Boston.

When she came back she was very happy, very excited to see everybody. Peppy danced around on three legs like a fool.

"Don't you ever leave me like that again," Dale held her by the arms and looked down at her.

"If you're good maybe I won't."

"Don't talk to me like that, Doreen."

"What's the matter? It upset the baby?"

She pursed her lips, snuggling against him.

"I don't like it when you act that way."

"What do you like?"

They fell into a big clinch. I had to leave the room before I puked.

Even after that, we kept going to the beach. But the games stopped for a while. At the beach, I continued to build forts and canals in the wet sand. I ran in and out of the humble little surf.

Dale finally noticed that I only went in up to my waist.

"Why don't you go for a swim?" said Dale one day.

I told him I didn't feel like it just then.

"You can't swim, can you?"

He was squinting against the sun, grinning at me, showing his cracked tooth.

Doreen turned the radio down.

"Leave him alone, Dale. Don't tease him."

"Boy that age can't swim. I'd be ashamed if I were him."

Dale was proud of his swimming ability. He'd lay his head in the water and slowly do what he called the crawl back and forth in front of our blanket for what seemed hours, his arms loosely rising out of the mildly choppy water in slow rhythmic motion, the O-shape of his mouth facing toward us on alternate strokes.

He'd come back to us after one of these demonstrations, smiling proudly, pushing the black wet rope of his hair out of his eyes, his dripping swimsuit slung low on his belly. He had the big shoulders of a swimmer and skinny, almost hairless legs. His bony knees practically touched as he scuffed up the beach.

"Well, if you won't swim, maybe you'll fish. You want to fish?"

I figured it was his money. We rented the fishing tackle and went out on the pier. We stood there baiting our hooks.

"Here," he said. "Turn around here. You're not doing it right."

When I handed him the fishing rod, he pushed me off the dock. I went over backwards, hit the water with a loud splat, and sank like a stone statue.

The next thing I remember was some lifeguard had me on my belly on the beach pumping water out of me. Doreen was there, right down beside me, her face practically in the sand.

"Thank God, Joey! Are you all right?"

"I was only trying to teach him."

Dale was kneeling beside her, still explaining how it had gone wrong.

"It worked for me."

"Well, it didn't work for him. You asshole. You sure you're all right, Honeyboy?"

I was sure. A crowd of faces peered at me but I didn't want to look back at them. I just wanted to get out of there.

"Get back everybody," said the lifeguard. "You sure you're all right, son?"

I said I was sure.

"Dale, carry him to the car," said Doreen.

"No! Keep away from me, you son of a bitch! You come near me, I'll kill you!"

I suppose I lost some crowd sympathy, talking like that.

Nobody said anything in the car on the way home.

Dale pulled into the driveway and turned off the key.

"Well, shit. You going to hold it against me for the rest of my life?"

Doreen drew his spiky head to her shoulder and tried to smooth his hair down. I got out and left them sitting there holding hands.

Dale and I avoided each other after that as much as possible. It is amazing how little you have to see of people who live in the same house if you work at it. I asked Doreen to feed me before he got home from work, which she did. Cooking was not her speciality; she was big on frozen food. So I learned early to do my own cooking. She put too much bleach in with the clothes at the Laundromat and regularly ruined one thing or another of mine. I got in the habit of doing my own laundry. I learned to sew on my own buttons and darn my socks. None

of this stuff came easy to her, and I had ideas about all of it.
So I did it myself, to make sure it was done right. I pretty much
came and went as I pleased. She never tried to set a time for me
or study hours or anything like that. She knew it wouldn't
work. She left me alone, and that was fine with me.

We lived together like that for seven years. They'd fight and
make up and fight again. Sometimes he would stay out late and
come home drunk. Doreen would accuse him of getting some
on the side. He'd deny it. They'd argue about it all night. Yes
you do, no I don't. Bullshit. Don't tell me, woman. The usual
crap. Some mornings she'd have a black eye.

"Where'd you get that?"

"I fell down in the bathroom," she'd say, or something like
that.

"Did he give you that?"

"Eat your breakfast. Mind your own business."

He got laid off when I was sixteen and hung around the house
all day reading the paper and drinking beer. Doreen was working as a hotel switchboard operator by then. With him around
the place all the time, I didn't bother going home. I'd stay at
some friend's place, or hang out in the park. I got to know some
bums that way. You'd be surprised, some of them are very
interesting people.

Hanging out like that, I met a whore who called herself
Pepper. What her real name was, I never did find out. When
business was slow, she used to take me back to her place. She
thought it was cool to make it with a kid. She never charged
me anything, except I did a few chores around the place for her
like take out the garbage.

One night when I came in, I found the two of them curled
up on the couch together watching TV. They grinned like a
matched pair of foxes.

"What's your problem?"

"Guess what?" said Doreen.

"What?"

"Guess."

"Oh for Christsakes, Doreen. Tell him."

"Dale and I got married today."

"That's something," I said, starting down the hall to my room.

He lifted his head off the couch.

"Why don't you give us a wedding present and move out?"

I guess Doreen thought if they got married things would go better. That's what women always think, and they're always wrong about it. It just makes a man, if he's no good, a little worse.

Dale still whomped on her pretty good, I guess. But he didn't try it when I was around. He knew I wouldn't take it anymore. Doreen was careful to hide her bruises. He was more careful where he hit her too. But every once in a while I'd see one, and I'd say, "I'll kill that son of a bitch."

"No, you won't. You're not going to jail for him. Sit down and drink your coffee."

They'd been married for a year when he made his mistake —or I made mine, take your pick. I was in the house that night. Dale came home after I'd gone to bed. They commenced to fight. The noise woke me.

I lay there listening. I didn't like the sound of it. He sounded ugly drunk. The more I listened, the more nervous I got. Then it quit suddenly. It went quiet back in there, and that was even worse.

I got up and crept down the hall by the light from the door to their room, which was open a crack. I heard Doreen sobbing quietly. She sounded like a broken-hearted little girl. I tensed against the wall, thinking maybe he could hear me or see my shadow on the other wall. When nothing happened, I kept moving, crouched Indian-style, steadying myself with my fingertips against the wall, slowly moving toward the light pouring through the crack in the doorway.

If he's hurt her, I thought, I'll kill him. I'll kill him.

Doreen was crouched on the big Hollywood bed in her lacy black nightgown. She was holding her face in her hands, her cloud of blond hair tumbling forward.

"Please, please."

Dale was standing in his underwear, swaying over her. Then I saw the gun and understood why she was acting so afraid.

"You puke," he whispered.

She shrank away. Her eyes looked even bluer now that she was terrified.

"Don't. Don't."

She closed her eyes as Dale put the pistol to her head.

"I ought to blow your brains out," he whispered, swaying.

"Dale, Dale."

She looked like she was praying to him.

"You creep. You puke. You been driving me crazy for years."

His arm stiffened, driving the pistol against her head.

"Dale. Please."

Doreen bit her lips, her eyes still shut.

"Why don't you beg? If you beg real good I might reconsider."

"Dale, don't kill me. Please."

"I got to kill you. You're driving me crazy."

"Dale." Doreen faltered. "It isn't right."

"Get down on the floor. Maybe if you're extra nice I won't kill you tonight."

He looked damned surprised when I came through the door. Then he recovered and went crazy. He had her by the hair on her knees in front of him.

"Get out of here! I'll kill her!"

He put the gun to her head again.

"Get out! He'll kill me!"

She was on her knees. He had her tightly by the hair.

I was looking him in the eyes, to see if he'd do it. I wanted to get to him somehow. I was going to get him for this sooner or later and he knew it.

"Do what he says, Joey!"

"I'll kill her! I swear to Christ!"

I started for him. His eyes changed like he couldn't believe it.

"Get back, you son of a bitch!"

Doreen started screaming. My head was full of the sound of her screaming and the look of surprise on Dale's face. I grabbed for the gun and put my elbow into his face. The gun went off. My head was full of the concussive explosion which went on and on and then the sound of Doreen came back only now she was in the corner and the wallpaper swimming with roses came back too and I was standing over the bed.

Dale was sprawled across it, straight back, his head over the edge of it, his arms dangling over his head. I stuck the gun in the back of my pants and jumped on him. I hit him a couple of times hard as I could. Blood spattered his cheek, squirting on the pink satin quilt. Doreen was screaming in the background.

"You'll never hit her again, will you," I said.

Peppy came out from under the bed and was barking shrilly. How many times I hit him, I couldn't say. I was choking him. I wanted to choke him to death. His teeth were stained pink with blood and it spouted out of his nose in black gobs, all very satisfying to me, as I sat on him choking the shit out of him.

Doreen tried to pull me off. When that didn't work, she beat me on the head with her slipper. That seemed to bring me back.

"Stop it, stop it! You'll kill him."

I let go. Dale fell on the floor.

She bent over him.

"Dale."

I had to admit he looked dead.

"Help me sit him up."

We got him propped up against the bed. He looked pretty bad. His nose was swollen, his eye was cut, his lip puffed out. Doreen pounded him on the back. Dale began to cough.

"Dale—are you all right, honey?"

I left the house without a word.

When I came back the next afternoon, Doreen met me at the door.

"You can't come in."

"Why not?"

"You're not welcome here anymore, Joey."

"Where's Dale?"

"He's not here. You better not be here when he gets back either. He'll call the cops. He says you belong in a reform school."

"Let me come in and get a few things at least."

"You stole his gun, Joey."

"That's all right. Tell him not to worry. I got it in a safe place."

"If you don't give it back, he's going to report it stolen."

"Yes? Well, tell him something for me. If he hits you again I'll come back and finish him."

"Don't talk crazy."

"You tell him."

She opened the door, looking worried.

"Come in and get your things. Only hurry."

Peppy wriggled a greeting in the doorway. As I bent to pat the dog, Doreen said, "You're going to get into trouble with that temper, Joe."

I straightened up, looking at her.

"Why do you stay with him?"

"He is what he is. I can't change him."

"You could do something."

"Where am I supposed to go? What am I supposed to do? I don't even have a high school diploma."

When I didn't answer, she smiled and touched me on the shoulder.

"Maybe someday. You never know."

I was in my room packing when she came rushing in.

"Here he comes! Oh Jesus! Go out the back door. Here, take this. It's all I have."

She handed me a crumpled ten dollar bill.

"Keep it," I said.

"Put it in your pocket. What are you going to do?"

"I don't know. Something. Take care of Peppy."

"I will. Get going."

"Keep his leg wrapped so he doesn't wear a hole in it."

"Will you stop worrying about the dog? Go see your grandfather," she said. "Maybe he'll let you stay for a while."

In the kitchen she tried to kiss me goodbye, but I told her to save it. She could kiss me hello sometime. I grabbed the last doughnut and went out the door.

Five

If I'd been shellac, I'd have had time to set up before he shuffled down the hallway and opened the door.

He opened it just a crack, his head bowed, his thin white hair in a disorderly cloud above his bony skull. His mustache drooped above his haggard mouth. He looked old and used up.

He frowned when he saw me and pulled himself erect.

"Yes? What do you want?"

A dog with warm friendly brown eyes stuck his black velvet nose in the opening. It was a different dog, I saw right away —a Labrador like the other, but this one was much younger.

I said, "You probably don't remember me."

He blinked his pale eyes, continuing to frown. It was plain he didn't know who I was, didn't care, and wanted me off his front steps as quick as possible.

I had to push my way up to the door through the wild rhododendron and other jungly bushes that were taking over the front gate, the frost-heaved brick walk, and even the granite steps leading to the front door. More bushes practically blocked the door to his office at the side. Apparently he'd given up any pretense of holding regular office hours. The front yard looked like a hayfield. The house was pretty much as I remembered it—big, square, and chalky white, badly in need of paint and general repair. A shutter had fallen off one of the windows near the door and lay in the weeds. The house was the only poor relation in the neighborhood. The other houses, equally big and imposing, were all in good repair.

"I'm Joe. Doreen's boy. Remember?"

He looked like he didn't want to. He had egg on the front of his shirt. One suspender dangled from his waist. He was still unshaven, his eyes red-rimmed as fresh cuts. He didn't act fully awake although it was nearly noon when I rapped on his door. I'd sat in the park across the street for a couple of hours to make sure when I knocked on his door he'd have had his breakfast. I wasn't going to start by showing up at mealtime.

"We visited you about nine years ago. We came up on the train and you met us at the station. You probably don't remember. We only stayed a couple of days."

"I'm not senile yet. What do you want?"

"I'm on my way to Quebec. I just stopped to say hello."

"Quebec, huh. Where's your mother?"

"She's at home."

"You traveling alone?"

He kind of sniffed at me suspiciously.

"That's right."

"You're traveling kind of light, aren't you? Don't you have a bag?"

"I left it on my bike over in the park. I thought I'd see if you were home this morning."

"Your bike? You've got your bike with you?"

"Yes, I do."

"Why is that?"

"Pardon?"

"Are you deaf? I asked why do you have your bicycle with you?"

"Well, I'm riding it, that's why."

"You rode it all the way from Massachusetts to my front door?"

"Yes," I said. "How else was I going to get here?"

"What are you—running away from home? Is that it?"

That seemed to satisfy his suspicions about me, which only made me mad.

"No, I'm not running away from home. Forget I knocked. Sorry to bother you."

I turned and started down the steps. He followed after me, the dog at his heels. I began to think maybe he was crazy.

"You're in trouble. Is that it?"

"No. At least I wasn't till I knocked on your door."

I started out the gate, wrestling my way through the jungle of overgrown bushes.

"Why don't you get somebody to cut these bushes back?"

He followed me out onto the sidewalk, looking wild as a hawk. I couldn't figure out what had him so agitated.

"What do you want from me?" his eyes wide, he spread his palms toward the elms. He was acting crazier than hell.

I turned.

"Listen, forget it. I'll stop again next time I'm in town."

I crossed the street. That old fool, I thought. I walked toward the trees where I'd left the bike chained to a bench. I stepped into the cool shadows under the trees. Right away it helped to calm me down. Who needs that guy, I thought. My front tire looked a little low. I detached the sleeve pump from its mountings on the down tube, kneeled by the silver dazzle of the spokes, and started to pump her up a bit.

"Come to the house," said this voice from the dead. I nearly jumped out of my skin.

"Don't sneak up on me like that! I hate when somebody does that!"

"You're an excitable fellow," he rubbed the knob of his sandpapery chin. "You always so excitable?"

At the house, he made me a cup of instant coffee and offered me a powdered doughnut. As we passed through the hall to the kitchen, I saw the door to the study was open. I noticed a rumpled blanket and pillow on the couch, a lot of books, a coffee cup, a plate on the floor. I figured he must be sleeping downstairs these days. From the looks of him he wasn't bothering to take off his clothes at night.

I blew on my coffee. He sat opposite me at the table, his elbow on the oilcloth, glaring nonspecifically into the middle distance. Although I think it was the strong light coming in at the window and not because he was annoyed about anything. Old people, I had noticed, have a way of glaring against the light.

Nobody said anything. I concentrated on my doughnut. How often things come and go in circles. Here the last thing I'd eaten two days ago was a doughnut. And now the first thing again was a doughnut.

The house had a musty, old man smell about it which clung to the curtains and the furniture. Henry smelled like his house. It was a case of the chicken and the egg. I didn't know whether he smelled so bad from lying around the house, or the house smelled bad because he stank it up. His aroma was concentrated, made up of tobacco, dog, body odor, and whiskey. Here's a man who likes one or two in the morning, I thought. Just to get him started on his way downhill. Whenever he shuffled close I stopped breathing till he moved away again. I wondered how you could let yourself go like that.

"How come you let the grass grow tall and those bushes at the front get out of hand?"

"I got other things to do. I can't worry about grass or bushes all the time."

"Looks like you don't worry about it at all. You too busy doctoring people, is that it?"

He scratched his head and looked off.

"I don't do much of that anymore. There's a young fellow in town. Once in a while I get a call."

"You still have hours over at the office?"

"I don't exactly have hours anymore. Some of the old patients still come around. I listen to their complaints. There's not much else to do. What they're suffering from is old age. I'm what you call semi-retired, I guess."

"You were semi-retired ten years ago."

"Yes, I suppose I was. I guess I've always been semi-retired."

"Then what keeps you so busy you can't cut the grass?"

"You're pretty damned nosy, aren't you?"

He smiled suddenly, showing me the crooked yellow horse teeth under his ragged mustache.

"Just curious."

"Well, I like to read," he pulled up his suspender. "I do a lot of thinking. Damned if the day doesn't get away from me."

"Can't you get anybody to take care of things for you?"

"I don't need any help. Guess I can do it myself, if I wanted to. You want more coffee? I got another jar around here someplace."

"Tell you what," I said. "How about I work on your lawn. Cut back those bushes before they attack somebody passing on the sidewalk."

"Oh yes?"

"You can pay me a dollar or two. Or feed me supper and

let me stay the night. What do you say?"

"You can't stay here long. I'm not set up for company."

"I can see that. I'd pay my way by doing some work for you. I could use a place to stay for a few days."

"You sure you're not in some trouble?"

"I'm not in any trouble."

"Well—I guess you can stay. Only for a couple of days, understand."

I brought my bike in the house and parked it in the study.

"What kind of a bike is that?"

"That's a ten-speed. A Motobecane. A French-made bicycle. A good one too. I can go a hundred miles in a day on that."

"Good Lord. That so?"

"I got that bike mowing lawns and doing odd jobs."

"It's nice to hear you're no stranger to work."

He told me to put my stuff in the same room upstairs I stayed in last time I visited—almost exactly nine years ago. I put a few shirts in a drawer, hung up my spare jeans in the wardrobe. Still wrapped in its oily cloth, I stuck Dale's gun under the mattress at the head of the bed so I could get at it fast if I needed to. Why I thought I might need to, I couldn't say.

If I'd been smart, I'd have flung that gun into the weeds down some lonely road. But I was a crazy kid in those days. I was sleeping in culverts and under bridges. I guess I was afraid of the boogeyman. I suppose in case of trouble I was going to pull that gun out of my pants and wave it around. I didn't exactly intend to shoot anyone. But I guess I thought if I showed the gun, trouble would just go away.

The grass was so tall I had to use a scythe to cut it down. I spent all afternoon hacking away at the bushes and the grass and hardly made a dent in things. But when I was finished you could swing open the gate and walk up the front walk without being assaulted.

As I washed up at the kitchen sink Henry asked me what I wanted for supper.

"Anything is fine."

I could have eaten a skunk, I was that hungry.

"I was thinking of opening a can of peaches. You particularly hungry?"

"You're not much for cooking, are you?"

"No, I guess not. There's only me to cook for. I'm not particular."

"The store's still open, isn't it? Why don't you send me down there to get some groceries. I'll cook you a real meal for a change."

"You cook too, do you?"

"Sure. Who do you think fed me all these years? Doreen?"

"No, I don't suppose she did."

"You're damn right she didn't. So how about it?"

"All right. If you don't mind cooking?"

"No, I like to cook."

I figured it beat sharing a can of peaches.

When I got back, I noticed he had shaved and trimmed the stained part off his mustache. He'd run a comb through his cloud of thinning white hair too. He'd put on a tie and jacket and looked almost presentable.

I cooked him a steak and mushrooms, some green beans and some homefries with bits of onion and bacon in them. He suggested we eat in the study. It seemed to be his favorite room, what with all the books and other paraphernalia he had in there. There was an oak table stacked with books behind the flowered drapes of the alcove. He put the books on the floor, dragged a cloth across the table, set out the plates and silverware while I got things ready in the kitchen.

We sat down to dinner. Everything tasted wonderful. I used

the bread and butter to sop up some of the steak gravy on my plate. Nobody said anything for quite a while.

"I see you got a new dog."

Because the dog was sitting there, watching us eat with a wounded look on its face.

"Nothing new about him. Cat's six years old. Aren't you, Cat?"

"What do you call that dog?"

He looked up when I asked him that.

"I call him 'Cat.' "

I thought it was a stupid name for a dog. I wasn't going to give him the satisfaction of asking how he came up with it.

"You got a lot of books in this room. You must like to read."

This made him laugh. He raised the gnarled claw in which smoldered his ever-present cigarette and went heh-heh behind it as if laughing aloud was a public disgrace.

"Yes, I like to read—greatly. And yourself?"

"I'm not much for it. I like to be out in the air."

"How old are you now?"

"Turned seventeen last month."

"What grade are you in?"

"I'd be a junior. Only I'm not going back."

"Sounds like you've been left behind a time or two," he puffed on his butt, making the tip of it glow orange.

"I've had a little trouble. Me and the teachers don't always see eye to eye."

"I gather as much. What are you planning on doing?"

"Figure to get a job or go in the service."

He nodded gravely. I could tell he disapproved of people quitting school. But it wasn't his life we were talking about, was it.

When we sat down to eat, he'd produced a bottle of whiskey from off the floor.

"Care for a drink?"

"Don't mind if I do."

I cut it pretty good with the water jug but it was still burny going down. He had two or three drinks with his meal. He kept a cigarette going in the ashtray. He lighted one off the other, puffing away till the smoke swirled blue around his head. Mostly he studied his plate, chewing rapidly, washing his food down with the whiskey.

"You always smoke through dinner?"

He looked up, stopping his fork midway to his mouth.

"Don't know. Never thought about it."

That was the end of it till he laid his knife and fork on his empty plate, patted his mustache with his napkin. He pinched his current cigarette butt between thumb and forefinger, automatically placed it on that black blister each time. I wondered if he had lip cancer.

"You're not a bad cook."

He sucked on his weed and exhaled. Nothing came out. He must have taken the smoke right in through the lining of his lungs.

"That's more than I've had to eat since I can't remember when. Hope I don't get sick from all that food."

"I like to eat well," I said. "Can't stand Doreen's cooking. French toast is about all she can make. What's that picture on the wall?"

A big gilt-framed photograph gloomed down from the faded wallpaper. At the apex of a group of soldiers was a bespectacled man in uniform holding in his hands an officer's cap that looked too small for his head.

"That's me. As a young officer in France."

"That's you?"

He was surrounded by his men, all looking no older than I was, crowded together on top of a small muddy mound or hill somewhere in France in 1918.

He said it was taken the same afternoon he had shot the German boy. They had badly frightened each other when Henry walked in on him as he was hiding in the remnant of some Frenchman's barn. Henry said he was so scared, he cried out for fear. He said the boy was just a boy, a smooth-faced blond boy with large blue eyes. When the boy went for his rifle back in the hay, Henry shot him in the heart. The boy lay back in the hay as though swooning. But he was very dead, said Henry.

In the picture, Henry is bareheaded. The sides of his head are shaved; the hair on top looks like a small thatched roof. His holstered pistol has slipped forward on his belt and points at his crotch. If it had accidentally gone off, likely the bullet would have taken his balls. Maybe his left kneecap as well.

"I killed him," he said. "If I'd played it smarter, maybe both of us would have gotten out of that barn alive."

"He went for his gun. You didn't have a choice."

"Oh, I expect I had a choice," he puffed nervously on his cigarette.

We had approached the picture as we talked about it. Henry was squinting at it, looking for a way to crawl back into it. He puffed his cigarette as he studied the problem. The hot little cigarette end began to sting his fingertips. He looked for a place to put it down but was baffled by this one too.

"That bullet traveled on," he said.

I didn't follow that part. He explained that his own son, Doreen's brother, whom I never even knew existed till then, abruptly left medical school to join the army early in World War II.

Henry said the boy was seized by a sudden attack of patriotism. Henry gave him his—Henry's—own pistol to carry with him, the one he'd used to kill the German boy. Henry thought it might bring him luck.

That was before he realized a gun that's killed somebody is unlucky. The realization that a pistol like that could only bring bad luck woke him up one night in a cold sweat. He wrote to his boy and told him to send it back.

But it was too late. The kid was killed at Monte Cassino, some place in Italy. Later, the army sent the gun back and here it was now—back home in its glass case, a little shrine to bad luck in the corner of Henry's library.

The pistol was cushioned on green felt. An engraved brass plate in the corner explained how Henry had carried the pistol in World War I and how his son, Donald, had carried the pistol in World War II, and that he'd been killed in Italy at the battle of Monte Cassino.

"I should never have given it to him. I should have known it was bad luck."

"It's not your fault."

He looked at me.

"Yes it is."

"Hell," I said. "It wasn't even the same war."

That amused him. He laughed till it brought on a coughing attack.

Finally he got it under control. He stood there gasping, leaning against the table with the glass box on it.

"Go to bed now." His face was blotched and feverish-looking. "You must be tired from your day's exertions."

"Okay. You sure you're all right?"

"I'm sure. I'm going to read a little before I turn in."

"Tomorrow," I said, "I'll finish mowing the front yard. Then I'll start on the back. This place could be nice if you'd fix it up."

"Good night," he turned from me.

"Good night."

Slowly he crossed the room toward the couch and the light and the softly glinting shelves filled with the books he seemed to like better than people.

Six

When I came downstairs at ten o'clock the next morning he was still gassed out on the couch. The light from the goosenecked lamp on the littered end table was shining in his face. His mouth was open and a book was spread face down on his chest. Next to him, on the floor, were the dog and the whiskey bottle.

The dog looked up when I came in the room.

"Hello, Cat."

I turned out the light so it wouldn't shine in his face and put the nearly empty whiskey bottle on the table. He was snoring through his mouth, dead to the world. The air in the room was stale. It was the worst-smelling room in the house, probably because he spent so much time in it.

He'd hung his suit coat over the back of a chair. His wallet was in the left inside pocket. He had thirty dollars in it. The bills were old and dirty, slightly waxen under my fingers. I stuffed the money in my back pocket and went out the front door.

I have to admit. I wondered how far that money would take me if I used it to buy a bus ticket. Probably I could have gone all the way to Quebec on that money. It wasn't likely he'd report it to the cops. So in a sense it was free money. Mine to choose what to do with.

Doreen had told me that the people in Quebec lived underground in the wintertime. They had hotels, apartments, restaurants, movie theaters, everything underground. All of it connected by subways and underground sidewalks. I was fascinated by the idea. Of course, I had it wrong. She had really told me about Montreal. Somehow I got mixed up and thought it was Quebec. It took some time for me to find out my mistake. I was always heading in the wrong direction in those days anyway.

So I walked along thinking, I don't owe him anything. He's supposed to be my grandfather. But he never even gave me a birthday or Christmas present. He owes me a few bucks. He's been getting off easy. I'd cut down his damned bushes for him. That was worth something too.

In the end, I went to the IGA to get some more groceries. But for a minute, the idea of heading out of town had its attractions.

I was back in the house before he ever turned over. When I heard him groan, I went in and handed him a glass of tomato juice with a slice of lemon and some Worcestershire sauce in it. I gave it to him as he sat on the edge of the couch nursing his head in his hands.

He looked up in surprise.

"What's this?"

"Drink it. It's what I do for Doreen when she's hung over in the mornings."

"What is it?"

"You particular? That's tomato juice. You've heard of that. It's got a slice of lemon in it and a little Worcestershire sauce. Drink it down."

He blinked at me.

"Here," he handed me the glass and began to pat his pockets. "Hold this abomination while I have a cigarette and think it over. This is a big change from my usual routine."

"No doubt. You still crumbling crackers in milk for your breakfast?"

"Where are my cigarettes?" he began to cough.

He coughed till he turned nearly blue, rocking stiffly from his hips back and forth on the horsehair sofa. The more he coughed the more pronounced the forked blue vein in the center of his forehead became. He ended this fit by spitting long and copiously into his handkerchief. It was disgusting. But I guess it was either that or choke to death.

After he slumped back, staring slack and palpitant at the ceiling, I held up his empty pack. I'd spotted it lying on the floor, half-hidden by one of the curved legs of the couch.

"Looks like you're out of cigarettes."

Turning his gaze from the wedding cake-like designs of the tin ceiling, the old man looked at the crumpled pack in my hand.

"Drink your tomato juice," I said. "I'll run out and get you some smokes. If I'd known you were out, I could have got you some at the store."

He paused in the act of pressing the glass of tomato juice to his lips and looked at me.

"I already been out for groceries. You had some money in your wallet. I used that."

"You're kind of light-fingered, aren't you?"

"I should have waked you up. You looked like you could use the sleep."

"I'll have to carry flypaper to keep you the hell out of my pockets."

"I got the receipt if you want to check it."

He tried to get off the couch, then thought better of it.

"What time is it?"

"Almost eleven. I'll fix some breakfast. You want a book or anything?"

"Get me some cigarettes. Since you're so damned all fired to do my shopping this morning."

"Okay."

So I went out the front door again. What a miserable old son of a bitch. It probably came from living alone. He'd been living in that big mausoleum all by himself for seventeen years. And I thought too: everybody he ever loved has either died or run away.

When I got back he tore the package open with stiff, trembling fingers, his eyes hooded, his face so sullen with greed that it shocked me into silence. I watched him paste one on the purple bug. The match hissed, sudden and sulfuric, conjured out of thin air.

"You got a bad habit there. It's liable to kill you one day."

He rumbled deep in his bony chest.

"You don't say."

He grinned at me, tapped the ashes off the end of his cigarette. The ashes sifted down, landing on the toe of his dull black shoe.

"Now you've had one, you ready for breakfast?"

He blinked like an old turtle. I started out the door.

"I don't want much."

"I'm the cook. You can't run the kitchen from in here."

"Don't get carried away."

"We'll eat in the kitchen. It's nice and sunny in there. You ever go outside?"

"Outside?"

As if I were talking about the Kingdom of Siam.

"Well, yes. Sometimes I do."

"You don't look it. You're goddamned ghostly white. You ought to go easy on that booze. How do you like your eggs?"

He didn't answer. To hell with him, I thought. He'll get what I cook.

I cut and sectioned half a pink grapefruit for him. From the looks of him, he could do with a few fruits and vegetables. If that's what old age comes to, I remember thinking, you can have my ticket.

I cooked him a nice thick slab of ham and a couple of eggs sunny side up and an English muffin. He didn't have a toaster. Neither did Doreen, so I cooked it in the oven just like I would at home. I made a pot of coffee too.

While I was doing this, I happened to glance in the hallway. Henry was hanging on to the banister for dear life trying to creep upstairs. He looked like a man trying to go up a rope hand over hand. He looked horrible, about a hundred years old. His eyes were bugging out of his head. He was the color of tooth-paste or worse. From the looks of him you would have thought he was locked in deadly combat with some invisible presence that was trying to lift him over the banister and hurl him to the hallway floor. I watched, speechless. Silently he crawled out of sight, knuckling the banister desperately.

After a pause, I heard the water running in the bathroom upstairs. Briefly. Just a modest little test to see if the plumbing still worked. Surely not long enough for a shower. Or to fill up a bathtub. Maybe long enough to splash a little water on his face and use what was left in the bowl to eke out a little shave.

Things were quiet up there. Then I heard him creeping around again. My guess was he'd gone into his bedroom to change his shirt. I heard a step creak, and turned to see him descending the stairs stiffly, his gnarled hand clutching the banister, his braces dangling, the fresh white shirt ballooning in the back at the waist where he'd tucked it in carelessly.

He came into the kitchen, shuffling by without a word, moving stiffly and silently with a grim determination toward the sink. Which he made. Which was an achievement he decided to savor. He hung on to the edge of the counter for a minute, pretending he was looking out the window at a sparrow hopping around on a tree branch out there like a windup toy gone berserk. But really he was trying to catch up with himself and all the effort he'd engaged in that morning, starting with that glass of tomato juice.

His legs were trembling. He bowed his head as if in prayer. The pant legs of his black trousers, the same ones he'd slept in all night on the couch, were vibrating noticeably. He was hooked up, submitting humbly, to the workings of some invisible diabolical weight-reducing machine. Only in his case nothing was left to reduce.

The seat of his pants hung down all baggy as if the mice had eaten his ass. You wondered how he had anything left to sit on. I watched to see what he'd do next. He looked ready to collapse.

He reached under the sink, pulled out a big tin cup. He turned on the hot-water tap and let it run till a haze of steam appeared above the faucets. He filled the cup halfway. Then he blew on it and slowly drank it off, still steadying himself on the sink with his free hand.

"What're you doing?"

"I'm minding my business," he turned sideways to glower at me, but still held on to the sink.

"Just making conversation. You like your eggs up?"

"I like them soft-boiled."

"That's tough. Today you get them sunny-side. You want cream in your coffee?"

"Just black, if you will."

He watched me put the eggs on the plate, absently nibbling at his mustache.

"I always drink a cup of hot water in the mornings."

He spoke extra loud as if addressing a crowd.

"Is that right?"

"Yes. It helps regulate me, I find."

"That's terrific. Your breakfast is ready."

"Ham," he slid onto his chair. "I haven't had ham and eggs for breakfast . . . for some time."

"Eat up. You like to read the paper? I bought the *Globe*. I like the sports section in the morning."

I handed him the front section. He acted for a minute like he didn't know whether to eat it or play it. I folded the sports section into thirds and pretended to ignore him.

"Red Sox won."

He wasn't interested. In fact, he didn't seem to know what I was talking about. He sat there, somewhat out of plumb, and stared vacantly at the wall behind me. He acted like he'd just fallen out of a balloon onto his head. Finally he started in on his eggs.

After breakfast he floated upstairs again. I did the dishes. Then I went outside and started to hack away at the jungle out back. All the flower beds had gone to seed and were shapeless and overgrown. I doubted if anybody had bothered with them for twenty years. I waded through the sea of tall grass to the end of the deep lawn. I found a little footbridge that crossed over a brook. A path led up into an old orchard and beyond that into the woods. I decided to scythe a path from the back door of the house to the footbridge.

It must have been nearly five when I quit for the day. I hung up the scythe in the barn and started around the corner of the

house to get my shirt which I'd left on the edge of the drive.
But I ducked back. I saw this fat cop in a cowboy hat and
sunglasses waddling up the front walk. He had a notepad in his
hand and he was wetting a pencil stub with the tip of his tongue.

That fucking Dale, I thought.

I sprinted around the corner of the house and shimmied up
one of the posts on the back porch onto the balcony off Henry's
room. I crept into the hall. I could hear Henry at the front door,
his voice, high and stringy, and the cop's gravel baritone. I
couldn't understand what they were saying, but they were both
excited. I didn't stop for details.

I got into my room. Quietly I emptied my junk out of the
wardrobe into my panniers. It didn't take a minute. I got the
gun from under the mattress. I didn't know whether to use the
downspout outside my window or go back to Henry's room
and slide down the porch post. The siding looked so rotten, I
was afraid the spouting might pull away from the house. The
bedroom door creaked on its hinges. I swung around, the gun
in my hand.

"What are you going to do—shoot me?"

Henry was standing there, his shirt still not properly tucked
in his trousers.

"Where's that cop?"

"He's gone. I did some lying for you. It ought to give you
a chance to get out of town."

I relaxed a little.

"Thanks. I appreciate it."

"I said, were you going to shoot me?"

He looked at me.

"What? It was just a reflex. Hell, it isn't even loaded."

I stuck the gun in the back of my pants.

"Is that the gun you stole from your stepfather?"

"What stepfather? He's not my stepfather."

"You stole that from him," he said. "You beat him up and stole his money."

"That fucker hasn't got a nickel," I said. "He just mooches off Doreen."

"What did you have in mind for me?"

"Nothing. I didn't have anything in mind for you."

"What did you need to see here before you made up your mind what to do with me?"

I didn't say anything.

He was breathing hard, even for an old man with emphysema.

"Well, I lied for you," he said. "At least I won't have the shame of having you arrested in the house."

"I'll go out the back. Can I reach the highway through those woods?"

"You better throw that gun away before you kill someone."

"I don't take advice from drunks."

"Trash," he said. One side of his mouth was jerking around. "Your mother's trash and so is your father."

"You smell bad," I said. "Try taking a bath sometime."

I started past him. He made as if to hit me with the back of his hand. I grabbed his wrist.

"Don't make any mistakes, Granpa."

"Get out! Get out of my house!"

He didn't follow me downstairs. I went out the kitchen door and down off the porch. I had the panniers slung over my shoulder. They tapped me on the back as I walked. I looked around for that cop, thinking maybe he'd doubled back. But he wasn't around. I got my bike out of the barn. I had a feeling the old man was watching me from one of the windows upstairs.

I walked the bike down the path I'd cut that afternoon. I rolled it over the footbridge onto the steep ground of the dying orchard beyond. I walked it along one of the paths in the woods, and it took me over the ridge to the highway.

Seven

I WAITED out of sight across the street till the sun rose above the edge of the roof. His car wasn't around. That's a piece of luck, I thought. Maybe the son of a bitch got a job.

I crossed over, shivering in the morning dampness. I rattled the metal gate till it gave in.

The place looked strange to me somehow. The wire fence still bulged where I'd leaned against it as a little kid to watch for the orange chow. The smelly sandbox rotted by the sidewalk. The swing set still kicked out with its rear leg like a headless stick horse. Nothing had changed at all in the week I'd been gone. But it looked funny now that I no longer lived here.

The porch door was locked. That's unusual, I thought. I knocked on it and waited. It was Saturday morning, Doreen's day to sleep in. The dog began to bark, muffled and distant, deep inside the house. I chafed my arms, trying to get the circulation going. Come on, sun, I said to myself. Part of the waiting I did gave Doreen time to check me out from behind the curtains of the living room windows.

"Who do you suppose that is?" If she didn't like their looks, she wouldn't open the door. "No use asking for trouble," she'd say. She was good at spotting bill collectors. Now I guessed she was looking at me out the window wondering: what kind of grief is he bringing with him this time?

I couldn't blame her. Here you kick your kid out, and he's back on the doorstep in a week.

It took her a while to open the door.

"Joey! What are you doing here?"

"Where's Dale?"

"How do I know?"

"He's got the cops after me. That son of a bitch."

"I warned you, Joe."

"Let me in for a few minutes, will you?"

She wasn't happy about it, but she opened the door wider.

"I bet I look a mess."

Peppy did a little three-legged dance at my feet. I bent down and petted the wriggling fat slug of a dog. Hah, hah, Peppy breathed. I'm just a fool for love.

"Hello, you silly dog."

Doreen pulled her cotton robe closer to her throat, nervously touching her frizzy hair.

"What are you doing here, Joey? Wouldn't he let you stay?" .

"Don't worry," I smiled. "I'm not staying."

"You can't stay anyway. Dale would go crazy."

"Don't get yourself worked up."

"Oh Joe. You're in big trouble."

"It'll be big trouble for him, if I catch him right."

"Did you bring the gun?"

"Why?"

"Leave it with me, Joe. Maybe I can talk him into dropping the charges."

"The hell I will. So he can blow your brains out? The son of a bitch."

"It's okay to leave it. He won't hurt me. Not really."

It made me laugh.

"Doreen, you're incredible."

Peppy was bumping against my leg, wanting another petting.

"You're just a glutton, aren't you old dog?"

Peppy hah-hahed right into my face this time, a blast of warm putrid air that nearly keeled me over.

"Phew, Fish Breath. What's Doreen feeding you anyway? Come here."

"Joe. Come on, Joe. You have to get out of here."

"Here, let me take a look, old dog."

I pried Peppy's mouth open, and peered down his throat. There it was, a little dirty white balloon in back of his tonsil on the left side.

"This dog's got a tumor in its throat."

"What are you talking about?"

"Come here, I'll show you."

"Honestly, Joey. You only have a few minutes and you fool around with the dog."

"See this?"

I pried open Peppy's jaw.

"See what?"

"Look to the left. See that white glob behind his tonsil?"

With a pained expression, Doreen peered into Peppy's throat.

"I can't see anything."

"Can't you see it? It's right in front of you. On the left side. What are you, blind?"

"Don't get fresh. I can't see it, okay?"

She patted Peppy on the head.

"Mommy can't see anything, can she baby?"

Peppy wriggled his backside and boogied around Doreen's feet as she leaned over, talking to him in a high voice.

"Nice baby dog. Yes, yes. You're Mommy's nice boy. Good baby."

She straightened up, her face flushed and happy from talking to the dog.

"What are you going to do now?"

"I don't know. Maybe I'll take a run down south. Didn't you say McCabe lives down there somewhere?"

"He lives in Florida, I think. Why? You going to see him?"

"Maybe. You have his address?"

"I think I saved a Christmas card he sent a few years ago. Wait a second."

Doreen went to look through the box of junk under her bed. She kept love letters in there from her old boyfriends. Letters from Henry in his spidery handwriting rejecting her requests for money, and then relenting later in the letter, and swearing at the end that he'd never again send another check. She had some snapshots of herself, very tan and blond, in a one-piece white bathing suit, sitting on the top of the backseat of Dale's convertible before it was repossessed. It was the only summer she ever got a decent tan. She had programs from stage shows, menus from fancy restaurants she'd visited on dates, and other dead stuff which I'd sifted through as a kid. All boring. While she rummaged through her box of trash, I looked at Peppy's throat again. If she couldn't see the tumor, I don't know how she could miss the smell.

"Here," she said, when she came back. "I wrote it down on this envelope. I put fifty dollars in there for you."

"I don't want your money."

"Take it."

She put her arms around me.

"Joe, I feel so bad for you."

"Hey. You worrying about me?"

I held her at arm's length. I could feel the grin spreading crookedly on my face.

"I've been taking care of myself for a long time."

"I know. But you're still a baby to me."

She touched my cheek.

"You'll always be a baby to me. That's the way mothers are."

Doreen's maternal attacks always cracked me up.

"Do me a favor."

"What."

"Take Peppy to the vet tomorrow."

"We're going to the White Mountains tomorrow. We have a cottage rented and everything."

"Well. Stop on the way."

"I'll take him when we get back."

"If you fool around, this dog could be dead."

"What are you trying to do—frighten me?"

"No, I'm saying it's serious."

"I don't like the way you talk to me sometimes, Joey. You take too many liberties."

"Doreen."

"What?"

"Quit the bullshit. Take the dog to the vet."

"I suppose so. God, if I get a minute. I wanted to go up there and relax. Now I've got to worry about the dog."

She smiled down at Peppy, who gladdened his brown eyes and began to wiggle ridiculously.

"You want to go to the vet, little doggems? Do you?"

Peppy went crazy when she talked to him in this porkchop voice, figuring some food must surely follow. He rocked around on three legs at her feet, doing all he could to keep from piddling on the floor with happiness.

"Dance, little doggems. Dance for Mommy."

Peppy did his damnedest.

Doreen smiled as she watched the dog. In that moment, she looked about twenty-one to me. I thought to myself, she's really more like a big sister.

"Going to the doctor is no fun. Is it, baby dog?"

Peppy got all breathy, agreeing with her so hard.

"I got to go," I said.

"Good luck, Honeyboy," she smoothed my hair down in the back.

"I wish every good thing for you, babyboy. If you don't mind, could you go out the back way?"

I decided to ride a little farther south before getting on a train. I figured the cops around there might be looking for me and I was better off on the bike. Besides I had only so much money.

It took me two days to ride down to Greenwich, Connecticut. I looked around till I found a bicycle shop. I had them take the pedals off and turn the handlebars. They gave me a box for the bicycle for free and I went down to the train station and bought a ticket for as far south as fifty dollars would take me and had them put the boxed bicycle in the baggage car.

South of D.C., it got to be a nice quiet ride through the countryside. I have to say I was enjoying myself, watching the country—pretty, pretty country—slide by from right to left, and me just leaning my elbow on the cool metal of the window ledge with my chin propped on my hand. It was like watching some elegant movie except there were no words or music. But fascinating all the same.

I'll never forget that train ride south. At night in my dreams sometimes I still see the dark pastels of that flat country south of Richmond sliding by.

It was the best part of the trip.

My ticket ran out in North Carolina. I got off the train and rolled my bike around the streets of Raleigh till I found a bicycle shop. I got the pedals put back on, and the handlebars straightened, and bought a spare tire.

Nights, I slept in the local cemeteries.

Nobody bothers you there.

Inside of two weeks I was in Florida, walking up a cracked concrete road called Valdesta Drive in some crummy little town in the middle of nowhere. I stopped outside a little square stucco house the color of Pepto-Bismol with the number 2605 on it. Leaning my bike against a sick-looking palm tree, I went up the crumbling walk and knocked on the door. The usual delay followed. Having lived with Doreen and Dale all those years, I knew the drill.

No doubt I was being checked out from behind the blinds of the picture window next to the door. I was ready to be patient. You have to think it through before you open your door to a stranger. I understood that. A couple of yellowed newspapers lay on the soggy welcome mat. Maybe he's away, I thought. Maybe he's moved on.

Finally some white-haired fellow with a fat gut, dressed in a ribbed undershirt and a pair of high-water khakis, opened the door.

"If it's about the paper, I never wanted the fucking thing in the first place."

He had on a pair of no-see-um sunglasses. The black lenses made an interesting contrast to his sore-looking nose. He had a cigar in his mouth and wore his hair in a pompador. It might be white but he had plenty of it.

"Your name McCabe?"

He took the cigar out of his mouth.

"No, he ain't here. He moved out."

"You sure you're not McCabe? Used to live in Revere Beach, Massachusetts, way back?"

It sure as hell didn't look like McCabe. McCabe had jet black hair and was as skinny as I was the last time I'd seen him. This fellow was old and fat and looked like an ex-con. He looked about sixty to me, a lot older than McCabe would be.

"Who wants to know?"

He looked at me suspiciously.

"You got a kid named Joe, he'd be about seventeen now?"

He peeled his sunglasses off, squinting his blue, raw-looking eyes at me. When he peeled off the glasses, I saw the connected black eyebrow, the family trademark.

"Is that you, Joey?"

"Sure, it's me. I've been me all my life."

"Holy mother of God, I can't believe it. How'd you find me?"

"I just found you, that's all."

"Yeh? So you did. How are you?"

"I'm okay."

"Good, good."

He gave my arm a squeeze.

"Jeez, I can't believe this. How'd you get here?"

"I rode my bike. That's it down there by the palm tree."

"You rode your bike all the way from Massachusetts?"

"No, I took the train far as North Carolina."

"You rode your bike from North Carolina?"

It really knocked him out. He couldn't believe anybody would do such a thing.

"Sure," I said. "No big deal."

"How 'bout that? Jeez, that's something. What brings you down this way?"

"Nothing," I shrugged my shoulders. "I never been to Florida before. Thought I'd look it over."

"Oh yeh? That's great."

He bit down on his cigar and grinned at me.

"It's pretty nice," I said. "I like the weather."

"Yeh, it's nice today. Usually it's hot and muggy as hell this time of year."

"How long you been living down here?"

"Me? I been down here about ten years."

"That so? What kind of work you do?"

"Oh, this and that. Hey, I can't believe this. You want to come in for a beer?"

"Sure. I could use a beer."

What I really could have used was a sandwich. I hadn't eaten for a couple of days. My money had run out just about the time I crossed the Florida line.

"Better bring your bike in," said McCabe. "Somebody steals it, you won't have a way home."

I stayed on with McCabe for a while. It's weird to meet some stranger who's supposed to be your father and have nothing in common with him except your eyebrow.

We didn't have much to say to each other. We ran out of conversation pretty fast. He was interested in the dog races and tried talking that with me. But I'd never seen the dogs run, so could do little more than listen and try not to act bored.

"We ought to go over to the track," he said.

He didn't go to work while I was there. He told me he was off that week. He never did tell me what he did for a living. He sat around the house watching anything they showed on TV. "Mr. Ed" was his favorite show. They got the Yankees down there, and he watched the ballgames too. He went out for beer and the papers and a few groceries, but otherwise he stayed in

the house. He lived like a spider under a rock. Which explained
his prison pallor. He said he got the sunburn on his nose out
fishing on one of the bridges.

"We ought to go fishing," he said.

In the mornings we soaked bread in our coffee and ate that
for breakfast.

One night he took me to a real Mexican joint where he knew
most of the people at the bar. We drank tequila that night. He
introduced me to tacos and Carta Blanca beer.

But mostly we ate at the local drive-in. He told me he loved
their cheeseburgers.

"Too bad they don't serve beer," he said.

If it had, he'd have given it four stars.

"How's your mother?" he asked me once.

"She's okay."

"She was some looker. Is she still a looker?"

"I guess so."

"She ever get married?"

"Yes, she married some guy."

"That's nice. She never liked being alone. Boy, she was some
looker when I knew her."

He smiled, shaking his head at the memory of Doreen, enjoying the sensation of loss and pleasure it gave him.

"I could really pick them in those days."

He guarded the facts of his life, past and present. He was like
a dog with a bone. What he didn't volunteer, you weren't
supposed to ask. He wasn't interested in learning what I'd been
up to. Maybe that was part of the trade: if you didn't ask him
questions, he wouldn't ask you any. He did, however, tell me
who was behind the lunchroom sit-ins.

"Communists," he said. "They pay those niggers to do that
stuff. Those nigger preachers are all Communists."

I listened to him babble. He had a habit of laying his head back in his chair and drinking off a full can of beer. He added the empty can to the pyramid he constructed daily by the side of his chair. When he placed a can on the pyramid without knocking it over, he looked so satisfied, as if he'd done something special. Since he'd switched from bottles to cans he couldn't paste labels on a lampshade anymore. So I guess he had to find this new way of accounting for his time. Despite the evidence of the connected eyebrow, I'd think: this dumbbell's not my father.

I could have stayed longer. But I was restless. I knew I didn't belong there. It made me uneasy to be around a stranger. And mooching off him at that. Which was funny, because I didn't feel like a bum when I was staying with Henry.

I wandered around town in the bright, hurtful sunlight. McCabe stayed under his rock drinking beer and watching "I Love Lucy," "The Ed Sullivan Show," and the test patterns, I guess, if that was all that was on. I thought about things. I decided I needed to find a town I liked and get a job.

So I left.

"Come back again, kid. Hey, anytime."

His eyes protected by sunglasses, McCabe opened the palms of his hands in a gesture of perpetual welcome.

I told him I'd be back sometime. But I was thinking: no way, José. I'm not coming back here.

I went over to the orange groves and got a couple of weeks' work.

The agent asked me, "You ever pick oranges before?"

I said, "Why? Does it take special talent?"

"A smartass," he said. But he hired me anyway.

When I figured I had enough money, I hopped my bike and got out of there.

It was so hot and miserable in the orange groves, I decided

living underground in the winter didn't sound so bad. So I set out for Quebec again, or at least my mythical version of the city.

On my way north, I swabbed toilets and washed dishes for a Greek who owned a greasy spoon in Harrisburg, Pennsylvania. I cut cord wood in upstate New York for a week. That was the hardest work I ever did, outside of the groves.

I could have gone on to Canada. But I decided to stop by Doreen's, to see how Peppy was doing. I knew Doreen would be all right. Doreen was the kind who hangs on somehow. Till somebody like Dale blows her brains out.

I waited out of sight, till Dale came out and drove away in his car. He was driving an old Cadillac which sounded in need of a muffler. Dale always thought owning a Cadillac would be the cat's ass. Now he had one—the fulfillment of a dream. I wondered if he'd gotten a job, or if he was still fulfilling his dreams by sponging off Doreen. Big man with a Cadillac. Some joke.

I went over, rattled the gate till it surrendered, took the porch steps two at a time. The sunporch was unlocked this time and I went in, picking my way through the junk till I came to the old wringer washer guarding the door.

When I knocked, Doreen opened wide. She was dressed in a blue negligee.

"Joey! What are you doing here!"

She hid herself behind the door. She was so sure who it was going to be, apparently, she'd dispensed with the habit of a lifetime and hadn't checked me out at the window.

"Expecting company?"

"Get out of here. I helped you all I could. Get out of here, before there's trouble. Dale's coming back any second."

"Really?"

I looked down at her feet but saw no sign of Peppy, who

ordinarily carried on like a fool possessed if anybody came to the door.

"Where's Peppy?"

"Get out of here."

She tried to close the door.

"You let him die, didn't you?"

"Let go of the door, Joey."

"You let your goddamn pal die, didn't you?"

"There wasn't anything anybody could do."

"Did you even take him to the vet's?"

"I didn't have the money. It wouldn't have done any good anyway."

"You let him die. So you could dick around in the White Mountains."

Doreen slapped me hard across the face.

"Shut your filthy mouth! I'm your mother! You don't talk to me like that, mister."

I just looked at her. The color drained out of her face. Her eyes grew big and filled with tears.

"Go away," she whispered. "Before you spoil everything."

Eight

In the end I drifted back to Dunnocks Head. Don't ask me why. Henry and I didn't have anything left to say to each other, I was pretty sure. I thought I was on my way to Quebec. But I guess I was just traveling in circles waiting for bad luck to catch up with me.

My idea was to watch the house for a while from the park across the street. If it looked friendly, I'd go over, knock on the door, and see if he was feeling civil enough to offer me a cup of coffee.

If not, I'd just slide out of town and no harm done.

That was the plan, anyway.

Till I saw the cop car in the yard with its red and white lights swirling and the front door flung open, and the same fat cop of a few weeks back standing on the front stoop.

I didn't even think.

I dropped the bike and started running toward the house. He's hurt himself, I thought. The damned old fool's hurt himself. I figured he'd burnt himself up with a cigarette. Or killed himself with booze. Or expired from an overdose of dirty underwear.

I really don't know what I thought. But even as I ran toward the house and the cop slowly, cautiously, rotated his bulk toward me like a gun turret, his body beginning to tense as if saying to himself: oh-oh, who's this lunatic? even then, it came to me there was no ambulance or fire truck around.

But I didn't stop to think.

I thought he was hurt. I knew he was hurt.

"Hold it, boy. Hold it right there."

"What the hell—"

"Just hold it."

"Out of the way," I said. "I got to see him."

This fatso grabbed me by the arm, pinching the skin. Together we waltzed down the granite steps onto the brick walk, where he held me close and looked into my face, breathing hard, and whispered menacingly, "Who are you?"

He was a husky fella, about my height, with a fat milky face and red hair under his cowboy hat. He had on his no-see-um sunglasses reflecting back little funhouse pictures of my face.

"Let go, don't mess me around."

"You got a smart mouth, boy. Over against the car. Move it fast, Smartass."

He balled my shirt at the shoulder, pushing me forward.

"Easy, Jack."

"Shut it, Wiseass. I'll shoot your balls off."

He made me straddle against the hood of his car.

"Lay off, for Christsakes. He's my grandfather."

"You the grandkid, huh? I got a warrant for you, boy."

"Bullshit. I didn't do anything."

I guess my naturally bad temper got the best of me. Nobody in his right mind would hit a cop otherwise, would they?

I didn't even think.

When he snapped a cuff on me, the finality of that metallic

click did something bad to my head. It must have pinched a nerve directly connected to my brain. I lost it for a second, feeling a suffocating dread and panic, like somebody had just shoved my head under water. I guess I hit him automatically.

The next thing I knew, he was on his back in the grass. I was over him. I was breathing again, ready to do anything to keep on breathing. But he was out, resting peacefully, his sunglasses still arranged on his face, his cowboy hat a few feet away. His wiry orange hair looked very bright and fake in the sunlight.

I found the key and shook that goddamn cuff off my wrist. I threw them and his gun as far as I could into the jungle of the backyard. The pistol and the handcuffs sparkled in a high arc over the hip-tall weeds before dipping soundlessly out of sight into one of the ruined flower beds. I could really breathe again with that thing off me.

But I knew I'd just bought a lot of trouble.

When I looked up, Henry was teetering in the open doorway, a black bag dangling from his hand.

"Henry! You all right?"

I was surprised to find him on his feet.

"What the hell have you done to Sam Summers?"

"This guy? He was trying to cuff me for no damn reason. I was trying to . . . I thought you were . . ."

He looked at me wildly, sucking in air between his yellow horse teeth. His wispy hair stood up in a soft white smoky explosion like the roof of his head had just blown off.

"Jesus. Can't you move without making trouble? You hit the wrong man this time. That man's got as bad a temper as you have. Plus he's got a badge. Come on."

He started stiffly down the steps.

"Where we going?"

"You can drive, can't you?"

"Sure."

"Well, I'm not sure I can anymore. Since you just knocked out my chauffeur, looks like you get the job. Besides, this is trouble. This is just what you like."

He bent awkwardly to feel Summers' pulse. He drew back his eyelids and moved his head from side to side.

"Well you didn't kill him anyway. Help me put him on the back seat of his car."

He did help, sort of, but mainly he was useless and just got in my way.

"Why don't we just take this?"

Henry looked at me, showing me some of his horse teeth.

"You really don't know right from wrong, do you, boy? You're in enough trouble without stealing a police car. When he comes to, he'll be madder than hell as it is."

We got Henry's old Dodge out of the barn. After some trouble, I got the thing in reverse and backed it around the idling cop car, its roof light still screaming in Technicolor. I almost hit the gatepost as we lurched into the street.

"I thought you said you could drive."

"I'm not used to this antique. Which way?"

"North."

"Which way is north?"

"Jesus. Don't you know anything? Turn right."

I peeled rubber halfway down the street.

"Where we going?"

"Turn here. We're going out to Judge Fiske's farm. Seems a young boy got kicked in the head by one of the Judge's thoroughbreds."

Shakily Henry lifted a pint bottle to his dry lips. He tucked the mouth of the bottle under his mustache, threw back his head, and took a good glug.

"Touch of the dragon interest you?"

"No thanks. You act nervous."

"I might be a little nervous. Since I haven't treated anything more serious than an ingrown toenail for five years."

"It's like swimming, isn't it? Once you learn you never forget. Isn't that right?"

He laughed, began to cough, and hung out the window gagging till he got control of himself again. We were passing Roaring Beach at that moment. The surf was up, tumbling in great foaming sunshot clouds, flattening out in a crash, sliding rapidly up the dark slick sand to the farthest band of seaweed.

"This isn't the usual housecall," he said when he could talk again.

He grinned, arranging his face into a million wrinkles. His fine hair was whipping all around his head.

"It isn't even the usual emergency."

"Don't worry. You'll do fine."

"No, that's not it. You see, the boy's father is the Judge's stableman. It seems he's gone crazy with grief. He's already shot the horse. Which was worth about fifty thousand dollars, they tell me. But no matter. He's got the Judge's daughter in the stable with him. He's holding her prisoner. The state police are up there. He says he'll kill her if they try to come in. He's asked them for medical help. They sent Sam down to get me. Pull over."

I pulled over.

He opened the door and puked, wretching horribly into the roadside weeds. When he was finished, he looked up. He was wiping his mouth with the ball of his dirty handkerchief and looking at me as if to say: now you know the truth. His eyes were red and watery from puking for so long and so hard.

"Haven't been this sober so late in the day for a long time. It's no damn fun."

He held out his trembling hand.

"Look at me. I'm like a damned baby."

"You'll be all right. Take another pull on that whiskey."

I didn't have to coax him. He took two or three good swallows, his adam's apple bobbing in his scraggly throat.

"You ready now?"

"I'm ready."

We drove on. When we came to the beginning of the white board fence on the left side of the road, he had to stop again.

"Don't worry," I said. "I'll be with you."

"I'm not afraid of him," he said, wiping his mouth. "Not afraid of some crazy stableman with a gun. I just don't know what I can do for a hurt boy with these hands."

"I'll help you. Hell, you tell me what to do. I'll do it."

He looked at me funny.

"You're not afraid, are you?"

I must have looked puzzled.

"No, you're not afraid. Of anything. You're too damned young and stupid to be afraid."

"I doubt this fella will bother us much," I said. "How old's the girl?"

"Kathleen? Jesus, I delivered Kathleen, back in the ancient mists of time. When I was a respectable practitioner of the art and science of medicine. She must be twenty, twenty-one years old by now. She goes to school in Boston. If she lives through this, she'll have some story to tell her friends. Turn here."

We went up the long driveway between the white board fences. The big house sat on the crest of the hill facing the ocean view. The drive separated at the top of the hill. We turned left toward the stables, dipping over the ridge into a semicircle of state police cars. An ambulance was there too with its back door flung open and they had the litter down on the ground, its pillow and crisp sheets very white in the sunlight, and the two attendants dressed in white were sitting on it, back to back like a pair of bookends, smoking cigarettes.

A lean white-haired man with a big nose darted at us, jerking open the door on Henry's side.

"Henry! For Godsakes, man! What took you so long?"

"I got here as fast as I could. Turn the car off, son."

Right away, I could tell Henry didn't like the man.

As I got out, a big state cop with a big gray jaw creaked up in his boots.

"This the doctor?" he asked the Judge solemnly.

He narrowed his eyes at us. He was wearing one of those Dudley Do-Right hats favored by the state police.

"Yes, it is. Let this man through, please."

Henry pointed to me.

"This is my grandson. He's going in with me."

The Judge looked up in surprise.

"All right. If that's what you want. Just get in there before he does something to Kathleen."

The big cop steadied a bullhorn against the roof of his car. Cops were all over the place. One lay on the roof of the wellhouse cradling a shotgun, his legs arranged as if riding an invisible unicycle. Another crouched behind the big welted tire of a tractor. Others knelt at the trunk lids of their cars as if in prayer. Between some cypresses on the hill behind the stable I saw a pair scuttling like crabs, trying to work themselves into position to cover the back.

"Mr. Michaelsmith," said the big cop into the bullhorn.

His voice, enlarged and hollow, sounded almost bored.

"Mr. Michaelsmith. We have the doctor you wanted for your son. We're sending him and his helper in now."

Two other cops were lightly touching our chests with gray-gloved hands. I took the bag from Henry.

"Let me carry that for you. It'll make me look more official."

He looked at me out of the sides of his pale eyes.

"It hurts my damned hand to carry that bag anymore."

Henry smoothed down his hair and straightened his shoulders.

"Mr. Michaelsmith? Do you hear me, sir? We're sending in the doctor and his helper, Mr. Michaelsmith."

At a signal from the sergeant, the cops tapped us encouragingly on our respective shoulders and we started forward toward the stable doors. We had about two hundred yards to cover.

"Take my arm," Henry said to me under his breath. "Don't let them see me stagger. My goddamn legs don't work right anymore."

Fifty feet from the stable, the door banged open and the barrel of a rifle glinted in the sunlight.

"Stop right there," a voice said. I heard a girl cry out. A little wrestling match seemed to be going on just out of sight, behind the door.

"I just want the doctor," the voice said. "Tell the other one to go back before I shoot him."

"You better go back," said Henry.

"Bullshit. You won't get ten feet before you fall on your face."

He wrenched his arm free.

"Get the hell out of here, you fool! You want to get shot?"

I grabbed his arm again.

"We're going in together. You tell him why."

He stared at me in outrage for a moment, his eyes wide and pale.

"Get the hell out of here. I can handle this. I don't want your damned help."

"You got it. Whether you want it or not."

When he saw it was useless to argue, he turned his face toward the stable.

"Mr. Michaelsmith."

Mr. Michaelsmith's rifle looked attentive.

"Mr. Michaelsmith . . . I'm an old man. I've got arthritis in my hands and feet and knees. In other words, I don't move so damned well any more. My grandson here helps me get around. So you either have to take us both or neither of us."

A silence followed. We watched Mr. Michaelsmith's rifle think it over.

"All right," said the voice behind the door. "But try something. Either of you. I'll kill you both."

We started forward again.

"You're a goddamn fool," he muttered under his breath.

"You're not much better. What's between you and the Judge?"

"Some other time," he said.

When we got inside, I saw the man Michaelsmith had the girl —tall and dark-haired, her ice-blue eyes open very wide—by the arm and the rifle at the back of her neck. She had a man's white shirt on and tan riding britches and boots and a wide leather belt. She had long dark hair and long legs and she was simply beautiful.

"Set that bag down," the man said in a whispery voice. He was a bald-headed, short, husky man with meaty shoulders and the sad, pleasant face of a bank clerk and he looked quiet-crazy, the worst kind.

I set the bag down on the dirt runway.

When I straightened up, the girl was looking right at me. "Nice day."

Mr. Michaelsmith gave the girl's arm a twist as if to say: don't answer him.

"Now open it," he whispered. "Let's see if you're fools enough to try to trick me."

"Kathleen," said Henry. "Are you all right, my dear?"

"I'm all right. What a mess I've gotten you into."

"Shut it," Mr. Michaelsmith twisted the girl's arm. "There's no call to talk, any of you. Just do as I say. Nobody'll get hurt. Step back from that bag, boy."

I did.

The man looked at me for a long time.

I looked back at him steadily.

"You ain't planning to be a hero, are you?"

"No, I don't have any plans."

"Good. Because I'll kill you all, if I have to."

He poked through the junk in Henry's bag with the barrel of his rifle.

When he was satisfied, he said, "This way. You and the boy go first."

He walked us down the hoof-hardened earthen runway. Just beyond the feed bin, a boy in jeans and a Mickey Mouse T-shirt lay on the dirt floor, a sack of grain under his head. I took him to be maybe eight years old. A thin red sauce leaked out of one of his ears. His eyes were swollen shut. A laceration was printed on the side of his head in the shape of a bloody horseshoe. He lay motionless as a snapshot. I thought he might be dead.

Mr. Michaelsmith sat down on an empty dynamite box not far from the boy on the floor, making Kathleen sit down in the dirt directly in front of him.

In the stall behind him, a black horse lay on its side in a sticky lake of dark blood. The other horses in the barn neighed and stamped nervously in their stalls. The smell of the dead horse had them spooked. Its hooves were curved stiffly inward towards its belly as if its soul had fled in full gallop at the instant Mr. Michaelsmith had begun pumping lead.

"All right, Doctor."

The man pressed the muzzle of his rifle against the base of Kathleen's skull.

"Now fix my boy."

Henry knelt awkwardly by the boy, putting a gnarled hand on his forehead. The kid's left eye was swollen almost twice its normal size. It looked like he had a tennis ball instead of an eye behind the lid. His mouth was puffy, his lower lip stained with dried blood. He looked dead to me.

"How you holding up?" I said to the girl.

"I could use a cigarette," she said.

"You don't want a cigarette. They're bad for you."

"You're kidding," she said. "When did that happen?"

Which I thought was a pretty spunky answer, considering a crazy man had her by the hair.

"Shut up," said Mr. Michaelsmith.

His eyes were black and shiny-looking.

"Don't talk to her. I'll kill her if you do."

Henry pressed the boy's lids back from his eyes. Both eyeballs were red as taillights. I'd never seen anything like it.

"Give me the bag."

I handed it to him.

"You need any help?"

"Not yet."

But I saw his hands were trembling.

He opened the boy's shirt and laid the stethoscope on his pale chest, adjusting the plugs in his ears as he did. He cocked his head like a parrot and listened for a long time. We others just watched him.

I hope he's not dead, I thought.

Because if he is, so are we.

Henry felt the boy's forehead. Gingerly he inspected the bloody flap of skin sodded with the boy's hair. The horseshoe shape of that flap was perfect, like it had been stamped out with a die.

Henry sighed, folding his stethoscope.

"Help me up."

He got up heavily, leaning on my arm.

He stood with his shoulders thrown back, facing the man, although his legs were a little wobbly.

"He's still alive. He's got a bad concussion at least. He might have a fracture. But I can't feel it. At least the bone isn't depressed."

"Will he be all right?" whispered Mr. Michaelsmith.

"He's badly hurt, Mr. Michaelsmith. I can't tell how badly. We need to get him to a hospital right away."

"No."

Mr. Michaelsmith shook his head, looking at us gravely.

"I promised his mother I'd have him home by his birthday. He's going to be ten years old on Tuesday."

He looked at us.

"She didn't want him down here. You know women, how they worry. Just for a few weeks, I said. He'll be all right. Boy's got to grow up sometime . . ."

His voice, slow and stupefied, just trailed off.

He looked at the boy on the floor, no particular expression on his face.

"The boy needs medical attention," Henry said quietly.

"More than I can give him in a barn."

"I'm taking him home," said Mr. Michaelsmith dreamily.

He looked at Henry.

"His mother wants him home."

"Where do you live?"

"Live?"

The question seemed to rouse him. Kathleen was bent over on her side in the dirt in front of him. He had her arm twisted so she couldn't very well sit up. He was still holding the rifle to the base of her neck. He studied the back of her head as if amazed it was still perfectly round and in one piece.

"We got a place in the woods north of here."

"You mean up around Jackson?"

"What do you want to know for?"

"Because your boy can't travel far, Mr. Michaelsmith. He needs medical attention."

"You fix him," Mr. Michaelsmith pulled Kathleen to a sitting position by her hair.

"Fix him so I can take him home."

"You don't understand. He may die if he doesn't get help immediately. There's an ambulance outside. We could have your son at the hospital in twenty minutes."

"No, I promised he'd be home for his birthday. Now you fix him. Fix him good. Or I'll shoot this girl. I'll shoot this boy and I'll shoot you too."

Henry sighed and glanced at me. He looked back at Mr. Michaelsmith.

"His brain is swelling in his head. We have to do something to relieve the pressure or he'll die."

"Do it. When he's fixed, I'll take him home."

"I don't have the right tools," said Henry. "It's called trephining. I'll have to drill a hole or two in his head to relieve the pressure. Do you understand what I'm telling you?"

"Yes," said the man. "If you hurt him I'll kill you."

"He's got a better chance if I do it than if I don't. You want me to try it?"

For a minute Mr. Michaelsmith, his bald head glistening, just gazed at Henry with his sad black eyes while the girl, Kathleen, and I exchanged looks. She looked scared but she still had her nerve, I could tell.

"Did you ever have a son?"

"Yes."

"Where is he now?"

"Dead. He's dead. Died in the war."

Mr. Michaelsmith searched his face.

"How do you live after that?"

"I don't know. I'm not sure I did."

"Go ahead," Mr. Michaelsmith said at last. "If it will fix him."

"If I don't do something, he will die. You understand?"

"Do it," said the man.

"I will need a drill. Some bits boiled in water. Clean linen and hot water. Some alcohol. A razor and some shaving cream. I'll have to shave some of his hair. Will you let Joe go outside and ask for these things?"

The man looked at me.

"Don't worry. I won't try anything funny."

"I've got to get Cal home to his mother."

"I know. I'm ready to help you out."

"All right," whispered Mr. Michaelsmith. "Get whatever your grandfather says. But remember. When you're out there. He's still here with me. And so's this girl."

"I won't forget," I said.

Nine

WHEN I reached the circle of police cars two or three people grabbed me all at once, including the Judge.

"Kathleen," he said. "Is she all right?"

"She's fine. She's holding her own just fine."

"Thank God. What's he want? Why did he let you out?"

"Henry needs some things to work on the boy."

"How is the boy?"

"He looks bad to me," I said. "Let's not fool around. I got to get these things and get back in there before—"

Someone hit me and I went down against one of the cars. Above me, the cops surged together and there was a sudden confusion of voices.

I must have blacked out for a second. When I came around, I was holding on to the tire of the police car. As I studied the mud in the tread, I heard the Judge yell, "What in the hell is wrong with you?"

I looked up groggily. The other cops were holding this one back. He was straining to get at me, panting hard and trying to push off the shoulders of his pals. He had his no-see-ums off, which is probably why I didn't recognize him right off. But there was that red hair, close-cropped against his big melon head, gleaming like copper in the summer sunlight.

"That son of a bitch suckerpunched me down in front of Doc's house," he surged against the others. They held him back gently.

"Let go! I'll teach him to hit a cop!"

"Did you hit this man?" the Judge asked me.

"I hit him," I said. "Is there a law against hitting a moron?"

"Let go!" said Summers. "I got a warrant for that bastard's arrest."

The Judge barely flickered a muscle, but the other cops dragged Summers away, taking him over behind the ambulance to calm him down. It was plain the Judge was the big bear in this part of the woods. Even though the troopers had him surrounded Summers stretched his neck around hats and shoulders keeping a hungry eye on me.

"I'll get you, you bastard," he shouted.

The Judge extended his hand.

"Here, son. Can you stand up?"

"I guess so."

I got up, feeling my jaw. My fingers came away with a little blood on them.

"Shit, I'm bleeding."

"Here, let me see," said the Judge. "Looks like you hurt yourself against the car. That's a pretty nasty gash."

"That'll just give Henry something else to do. Keep him out of trouble."

The Judge gave me a brief, sharp-eyed smile. He looked like a man who was shrewdly considering an investment.

"Why did you hit that man?"

"Because he was slowing me down. Just like you're doing

now. I got to get that stuff and get back in there before that
fella decides to shoot Kathleen and Henry. I don't know why
people can't see what comes first sometimes."

He looked at me.

"Yes," he said. "What do you need?"

I told him what Henry told me to get.

"All right," he said.

"Fast," I said.

"All right. Promise me one thing."

"What's that?"

"Promise you'll help Kathleen, if you can. She's the only
child I have. If you're ever a father yourself, you'll know what
that means. She's a wonderful girl with a bright future. Promise
me you'll help her if you get the chance. I'll make it worth your
while."

"What will you do?" I smiled. "Give me one of your Ara-
bian horses?"

He didn't know how to take it.

"I tell you what you can do now. Get those others to keep
that red-headed cop out of my face."

"Yes," he said.

He raised his big nose, studying me out of the sides of his
blue eyes, the same icy blue as Kathleen's, with a movement of
his head that reminded me of a hunting dog trying to pick up
the scent of something strange and foreign in its experience.

"They'll keep Sam away. You can be sure of that."

"Tell them not to try anything fancy either, like rushing the
barn. This Mr. Michaelsmith is crazy with grief. He'll kill your
daughter if these cops try anything."

"Yes, all right. These men won't do anything. You remember
what I told you. Do what you can for Kathleen."

"I'm not running things in there, Judge."

"Yes, I understand that. But do what you can."

It seemed to take forever. Finally the Judge's cook came out the back door of the house carrying clean sheets, a bucket of hot water, the sterilized drill bits wrapped in a piece of sheeting, the drill itself, plus an extension cord and the other stuff packed in a basin.

"What does Henry want with these things anyway?" asked the Judge.

"He says the kid's brain is swelling. He's got to drill some holes in his head to relieve the pressure."

"He's going to do what? I never heard of such a crazy thing."

"Neither did I."

"I don't mean any offense, but it's been a long time since your grandfather has practiced any real medicine."

"That's what he said."

"If Dr. Williams had been in town instead of away on one of his damnable AMA meetings . . ."

"Yes," I said. "I guess you wouldn't have sent for a drunk like Henry, if you had a choice."

"I didn't say that," said the Judge. "I know he's doing everything he can. But a mistake could be fatal for more than just that boy. I hope he knows what he's doing."

"We'll find out pretty soon, won't we?"

But I was nervous too. Henry wasn't my idea of a brain surgeon.

When I got back inside, Mr. Michaelsmith wanted to know why the red-headed cop had hit me.

"He doesn't like me," I said.

"Here let me look at that gash on your jaw," said Henry. "Ouch."

"I see you talking to the Judge," said Mr. Michaelsmith. "Why were you talking so long?"

"He wanted to know how his daughter was."

I looked at Kathleen.

"He was happy to hear you were doing okay."

"I ought to kill you," Mr. Michaelsmith whispered. "You keep breaking my rules."

"I guess you'll live," said Henry. "I can patch you up later. I told you Sam Summers had a temper."

"Yes, you did."

"You'll hear from him again, I'm sure."

"Maybe I'll be ready next time."

"Looks like you've got everything. Let's get this done so Mr. Michaelsmith can get the boy home to his mother."

"Yes," said Mr. Michaelsmith.

We walked back along the runway, Henry and I in front. I had him by the arm, to steady him.

"You're a damn fool," he told me. "To mix it up with Sam Summers."

We got to where Cal lay sedately on the packed dirt, his head propped up on the grain bag.

"Plug in the drill," said Henry. "There's an outlet, right there in that post by the boxstall."

I did what he said.

"Now come over here, son, and spread the things out right here, right above Cal's head."

I set down the bucket of hot water and laid the piece of folded sheeting in the dirt above the boy's head, unwrapped the sterilized drill bits, and placed them and the basin containing the rest of the things on the sheet.

Mr. Michaelsmith sat down again on the dynamite box, with the rifle at Kathleen's back while holding her erect, it seemed, by her hair. She had dark circles under her eyes. But other than that, she really seemed to be holding up pretty well.

"You ever use a hand drill before?" said Henry.

"Couple of times," I said.

But I didn't say, I never used one to do brain surgery before. I didn't think Mr. Michaelsmith would find it funny.

"Mr. Michaelsmith," Henry said. "I got arthritis in my hands, sorry to say. My goddamn fingers hardly work any more. My grandson is going to have to do the drilling. Do you understand?"

Mr. Michaelsmith looked at me.

"If you hurt Cal, I'll kill you, all three."

"I'll do my best not to hurt him."

"I will need Kathleen's help too," said Henry.

"No," said Mr. Michaelsmith. "She stays with me."

"I need her to hold down Cal's arms while I steady his head," Henry explained patiently.

"No," said Mr. Michaelsmith.

"We don't have time to waste, Mr. Michaelsmith. The sooner we start, the sooner you can get the boy home to his mother."

Mr. Michaelsmith released his grip on Kathleen's hair.

Kathleen hesitated.

"Go," he said.

Kathleen crawled across the floor to us.

"I'm going to ask you to hold his arms while we do this, dear," Henry said. "You think you can do that?"

"Yes."

"Good. Maybe you can help me get things ready too."

He looked at me.

"Now son. I want you to drill a nice neat little hole in this boy's head. Not too deep mind you. Just enough to break through the bone. Can you do it?"

"I suppose so."

"Fine. Wait till I turn his head and shave him."

Henry held the loose flap of bloody scalp to the boy's head and turned the head so that the undamaged side faced up.

"You want me to drill a hole in this side? This side isn't even hurt."

"This is the side we drill to relieve the pressure. First we're going to shave the hair off this side of his head. You hold him while I do that. Kathleen, honey, pour some of that hot water into the basin, please."

I watched Kathleen take the stuff out of the basin and pour the hot water. She was pretty steady. She had dirt all over her white blouse and the knees of her riding pants were practically black but she was doing okay, it seemed to me.

"Thanks, dear. Now come around this side again."

Kathleen obeyed him quietly, Mr. Michaelsmith watching her every move from his dynamite box.

Henry plunged his hands in the hot water, playing pattycake with the bar of soap for a while, then dried his stiff, misshapen fingers on a piece of the cotton sheeting.

"Not exactly sterile conditions, but I guess it'll have to do."

He poured some alcohol on his hands, rubbing it in good, then dried his hands again.

"Now you do the same thing, son."

I did what he said.

"Hold his head for me."

I held the kid's warm, sweaty head in my hands, a rigid cage full of ballooning brains. Henry cut the boy's hair close to the scalp with the straight razor. Henry was kneeling in the dirt leaning over the boy. I could hear the old man's tortured breathing and how it stopped altogether at the tricky moments and then how he let it out all at once like a seal coming up for air.

I was so close I could see the individual gray hairs, coarse and springy, growing out of his purplish nose. The blood blister on his lip had turned very black. Everything seemed sharper and clearer to me in that moment, everything somehow magnified in size and sound like never before.

Henry was holding his breath, concentrating so hard he looked crazier than Mr. Michaelsmith. The blood on my fingers was hot and sticky as I held the kid's head while Henry, breathing hard, finished shaving him. I could feel the furry wet flap of skin from the horse kick lying heavily in the palm of my hand.

When Henry finished, the kid had himself half a Mohawk: bald on one side, right down to the dead-white skin with its faint blue network of underlying veins.

"Now son. You ready?"

No I wasn't. But I started anyway. I steadied the whining drill against the kid's unbelievably hard head. The bit twisted the smooth shiny skin beneath it into red shreds and vibrated against the tough gray bone underneath.

"Easy," yelled Henry. He put his hand on mine. I let up on the trigger. We looked at each other. His mustache was trembling. Kathleen was still holding the kid down and had her head turned away so as not to see what we were doing.

"When you feel it break through just slightly, stop drilling."

I nodded. He took his hand away. Kathleen was holding the kid good by the arms. Henry was holding his head down. The kid hadn't moved, except from the vibration caused by the drill. I started again, holding the bit against his skull, ready to stop the second I felt it break through. When the break came and I let off, clear fluid squirted out of the tiny hole about a foot in the air.

I damned near fainted, I was so surprised. A salt sea smell hit me in the face, only more sweetish, more like the smell of oysters on the half shell.

"What have you done to him?"

Mr. Michaelsmith started up from his box.

"It's all right," said Henry. "That little hole relieved the pressure on Cal's brain considerably."

Henry looked at me.

"You aren't going to faint on me, are you?"

"Jesus Christ," I said. "This is nice work you do."

"Drill another," he said. "Two ought to do it. Then we'll bandage him and hope for the best. Kathleen, honey. You got his arms?"

"Yes."

"That's good. You hold him while Joe drills another hole."

Afterwards Henry quickly closed the laceration with catgut from his bag, using a stitch not unlike what you see on the seam of a baseball, and then he finished bandaging Cal's head with strips of the clean bedding which the Judge's cook had provided. Before Henry was finished, I thought I could see some reduction in the swelling in the kid's left eye. He certainly felt cooler.

"Mr. Michaelsmith."

"Yes?"

"I've done all I can for your son."

"Is he better?"

"I don't know. We've relieved some of the pressure on his brain, but it is hard to say how extensive his injuries are. Let us take him to the hospital."

"No," he whispered. "We're going home now. Kathleen. Come here."

Kathleen began to shake.

"Oh God, no. Please."

"I got to keep you with me, Kathleen. They won't let me go home unless I keep you. Then Cal won't get back in time. His mother'll be mad. She'll never let me take him anywhere again."

"Please," said Kathleen.

"I explained it to you. Now get over here. Before I get mad."

"I got a good idea," I said.

"I'll tell you a good idea," he said. "You shut up. Before I kill you."

"No, I got a better idea than that. Take me instead of Kathleen."

"No, no tricks. Kathleen goes with me."

"Look, I can be of help. That girl is just scared. What good is she to you? I'm on my way north anyway. You could give me a ride partway. You'd be doing me a favor."

"Shut up," he said. "I don't like your voice."

He had Kathleen by the hair again. Her eyes were growing big as he tightened his grip.

"I could drive," I said.

"No," he said.

I wasn't getting anywhere with him.

"We can take Kathleen along, if you want. Once we're clear of town we can just let her off somewhere. I'll stay on with you till you get home if you want me to."

"Are you crazy?" Henry whispered.

"No whispering," Michaelsmith said. "Don't you whisper around me."

He looked at me.

"Cops are outside. They want to stop me from taking him home."

"I know. I can get rid of them for you. I can get a car down here, back it right up to the door."

He looked at me some more.

"Are you lying?"

"No, I'm not."

"You going to try something?"

"No."

"All right. Get us out of here. Maybe I'll let her go."

"Come on, Henry," I said.

"Go," said Michaelsmith to Henry. "His mother will take care of him. When I get him home."

Just before we stepped out, he said to us, "Remember. I'll kill her. If you try to trick me."

"I won't trick you."

Kathleen had her head back against Mr. Michaelsmith's fist. She was crying silently.

I looked at her.

"I'll be right back."

She nodded slightly. I could see she was scared but still holding on.

Henry and I stepped out the door into the blinding sunlight.

"You damned fool," Henry muttered as we walked toward the police cars.

Out of the chimney of the Judge's big house, a stream of white smoke was flowing peacefully into the wider river of the blue sky.

"You damned fool. What are you up to now?"

"Nothing, I just made a deal. I figure if I get Michaelsmith and his boy out of here, we can go back to normal."

"If you don't get killed in the process," he said.

"He looks like a man who keeps a deal," I said.

"He's crazy," said Henry. "Can't you see that?"

We reached the semicircle of cars and I leaned Henry against one of the cars before turning to the Judge. Henry looked all used up. I knew he was dying for a drink. But he was too proud to pull that pint bottle out in front of all those people.

"Yes?" said the Judge. "What's going on now? How's Kathleen?"

"She's okay. He wants a car. I think I worked out a deal with him to let Kathleen go."

"You did? That's wonderful. I won't forget this, young man."

"Wait a minute," I said. "Nothing's definite. You got to get these cops out of here."

"Yes, all right."

"No tricks. Get those monkeys off the shed roof. We don't want any accidents. We got a chance of getting out of this without anybody getting hurt."

"Gentlemen," said the Judge, turning to the police. "I need your assistance."

The big state trooper who was supposed to be in charge of things gave the Judge a deadpan look. I saw Sam Summers glowering over the big cop's shoulder, just bulging out of his skin to get at me.

I went over to Henry.

"Come on, Henry. Maybe one of the cops can drive you home."

"Why don't I go along with you?"

"You don't want to do that. You look like you been through a knothole already. Go home and take a hot bath."

"I wouldn't be able to get out of the tub again."

He said it so solemnly that it made us both laugh.

"I'll be home before you know it and cook you some supper."

"Be careful," he said.

"Hell, this man's a maniac," I said. "I've lived with maniacs all my life."

The Judge got the cops to clear out fast. I told him, no roadblocks and no pursuit. And he agreed, he said they wouldn't. I said, if we just leave this fella alone and let him do what he wants, nobody'll get hurt. The Judge allowed I was probably right.

I didn't tell him Mr. Michaelsmith wanted to take Cal home. I didn't trust the Judge far enough to tell him what Mr. Michaelsmith's plans were. I figured he and the cops might cook up something clever if I did and then there was no telling what might happen to people, including me.

Living with Doreen was good training for later life. You learn to tell folks no more than they need to know in order to be helpful. Tell them any more than that, they're liable to get ideas of their own. Then everybody's in trouble. People have room for only one idea at a time, is my opinion.

Ten

"WHICH way?" I said.

"North. Turn north."

We were at the bottom of the Judge's drive. Mr. Michaelsmith was on the floor in the back. He had Kathleen on the floor with him and the boy on the seat with a pillow under his head and he'd made Kathleen put the end of the rifle in her mouth. He told me he'd blow her head off if the cops tried to stop us.

"Left or right?" I said.

"Don't you know which way north is?"

"Not yet," I said. "Left or right?"

"Go left."

We drove along the coast, the surf exploding in white foam against the gray fortress ledges jutting into the sea.

"You see any of them?"

"No, I don't see any. I think they listened real good."

Mr. Michaelsmith eased into view in the rearview mirror, looking over his shoulder out the back.

"Get up, Kathleen. Keep that barrel in your mouth. If your pa's playing tricks on me, I'll blow you right out the door."

I couldn't see Kathleen. I could imagine she was terrified, but she wasn't making any noises like she was. I thought she was an extraordinary girl. In a similar fix Doreen would have been out of her mind.

"When you come to the next road to the left, take it."

"All right," I said. "Gee, this is a nifty car your dad has, Kathleen."

I thought it might help to break the tension for her if I made a little small talk. We were traveling in the Judge's big four-door Cadillac, not really my kind of car, it being kind of mushy to drive really. But I thought, let's lighten it up. Poor girl must be frightened to death.

"Don't talk to her," Mr. Michaelsmith whispered. "How many times do I have to tell you?"

We came to the road and I turned left. Still we hadn't seen any cop cars. We went through a little village that seemed perfectly empty.

"No cops," I said. "See? The Judge is an honest man."

"Keep driving," he said. "And shut it for a while."

No sense making the man mad, I thought. Then he said, "Cal? Cal, you all right?"

I held my breath on that one, afraid that maybe the boy had expired right there on the backseat with Mr. Michaelsmith holding that rifle to Kathleen's mouth. I thought I heard her whimper a little.

"I'm taking you home, Cal," said Mr. Michaelsmith. "It won't be long now. You can tell your mother what happened. When you're better," he said. "You explain. It wasn't my fault you got hurt. Will you do it?"

Naturally the kid didn't say anything. But Mr. Michaelsmith seemed satisfied.

We drove on.

We stayed off the Interstate, traveling through little towns and villages, heading north. We didn't see any cops. Both Mr. Michaelsmith and I kept a keen eye out for them for different reasons. But I had an idea, even though we couldn't see them, the countryside was swarming with them.

After we'd been on the road for about an hour, we came to another little town.

"How about we let Kathleen out here?"

"No, she stays with us."

"We don't need her. She's just going to get in the way if things get tight. Come on, we'll set her down outside the post office."

"You just shut it and keep driving."

"Come on, be fair. I'm willing to help you get Cal home to his mother. I'm all the hostage you need. The Judge is keeping the cops in line. You can let her go."

"She'll tell the cops. They'll try to stop us."

"No, she won't. Will you, Kathleen?"

I didn't hear her answer as she still had a good deal of rifle in her mouth.

"Her father won't turn the cops loose either. He owes me one, Mr. Michaelsmith. In fact, if you let Kathleen go, he'll probably forget all about that racehorse you killed."

"I shouldn't have done that. But I was so mad."

"Anybody would have done it. I would have done it. The Judge would have done it, if it had kicked Kathleen. He'd have probably taken it out and had it hanged."

"I shouldn't have done it," he whispered.

I decided to take a chance. I pulled over in front of the post office. There was nobody around, not a soul. It seemed like a good place to take a chance. If there'd been people maybe he'd have panicked.

"What do you say, Mr. Michaelsmith? Let's let her out here."

"You won't tell?" he asked her.

I heard her say, "No."

"Don't call anyone, Kathleen. Promise me that. Mr. Micha-elsmith here is liable to shoot my ass off, if you do. Will you agree to that?"

"I won't call anyone. I promise."

"Good. Isn't that good, Mr. Michaelsmith? We all got to trust each other so nobody gets hurt."

"I understand," said Kathleen.

Mr. Michaelsmith swung the door open and Kathleen crawled out.

"Tell your father I'm sorry," said Mr. Michaelsmith. "I just got mad is all."

I put the car in gear. I could see her in the rearview mirror. She was looking after us, brushing the hair out of her eyes, her clothes so filthy it looked like she'd been working on a tractor all day.

We drove on without a word for some ways. We were somewhere outside of Augusta on one of the back roads. Then he directed me off into a series of more remote roads and then finally we were on a dirt road, the gravel stoning the underside of the big car with a sound like hail on an iron roof. We drove probably five, maybe six miles before he told me to pull over.

"Why we stopping here?"

"Because we're almost home."

"Really?"

There weren't any houses around. On the left side of the road were the woods. On the right side sprawled some scraggly pasture dotted with little Christmas trees, the edge by the road set off by a single strand of rusty barbwire.

"You can go now," he said. "I don't need you anymore."

"How far have you got to go from here?"

"Two miles from here."

"Why don't I carry the kid? We better hide the car too."

"I said you can go."

"I can go later," I said. "I told you I'd help you get him home to his mother. I'm just keeping my part of the deal."

He looked at me.

"Park it in the road."

He nodded faintly in the direction of the trees. Now that he'd pointed it out, I could just make out a shadowy indentation below the hanging branches. I pulled the car in there and the woods immediately swallowed it up.

I collected the boy off the backseat while Mr. Michaelsmith watched me, holding the rifle slack at his side. I guess he'd started to believe I was being honest with him. We started up the steep trail through the woods.

"You live in here?"

"Yes."

"How do you get out of here in the winter?"

"No cause to get out in the winter," he said as if anybody with any sense ought to understand that. "We got snowshoes if we want to use them."

The boy was light as straw. He was pale looking, ghostly in the eerie underwater shadows cast by the tunnel of trees we were walking through. But so far as I could tell, he was still alive.

We walked about a mile.

"Wait a minute," I said.

I knelt down, letting the lower half of the boy's body rest on the ground, still cradling his head and shoulders on my arm. I didn't want his head touching the hard ground.

Mr. Michaelsmith stood over me.

"It's only a little ways," he said.

"I got to rest a minute," I said.

He looked back over his shoulder, studying the slanting green
tunnel up which we'd just climbed.

"What's that?"

I listened. Somewhere off to the right, a bird twanged like
a broken guitar string.

"I don't hear anything."

"I thought I heard—listen."

We listened.

"I don't hear anything now," he said. "I thought I heard
something."

"I'm ready."

I raised the boy in my arms. We started up the rocky hill
again.

In about fifteen minutes, we broke into a clearing. Over to
the left was a shack, weathered silver-gray, about as long as a
boxcar. In front there was a garden, the corn about four feet
tall and the beans neatly trained to the poles. A wisp of smoke
was coming out of the chimney.

It was like something you see in a movie about the Indian
frontier, as if, when we'd stepped out of the woods, we'd gone
back in time three hundred years and it was very peaceful too
with that long ribbon of blue smoke hanging motionless against
the green haze of the woods behind the house and that neat
garden. I almost understood why Mr. Michaelsmith wanted to
get his boy back here.

"Here we are. His mother's probably watching us out the
window."

Carefully I shifted Cal into his arms. He found it a little
awkward to carry both the boy and the rifle but he was managing.

"Tell the Judge I am sorry about his goddamn horse. But I
would kill it again."

"I'll tell him."

"Goodbye."

He started for the cabin with the boy in his arms. I watched him for a second. Then I started down the hill into the trees.

I was thinking about Mr. Michaelsmith and his wife and kid. When I sank back into those woods I seemed to sink into a green dream. I thought about them moving about the cabin back there in that little fragment of frontier life that somehow still existed on a hilltop in the middle of these woods.

They were moving from room to room, murmuring to each other. I couldn't hear the words they said. They tended to the boy. He was conscious now, lying groggy and quiet in his parents' big featherbed. I could see he was going to be all right.

In this daydream of mine, or wood-dream or whatever you want to call it, the woman's hair was done up in a bun. She was some years younger than he was. Crazy how plain I saw it all, just as if it were real. She had on a long-sleeved print dress. The hem brushed the wide bare floorboards as she walked back and forth doing for her son.

It seemed like it took me no time to get back to the car.

I put my hand on the door to get in and they jumped me, two or three of them.

Sam Summers wasted no time hitting me alongside the head with the butt of his sawed-off shotgun. I went down and he started kicking at me, then he tore the shirt off my back, pulling me to my feet and spinning me around against the fender of the car.

"Spread your legs, Dogshit," he said. "Come on!" he whacked me in the spine with the butt end. I nearly went down.

"Try something. Come on, try something. I'll shoot your balls off."

"Easy, Sam," said one of the cops with him.

"This fucker likes to punch cops," Sam said.

"Easy, Sam. For Christsakes."

Sam felt along both legs then pulled Dale's pistol from under my shirt out of the back of my pants just above the crack in my ass where I'd had it hidden all the time. In fact, I'd even forgotten it was there, it had become so much a part of daily life. Summers held the gun up for the other cops to see.

"See? What'd I tell you? Turn around, Dogshit."

When I turned, he hit me in the mouth with the pistol. My knees buckled. I rapped the fender of the Cadillac pretty good on my way down.

"Get up, you little prick. Get up before I kill you."

He kicked me. I was so groggy I didn't even cover up. Then he kicked me again and I was gone.

I must have come to when he pulled me to my feet.

"Come on, you little prick. We're going back up the hill for your friend."

He cuffed my hands behind my back.

"Why don't you leave him alone? He doesn't want any trouble with you."

"See?" he said to the other cops. "I told you this little prick was in with him."

They dragged me up the hill. I kept falling down and they kept picking me up, dragging me along. I was bleeding pretty much and was dizzier than hell. When we got to the clearing Summers and one of the cops went over behind a big beech tree that stood by itself in the open while the other cop and I waited back in the trees but with a clear view of Mr. Michaelsmith's shack.

They called him by name.

Nothing happened.

They called him again.

Out of the shack's chimney the smoke rose silently straight

up on the mild evening air. Everything looked peaceful.

The door opened. Mr. Michaelsmith stepped out on the porch with the rifle in his hand. With his free hand he made a gesture as if trying to quiet a crowd.

Summers shot him three times, flattening Mr. Michaelsmith against the door. I thought I heard a woman cry out. Mr. Michaelsmith staggered forward, his hand raised palm outward as if still appealing to an unruly crowd. He pitched headfirst into his garden, pulling down some bean poles as he fell.

Eleven

SUMMERS took me back to the jail in the basement of the firehouse and threw me in one of the cells. I was so messed up I hardly knew what was going on.

I woke up naked on a cot under a rough blanket. That bastard must have taken my clothes, but I don't remember. I was in a cold sweat, trembling so bad it seemed like the cot was trying to shake me off, and after a while it succeeded. The damned thing bucked me off. I slid to the floor, my little bag of balls touching the cold concrete first.

That was when I heard it: the sound of a trapped or wounded animal in the cell there with me. But I couldn't see it. By the dim light from the hallway, my eyes rifled the thick shadows of the cell looking for whatever was making that horrible noise.

Slowly it came to me: that horrible sound was coming out of me. My shoulders quaked against the iron rail of the cot. I couldn't breathe. I was damn near ready to choke to death. Slowly the sound and the spasms quieted. I found I could breathe again.

I was tired, I tell you. I laid my head back on that wafer-thin mattress and went right to sleep, my hands between my sprawled thighs, my balls still resting on the cold floor.

How long I was like that, I can't say. Not long, probably. When I woke, I couldn't lift my head off the mattress at first. It felt heavy as a cannonball. Finally I managed to get to my feet, and staggered dizzily across the cell, intent on relieving myself. The toilet was broken but they had a slop bucket.

At first I thought: good Christ, I'm pissing ink. But then I guessed it was blood. Something inside is broken, must be, I thought. But nothing hurt especially and I was grateful for that. I figured whatever it was would heal on its own if I could get some sleep.

I fumbled back to the cot, crashing down on it. Instantly I fell into a black numbing pit, beyond all pain or dreams. How long I slept is anybody's guess.

The next thing I heard was Summers banging his nightstick on the bars.

"All right, you son of a bitch. Get off your ass."

He tossed my clothes in between the bars. When I reached for them I made sure I was out of range of that nightstick.

Summers watched me as I pulled on my pants and buttoned my shirt, grinning as if to say: well now, haven't things switched around since you came back to town.

One side of his smile was flecked with breakfast egg. He watched me quietly, his steely little pig's eyes glinting as he squeezed that billy club between his fingers.

When I was dressed, he unlocked the cell door and opened it.

"Out here in the hall, Dogshit."

"Where we going?"

He had the leather thong of the nightstick looped around his wrist. He tapped the head of the nightstick with a dreamy metronome-like beat into his free hand. He just stood there looking at me, smirking.

"Don't ask a bunch of questions, Dogshit. Just do as I tell you. Now get out here."

"I'm not moving till I know where we're going."

He thrashed the bars with the club.

"You ain't the doctor's kid in here! You're my prisoner! Now get over here like I say."

"Tell me where we're going."

Summers started in through the door.

"You're getting stubborn again. You know what happens when you get stubborn."

I backed away.

But I told him. I said, "You better not hit me with that stick."

He stopped in his fat tracks as if he knew there was more.

"If you use it, you better finish me. Because if you don't, I swear to Christ I'll kill you."

Summers hesitated, looking at me, searching my face to see how much he had to worry about. You could almost see him thinking: can this kid really get me? Don't I really hold all the cards?

Well, I guess he did hold all the cards. But it didn't matter, did it? Lots of times it doesn't matter. Because I meant what I said. And if I lived through another beating I knew one way or the other some day I'd catch up with him and when I did I'd kill him.

"You threatening me, is that it?" said Summers. "You never learn, do you, boy?"

He came at me slowly, watching my eyes. I backed up, looking for something to hit him with. The only thing in reach was the slop bucket. I kicked the cot into the middle of the floor between him and me and cocked the bucket.

"Put that down," he said.

"Like hell I will."

"You don't give me much choice," he said, slowly starting his meaty hand for his holster. I thought to myself, well it's over. You had a short career, didn't you? I figured to hit him right in his fat face with the bucket, follow up with a kick in the balls, and ad lib the rest. I was damned if I was going to let him beat up on me again. I'd rather have him shoot me.

"Hold it there, Sam."

It was Judge Fiske and Henry was just behind him.

"Joe," said Henry. "What the hell did he do to you?"

"Put down that bucket, son," said the Judge. "Sam, get out of that cell."

"Look at him," said Henry. "What the hell did you beat him for, Sam?"

"He was resisting arrest. Ask the troopers if you don't believe me."

"You didn't have to arrest him, did you?"

"He had a gun on him," said Summers. "I got a damn warrant for his arrest. Sure, I had to 'rest him. It don't matter what he did yesterday. I still got a warrant on him."

"How did this happen?" Henry turned to the Judge. "Don't you own the police force in this town? As well as the fire department, the water company, and every other damned thing? Can't you control your own gorillas?"

"Go upstairs, Sam," said the Judge. "Wait for us. Mr. Preble has some papers for you to look over in connection with this boy."

"You're going to get him out," said Summers bitterly, squinting at the Judge. "It don't seem to mind if some people break the law, does it?"

"Sam."

Summers ducked his head and pushed past Henry. Then it was just the three of us.

"Sit down," said Henry. "Let me look at you. Good Christ, what'd he do to you?"

"How's Kathleen?" I asked the Judge.

"She's fine," the Judge smiled. "She's a little shaken. But she's going to be all right. We're very grateful to you."

Henry got the towel over by the sink, dampened it, and began to swab my face and throat. The dried blood on my chin and throat came off on the towel thick and black like tree bark. My mouth was a bloody balloon. I could feel one tooth was knocked crooked. I could wiggle it with my tongue. I was blowing bubbles strawberried with blood out my nose. It was hard to breathe. I was doing most of it through my mouth, figuring very likely that my nose was busted.

"You look a mess, son," said Henry, wiping my face with the damp towel. It felt cool and good, although it hurt some too. Suddenly I was beginning to feel awful sleepy. My head was starting to droop to one side as if it had a sash weight tucked in it. I was trying to hold it up but I couldn't do it.

"Were you carrying a gun, as Summers claims?" asked the Judge.

"Yes," I said.

"That damned pistol again," said Henry.

"Where'd you get it?"

"I took it off Dale."

"He means his stepfather," explained Henry.

"Not my stepfather. That skunk is nothing to me."

"Why did you take it?"

"Because he offered to kill my mother with it, is why."

"Yes," said the Judge with that absentminded air of his.

"You didn't tell me that," said Henry.

He looked painfully embarrassed.

"You didn't give me time."

"No, I guess I didn't, did I?"

"Did Sam beat you?" asked the Judge.

I thought it was a dumb question.

"What's it look like?"

"Answer me. Did he beat you?"

"Yes."

"Were you resisting arrest?"

"It happened too quick for me to resist anything."

The Judge sighed and shook his head.

"Sam Summers gets carried away sometimes. Hot-headed. But a good man, basically. We'll have you out of here in a few minutes."

"He's a goddamn cowboy. He shot Mr. Michaelsmith. He didn't have to do that."

"Sam Summers is a sadistic son of a bitch," said Henry. "And you damn well know it."

"The others say Mr. Michaelsmith fired first."

"That's a lie. Summers shot him cold."

"There'll be a police report. If there's anything irregular in it, I'm sure the district attorney will look into it."

"Sure he will," said Henry.

Henry looked into the slop bucket.

"You're bleeding inside. We got to get you to a hospital."

"I just need some sleep," I said.

"Judge, will you tell them upstairs that we'll need the ambulance."

"Surely. We'll talk later, young man."

He nodded and went out.

"I'm not going to any hospital," I said.

"You're going to shut up and do as I say," said Henry.

"I just need a little sleep. Let me get in my own bed and sleep it off."

"Just rest," said Henry. "That damn son of a bitch kicked you silly, didn't he?"

I didn't feel much like talking about it. I ached all over and was beginning to fade fast.

They got the litter down there in a hurry. Everybody in town jumped when the Judge barked. I thought it must be nice to have people listen to you like that, whether what you said made any damn sense or not.

Two fellows laid me gently on the litter, covering me up with a gray wool blanket. Few times have I felt such sweet relief in my life as that moment when they laid me on the litter. Nor so near death either.

"Tell them to take me home, Henry. I'm not up for any hospital."

"Hush, I'm in charge now. Careful, boys."

"It's my damn life," I said.

But he wasn't listening anymore, he was too busy directing traffic.

They got me out of that cell and somehow navigated me up those narrow stairs. But I was pretty well gone before we got to the top.

The next thing I remember was they were putting me in the bed at the hospital in Bath.

"Hello," said the pretty nurse. Thick curly black hair stuck out around the edges of her white cap.

We were alone together in the silent, dimly lighted room. For some reason, as she felt for my pulse, smiling down at me, I came close to blubbering. I would have stuck my fingers in my mouth if I could have gotten my arm up that high. I felt the tears in my eyes as she smiled down at me, sweet and pretty.

And then she blurred till I blinked my eyes. I don't know what happened. I was suddenly so damn grateful to her for taking care of me.

A doctor with thick glasses and a gray crewcut came in. He asked me in a deep voice how I was feeling.

"I'm feeling totally shitty and worse by the minute. Where's Henry? How come he's not taking care of me?"

The doctor smiled and probed my abdomen.

"Cut that out. That hurts like fire."

He turned, conferring quietly with the nurse. The doctor left, assuring me that he'd be back soon. The nurse helped me undress and slid the soft warm bag of the nightshirt over my head. She gave me a shot of some kind and hooked me up to a glucose bottle. Then she lowered the shades. I could hear the starched whisper of her uniform as she moved quietly around the room. Before she was out the door I was asleep.

What time it was when I waked, I couldn't say. It felt like the deepest part of the night. The nurse was there in a chair by the foot of my bed reading a paperback. A little high-intensity lamp sat on the metal table next to her.

Where's Henry? I asked.

But as she didn't look up, I guess I hadn't managed to say it aloud.

But he was there when I woke up next morning.

"Well now, you look some better today."

I have an idea I smiled. Then I was gone again.

When I waked again, the white ceiling, soft and fuzzy as an angora sweater, was miles away. The bottle of glucose loomed over me like a threat. I wanted to get out of that place, go home, crawl off into the woods, anything but lie there hooked up to that rubber snake.

I listened for noises from the corridor. Everything was quiet.

I pulled the needle out of my arm. The sting of its sudden withdrawal marked a hot line from my wrist to my elbow, but I felt better right away. After that I rested, listening again for sounds from the hallway.

After a while I swung my legs out of bed. My feet went leaden with a sudden rush of blood. I lay back, my eyes shut, waiting for the dizziness to pass, breathing hard against my pillow. It seemed to breathe back warm. When my head cleared I stood up, waiting for the room to steady and my legs to stop wobbling like a baby's.

Then I pushed off into the wide ocean of the room. I reached a chair and held on. The damned thing seemed to tap dance under my hands, but gradually it quieted. I groped for the wall and made it. For a minute I laid my head against the cool plaster. When I'd rested, I made for the bathroom.

I hung on to the sink, peering into the mirror curious to see what I looked like. They'd wrapped my head in a turban of gauze. My ears were tucked under the bandages, my eyes were just two burnt-out dark smudges, my lips bruised and purple. My whole face was bright as a watch dial with sweat. I needed a shave. It looked like somebody had caught me full in the face with a shotgun full of pepper. My mouth was hanging open, my lips caked white around the edges as if I'd been frothing at the mouth. I looked like a damned idiot. Aren't you some damn sight, I thought.

My elbows started to wobble. I lowered myself to the floor. Cold sweat crawled across my belly. My nightshirt was soaked under the arms and across my back. So was the crown of my head under my bandages. I decided the best thing to do was to hold on to the commode and rest a while before my next move.

"Mr. Bigler! What have you done to yourself!"

The nurse's high-pitched voice forked deep into my head,

making my elbows twitch spastically, waking me violently as I lay peacefully asleep, my cheek cool against the smooth tile floor.

They gathered me up, laying me gently back into the sun-warmed sheets of my bed.

"Don't hook me up to that thing again," I said.

"The doctor says . . ."

"Don't do it. I'll pull it out again. I don't want that thing in my arm."

"You're a stubborn young man," she told me.

But that seemed to settle it.

A couple of days passed. I don't know how many. They were giving me some kind of pills that knocked me silly. Mainly I slept, interrupted by mealtimes and visits to X ray. They liked to wake me up to take my temperature. A little roly-poly nurse took care of me in the daytime and then the tall, handsome nurse with the dark hair at nighttime.

Often when I waked Henry would be there.

"How you feeling, son?"

Another time I woke to find Kathleen by my bed, holding my hand and smoking a cigarette.

"You shouldn't smoke. It's bad for you."

She kissed me on the cheek.

"You've been away on a long trip. How do you feel?"

Fine, I said. But the word was blown out like a match and I was gone again before it ever had a chance to flame on the air.

The first meal I really remember having in the hospital, the nurse and I had quite a time agreeing on just what it was they were trying to feed me.

"What's this? Fried sawdust?"

"It's a balanced meal. Now you eat it up like a good boy."

"Who balanced it? A seal? I'll eat the sawdust and the brownie too, if that's what it is. But I draw the line there."

I told her she could give the peas and carrots and the applesauce back to the seal. That stuff looked as appetizing as baby food. The fat nurse told me I wouldn't get well if I didn't eat my vegetables. I told her that was a lie, and she laughed.

After lunch, she obliged me to get out of bed and put on the slippers and robe which I was made to understand the Judge had bought for me and she took me for a little stroll down the hall. I was still light-headed, afraid I'd take her down with me, but she was stronger than I thought, keeping her arm firmly around my waist and her burly shoulder in my armpit.

On cue, I peed daily into a little beaker. There was hardly any blood in the urine anymore.

The fat nurse gave me a sponge bath each day. She asked me a lot of motherly questions most of which I ignored. I didn't want anybody knowing my business. She talked in a loud voice as if I were deaf or simple-minded. She was one of those people who laugh a lot, I noticed, although I don't remember saying anything that was particularly funny. But she was an okay lady.

One morning a skinny little guy with spectacles and dressed in a tight dark suit came into the room.

"Mr. Bigler?"

"Wrong," I said.

He looked puzzled.

"They told me at the nurses' station I'd find the young man in this room who was involved in the Michaelsmith shooting last week."

"That's me. Only my name's McCabe."

He looked at a piece of paper he was holding.

"Why have they got you down as Bigler?"

"A mistake. That's my mother's husband's name."

"Oh."

He looked around the room and then sat down on the chair by the bed. He smiled.

"Mind if I sit down?"

"What do you want?"

"I won't stay long."

"Who are you?"

"I'm Gorman—district attorney? What can you tell me about the shooting last week, Mr. McCabe?"

"Nothing," I said. "Goodbye."

He stood up and pushed his spectacles back on his nose. Spectacles was the only word for the kind of glasses this little dink was wearing.

"I have a few questions. Would you like to answer them now or later?"

"You got a piece of paper that says I have to talk to you?"

"No," he said.

"Then get out."

Because I wasn't telling anybody anything till I knew what was going on.

"I have a police report on my desk," he said. "Everything looks in order. One cop swearing what the other cop did. Only I wonder. I wonder whether that man really had to die. Or whether an overzealous cop shot him. You care to tell me?"

"Unless you got the paper on me, you better get out. I don't even know you, mister."

"Well, I'll get 'a paper,' Mr. McCabe. We'll have a hearing. You can tell a judge what you saw."

He nodded curtly, turned his back, and walked out. Who the hell was that? I thought. The fact that he'd called himself the D.A. only told me he was out for trouble. I wasn't telling him or anybody else anything till I knew what was going on. What's going on, I wondered. What's really going on? I didn't like lying there, not knowing what was up.

That afternoon, the Judge came to see me. He patted me on the hand.

"How are you feeling?"

"I'm okay."

I wasn't telling him anything either.

"Good, good. That's good to hear. They're taking good care of you?"

"Sure."

"That's good. Come out to the farm when you're feeling better. We'll have a talk."

I wondered what he was up to.

"I heard you had a visitor this morning."

"That's right."

"What did our district attorney have to say for himself?"

"He wanted to know what happened."

"And what did you tell him?"

"Nothing. Why should I tell him anything? I don't even know him."

"You're a smart boy. You're very clever. Most young men wouldn't have your presence of mind. I'm doing what I can to keep this incident out of the papers and this fool and his Republican friends are doing what they can to get it in. It would be nice, wouldn't it, if our elected officials spent their time going after criminals instead of using their office for political ends?"

"I guess so," I said.

"What did he say when you wouldn't answer his questions?"

"He said he'd get me in front of a judge."

"That's ridiculous. I've seen the police report myself. It's in perfectly good order. There's no reason for a hearing."

"That's what he said."

The Judge laughed appreciatively.

"That son of a bitch," he wagged his big nose at me, smiling. "We'll deal with him. I'd better let you rest. Now remember. When you're feeling better. I want you to come out to the farm. Both Kathleen and I want to thank you. Will you do it?"

"Sure."

"Good, good," he said, patting my hand again.

I didn't like any of this. I wanted to know what was going on. I lay there, very uneasy, thinking about it.

A few minutes later, Henry came in.

"Hello, young man. You feel well enough to go home?"

"I was always feeling well enough to go home. You got me into this. Lucky you came in when you did. I was getting ready to walk out."

He looked at me.

"I bet you would."

"You're damned right I would. I've had enough of this place."

"Well, get on your clothes. At least I can give you a ride home."

"Good," I said. "Get me out of here."

Twelve

THE next couple of weeks I didn't do much but rest up. Henry did his best to take care of me, even took up cooking again. And he didn't do too bad. He tried his hand at bacon and eggs. His eggs were hard and his bacon too greasy, but it wasn't a bad try for a fellow sadly out of practice.

He fixed me up on the sofa in the library, his favorite room. After breakfast, he'd come in and we'd chat or he'd read and, content to think my thoughts, I would stare at the ceiling or look around at the books and pictures on the wall.

Now that I was out of the hospital, I wasn't particularly restless anymore. But I sure seemed to need a lot of sleep.

I was more or less okay by that time. My balloon lips had deflated. My loose teeth rooted more tightly in my gums with each day that passed. The bruise at the corner of my mouth turned from purple to a faded brown and yellow. And no blood showed in my urine anymore.

But when I stood up, I was dizzy more like than not. And I tired easily. Very easily.

Henry was going through a convalescence too. Although he

still was smoking and hacking as much as ever, I didn't see him take too many drinks, maybe one or two before dinner. He was steadier on his legs. He was plainly more alert than he'd been when he was clobbering the sauce.

I got him in the habit of fixing something for himself whenever he prepared a meal for me. I told him he'd have to, otherwise I wouldn't eat.

"I'm not hungry," he said the first morning after my return from the hospital. "I'll just sit here and have a smoke while you eat your breakfast."

"Fine. Take this mess and throw it in the jungle out back."

"Don't act like a sap. I'll get something later. I promise. Now eat your breakfast."

"Get a plate and we'll split it."

"What the hell is wrong with you? Can't you ever leave a thing alone?"

"Get a plate."

He stared at me, his eyes large and fierce like an old eagle's.

"Don't give me that phony stare. You're not scaring anybody. Now go get a plate. Look at you. You're all skin and bone. How the hell you going to take care of me if you don't take care of yourself?"

He began to cackle, shaking his head at me as if he couldn't believe what was happening. The cigarette smoke twined in twin ribbons through the slots between his knobby yellow fingers.

"You are the damnedest kid I ever met. I used to think your mother was stubborn."

I wasn't going to argue with him.

He stubbed his cigarette in the ashtray.

"All right. You win. I'll get a plate. You know, I wouldn't do this if you weren't sick. Remember that. You couldn't get

me to do a damned thing I didn't want to do, if you weren't
sick."

"I know. I expect nobody ever got you to do anything you
didn't want to do."

He wheezed a little at that one, giving me one of his famous
wrinkly smiles.

"You're damned right about that."

So by holding out against him, using my own inherited
mulishness against the impenitent fountainhead and source of all
my own gift for stubbornness and Doreen's too, I finally got
Henry to take modicum care of himself for a change. He needed
more nursing than I did, was my opinion.

I said to him once when he handed me my lunch tray, "Why
do you sleep in your clothes at night?"

He seemed surprised by the question.

"It saves me time in the mornings. I don't have to waste all
that time getting dressed."

"That isn't healthy," I said. "It's not even sanitary. I get tired
of you smelling bad."

He didn't say anything, just looked a little sheepish. But I
noticed after that he managed to look a little neater in the
mornings. He owned six black suits, all of them exactly alike,
so it was hard to tell whether he changed his clothes or not. But
he'd commenced shaving every day again, that I could see, and
I heard him running water in the tub up there so I guess he was
taking a bath once in a while.

These days he didn't just drag around the house. He put on
his tie and vest and fixed his watch chain with the Phi Beta
Kappa key in his buttonhole. He tried to tame his hair. I could
see that he was combing his mustache regularly and trimming
it neatly free of its persistent residue of tobacco and coffee stains.
He no longer treated the outdoors as a foreign country for

which he lacked the appropriate visa. He left the house on errands as naturally as you and I, mainly shopping for groceries —real food instead of the junk he used to live on.

If I'd had to, I could have done more for myself than I did. But I figured it was just as well for Henry to have somebody to take care of. It seemed to do him considerable good to have me to worry about.

Although Henry was now eating more or less regularly, he was still the skinniest person I've ever seen outside of pictures of Mahatma Ghandi. You could have balled up the extra material in the seat of his pants and had enough left over to make a hat.

It always fascinated me to watch him walk. He reminded me of a big black crane, his legs moving like scissor blades, precise, almost prissy, as he clipped off his slow, measured steps around the house.

His neck, stamped with a diamond-shaped pattern of wrinkles, was so skinny I wondered how it could hold up his head. He worried me he was so skinny. Yet he held himself very erect, his shoulders back. He was a fine-looking old man when he got all dressed up to go after the groceries.

Late in the afternoons, he'd get tired. I'd know he was tired because he'd begin to stoop at the waist a little and his shoulder blades would stick out through the back of his black suit coat. He'd sit down in his old leather chair opposite me on the sofa and, handing me my drink, he'd sigh a great sigh of relief, tinkling the ice in his glass of whiskey and water.

"Ah," he'd sigh. "Drinkie time for the old doctor."

We'd have a couple of quiet drinks together. The late afternoon sun poured in the windows. On the wall the bindings of the books glowed in the mellow light, the sun picking out the ones with the gold lettering for special attention. The tables, the

Tiffany floor lamp by the couch, the armchairs, were all brushed
with gold. I remember that room perfectly, how it looked in
the late afternoon light, and how good I felt being there. The
conversation and the whiskey always revived Henry sufficiently
so that he'd get up after a spell and make us supper.

And then, after we'd eaten, we had the long night ahead of
us. We sat together in the study. Henry would fall down the
well of one of his books and disappear from sight for the
evening. It was quiet in the room, very peaceful. I wasn't much
of a reader in those days. I was content to sit there and think
my thoughts. If it was chill enough for us to have a little fire
in the grate, I watched it till I dozed off. Occasionally I would
pick up a book myself just to make Henry feel good. A page
or two was as good as a sleeping pill. I dreamed against the
printed page much as a derelict might sleep against a fence. We
hardly ever spoke to each other, but I remember those evenings
as the best and most peaceful of my life.

One day the Judge came to see me.

I heard them talking at the front door.

"Hello, Henry. May I come in?"

"What do you want especially? Have you decided to buy the
street and want to look over the property, is that it?"

I heard the Judge guffaw humorlessly.

"I'd like to see your grandson. I won't stay long. I'd like to
thank him for what he did."

"Wait here. I'll ask him if he feels up to a visit."

Henry came in, flushed and irritated, and saw I'd overheard
what had gone on between them at the door. I nodded it was
okay. Without a word he went out into the hall again and
brought the Judge in.

"Well, well," he began heartily, surveying the room, the
books and pictures. From his place on the floor beside the couch

Cat growled, soft and tentative, and I told him to be still. "Yes, well," said the Judge, beaming at me. "How is your patient doing, Doctor?"

"Fine. Tame as a denutted fox these days."

The Judge laughed, this time genuinely.

"I want you to know I've taken care of the hospital bill, so you don't have that to worry about."

"There was no need to do that."

"It was the least I could do for this young man. No reporters have been hanging around, have they?"

"No. That's right. You own the paper and the radio station. So you fixed that too, did you?"

"You can understand," said the Judge. "I don't want every nut for miles around teeming about the farm, looking for ways to get their picture in the papers. Poor Kathleen's had a bad enough time."

"Yes," said Henry. "I can understand that. I suppose the reporters and the state police and everybody have been very sympathetic."

"There are advantages to living in the country," said the Judge. "News doesn't spread so fast out here. If you have friends in the right places, the news doesn't spread at all. Besides in a few weeks we'll have some of Jack Kennedy's people out at the farm for a strategy session. It wouldn't do to have the farm splashed all over the papers and on radio and TV just before such a visit. Would it?"

"Certainly not," said Henry. "You going to deliver Maine. Is that it?"

The Judge laughed again.

"I'm going to do my damnedest. He'll make a great president, one we can be proud of. The first from New England in a long time."

"Yes," said Henry. "No doubt."

"You mind if I have a few minutes alone with the boy?"

"Of course not. This is the morning when I usually rearrange my sock drawer anyway."

"You don't have to leave, Henry," I said from the couch. "Anything the Judge has to say to me, he can say in front of you."

I tried to make it sound pleasant, but I was damned if the Judge or anybody was going to come into Henry's house and begin ordering him around. I hate that big deal stuff.

"That's all right, son. I want to get a little fresh air anyway. Come on, Cat."

After Henry and the dog went out, the Judge sat down in the old leather chair opposite the couch.

"Your grandfather doesn't like me."

"No, he doesn't."

"Our families have had differences in the past," the Judge explained. "Unfortunate occurrences."

"Is that so?"

"I hold nothing against your grandfather."

"That's good. He's a good guy."

"I'm sure he is. What's past is past."

"Yes," I agreed.

"And what's now is now," he said.

"No doubt."

"I hold to a very simple philosophy. I believe in rewarding my friends and punishing my enemies. You'd be surprised how far a man can go in politics and business with a simple idea like that."

"I don't know much about it," I said. "But I guess you're right."

"I'm right. Take my word. Now you've done me a favor. A big favor. Not one I'm likely to forget. Nothing's more precious to me than Kathleen."

"She seems like a nice girl."

"She likes you," he smiled.

"Well, that's nice," I said.

The Judge laughed again, this time faintly, raising his big nose as if trying to catch my scent on the wind again. He studied me out of the sides of his eyes. He had big powerful-looking hands and wore a fancy wristwatch.

"How are you feeling?"

"Lots better. I'm just faking it now, getting Henry to wait on me."

"As soon as you're ready, I hope you'll come out to the farm and visit us. Bring your swimsuit. We'll make a day of it. Will you come out?"

"You got a swimming pool out there?"

"Yes. Kathleen loves to swim. Do you like to swim?"

"Not much."

"But you will come out to see us, won't you?"

"Surely, thanks very much. How's Kathleen?"

"She's still shaken by her bad experience. She's not sleeping well, I'm afraid. She won't go near the stables. She knows it's unreasonable, but she's just scared to death of the place."

"That's too bad."

"Kathleen is a strong girl," said the Judge. "Given time. . . . She said she's planning to come to see you tomorrow, if it's convenient. She wanted me to ask if she could bring you anything. Books or . . . fruit, or something?"

"That's nice but I can't think of anything. I'll be happy to see her."

"I will tell her. Now I have a question of my own for you."

"What's that?"

"I want to show my appreciation for what you did for Kathleen."

"I don't want any reward, Judge."

"I understand that. But I would like to do something for you. God knows what would have happened to Kathleen without your help."

"I don't need a damned thing, thanks."

The Judge studied me kindly for a minute. His eyes were pink-rimmed and very blue. His hair, white and unnatural-looking as a domestic rabbit, was glued neatly to his scalp. You could see the lines made in his hair by his comb, like the grain in a piece of wood.

"Kathleen tells me you plan to quit school and go in the service."

We'd talked about it one day when she'd visited me at the hospital.

"I've been thinking about it."

"You seem like an intelligent young man," he said. "Have you considered continuing your schooling? Perhaps even going on to college?"

"No, I haven't considered it. Mainly because I hate school."

"Oh? Why is that?"

"Because somebody for no good reason is always trying to get you to do something you don't want to do. I never liked school. I never liked a damned teacher in my life."

"Maybe you haven't had the right ones. Maybe you need a tutor or the right private school. You might change your mind about school. How were your grades this last year?"

"All right, I guess."

"You didn't flunk anything?"

"No, I guess not. I don't know. I didn't bother to look at my last report card. Doreen didn't say anything, so I guess I didn't fail anything."

"Did you study?"

"Hell, no. I never ever did study. I hated school. Just hated it. They treat you like a simple-minded baby at school."

"Well, continuing in school is a thought, an idea," said the Judge. "Maybe you ought to consider it."

"Why?"

"Because it's the road to everything else. You go to the right school, you'll meet the right people. People who can be of use to you many times later in life."

"No kidding."

"Joe, I'm a rich man. I have only Kathleen to provide for, and she's well on her way to becoming a fine, well-educated young woman. I would like to have had a son as well. I own a great deal of property, besides the farm. I'm one of the principals in an electronics company in Boston. I figure after the election, that company will make a great deal more money for me. I'm a fortunate man. I'd like to share some of my good fortune with you. Kathleen tells me you haven't had very much good luck. I'd like to change that."

"I appreciate it, Judge. I really do. But this comes on me all of a sudden. I don't know what to say."

"Think about it," he said. "I'm not surprised you don't know what to say about it now. But I want you to understand that this is not the only thing I have in mind for you. I have a lot more in mind, but whether they are the right things or not will only become clear to me as I get to know you better. I do hope you will spend some time with me when you're well so that we can become better acquainted."

"Sure," I said. "If you want."

"Incidentally," he smiled. "I got the authorities to defer that warrant your stepfather put out on you. And the one Sam drew up for assault."

"Thanks. What's that mean?"

"It means that Sam Summers will leave you alone."

"That's good. I hate that bastard."

"Sam's useful," said the Judge. "He's like a pit bull. He does a few things very well. You have to look at him like that."

"I don't have to look at that bastard any way," I said.

"Well," said the Judge. "You don't have to worry. Those charges are in limbo. I don't think it'll be too difficult to get them lost permanently."

"Good, that'd be a relief."

"Now one other piece of business," he smiled at me. He put his hand in his blond corduroy jacket and withdrew a pipe.

"Mind if I smoke?"

"Go ahead," I said. What was the use of arguing?

"I'd like you to keep this confidential."

"I'll keep it confidential. What is it?"

"It looks like there'll be a hearing after all," he smiled. "People have tried to convince Mr. Gorman that it isn't necessary. But elections are coming up, and he'd like a little show. I'm sure he'll ask you to testify."

"I'm sure he will too."

"It won't be bad," he said. "You just tell them that Michaelsmith was armed and that Chief Summers shot him in self-defense."

"Lie, in other words."

He looked at his pipe and then at me.

"I don't think you'd be lying, would you?"

"Yes I would. That's what you want me to do, isn't it?"

"I want you to tell the truth," he said. "Sam Summers shot a dangerous man in the line of duty. A man whom I'd befriended and treated decently. Who shot one of my horses and kidnapped and terrorized my daughter. Sam has a bad temper, we all know. But he was doing his job. He's the best law enforcement officer this town has ever had. You'll find there's no crime in this town, no matter what you think of him. I'm asking you to use your head. Do the right thing. Instead of taking your differences out on Summers."

"He shot him," I said. "He was just trying to wave him away the way he would a horsefly. And Summers shot him three times."

"Michaelsmith had a rifle didn't he?"

"He wasn't pointing it at anybody."

"That son of a bitch kidnapped my daughter," the Judge said quietly, looking at me. "He put her on the floor of my car. He forced her to put the muzzle of that rifle in her mouth and threatened to blow her head off. You're telling me he was harmless?"

I could see he was good and mad.

"I thought everybody was entitled to a trial," I said. "Even in Sagadahock County. Or do you decide that too?"

That cooled him off a little.

"The troopers say he fired first."

"That's a lie," I said.

"The rifle had been discharged," said the Judge. "That's been established by the laboratory people."

"Somebody did it later then."

"Maybe you just didn't hear it go off. You were pretty groggy, weren't you? Didn't one of the troopers have to hold you up to keep you on your feet?"

"Maybe, but no rifle went off. Summers potted him right off his front porch."

The Judge looked at me, puffing on his pipe.

"Well, you stick to that story, if that's the right one. That will be fine. That'll be the truth as you see it. But I can tell you this. It won't do a living soul any good. Least of all, you."

"You mean it won't do Michaelsmith any good. Isn't that what you mean?"

"No," he said. "It won't do him any good either."

"All he wanted was to get that hurt kid home," I said. "He wasn't going to bother anybody. If people had left him alone he'd be alive today."

"It isn't that simple," said the Judge. "You can't shoot race-horses, hold people at gunpoint. You pay for all that according to the law."

Who's law, I thought.

"Isn't it a shame," I said.

"No, it isn't," said the Judge. "It's called civilization."

"What happened to the kid?"

"He and his mother are being taken care of. He's receiving the best medical care."

"Oh yes? Where is all this happening?"

"I had him flown down to Massachusetts General by helicopter. His mother's staying with him."

"That's good," I said.

I wondered if he usually had this much mopping up to do when he turned Summers loose.

"You see," he said. "I'm not forgetting there were innocent people involved."

"How's he doing?"

"He's doing well. The doctors say you and your grandfather saved his life. That's something else you can be proud of."

He smiled at me. He narrowed his eyes but never showed his teeth when he smiled.

"Think over what I said. I want you to do what you think is right."

"Okay," I said.

"Good," he patted me on the arm. He stood up and smoothed his hair down with the palm of his hand.

"Tell your grandfather, let bygones be bygones," he smiled again. He smiled too much. It made me want to look down to see which one of my pockets he had his hand in.

"I'll tell him," I said.

Thirteen

W H E N Henry came back from his walk he wanted to know what the Judge had said.

"He says, 'Let bygones be bygones.' "

"Shit," said Henry.

"He says he flew the Michaelsmith kid to Boston so he'd get the best medical care. He says he's doing all right. The doctors say you and I saved the kid's life. See? You're a better doctor than you thought you were."

"Just dumb luck," he said, but I could see he was pleased. "What's he want from you?"

"He wants me to say Summers shot Mr. Michaelsmith in self-defense."

"Do it," said Henry.

"Why?"

"Get something out of this," he said. "What's that son of a bitch offering?"

"He says he'll send me to college. He'll get them to drop all the charges against me. He's already got them delayed."

"Delayed," Henry said. "Just like him. Dangle that sword over your head by a thread to get you to do what he wants.

I don't like that whole crowd. They're all in it together."

"Who is?"

"Everybody. Everybody who runs anything in this town. The Judge, as they call him, owns everything. He has a little nonprofit company called Servco. It funds the library. It underwrites the cost of the police department and the fire department. Our taxes are wonderfully low, thanks to that man. He owns the water company, controls the bank. He throws a Christmas party for the children in town every year at the firehouse. People think that new friend of yours is a wonderful man. The town commissioners practically wet themselves when he says hello."

"So?"

"So now this wonderful son of a bitch who I can hardly stand steps forward and offers to change our luck. I guess we shouldn't look a gift horse in the mouth."

"What the hell are you talking about?"

"Maybe I'm just old and tired," he said. "But I want the bad luck to be over. I want something better for you."

"So you think I ought to do what he tells me to do."

"Maybe this time. Just this once. Then let him pay for your schooling. Call it blood money. You earned it. Maybe it'll change our luck. Maybe just this once he'll do some real good."

And he didn't want to talk about it any more that day, so I let it go. He seemed real depressed.

Henry's reaction puzzled me. It wasn't so much that I didn't know what he was thinking. I just wasn't sure I knew why he was thinking it. So the next day we talked some more about it.

"You think I ought to lie at the hearing?"

"Yes," he said without hesitation.

"I thought you would tell me to be honest. That fat skunk killed a man for no good reason."

"I know that."

Henry gnawed on his mustache for a second. He decided to have a weed. He blew smoke at the wedding cake ceiling, then looked at me. He looked like his insides pained him, and I was about to ask him was anything wrong, when he began to speak in a hoarse, strangulated voice.

"I don't give a shit about what's right or wrong anymore. I want you to save yourself. You're a young fella on your way to hell in a hurry. Till this happened. Till you came busting in here at exactly the right moment to set your life straight. So I say: Do it."

"That would be easy," I said. "To let that slimeball off the hook."

"Try something easy for a change," said Henry.

"Summers shot him down, Henry. The man didn't stand a chance."

"I know that."

He ran a hand through the pneumatic cloud of his thinning hair and looked at me. He smiled faintly.

"That man took the wrong hostage, didn't he? We can't do anything about it. Now we got to help ourselves. We don't need any more bad luck. I started it all, when I shot that poor German boy back in 1918. Now I'd like to get rid of it."

"You're talking crazy. You know that?"

"Maybe so. But there's something dogged about certain kinds of bad luck. Especially the kind you make for yourself. If your mistake is big enough, it follows you around for the rest of your life. Your family even inherits it, horrible as it sounds. I've paid for it. Your mother's paid for it. Poor Donald paid for it with his life. And now you're paying for it. I'll tell you another thing I believe."

"What's that?"

"I believe time is circular, that everything comes around again. But never fast enough for us to do anything about it. Only our children or our children's children, if they're lucky enough to read and interpret the signs. The sun is a circular mass of burning gasses. The planets are round. They travel round the sun endlessly. Under fire, frightened soldiers huddle together in circles. When lost in the woods men wander in circles. A man's life is a circle. The entrances to his body are called orifices. His stomach's round. His guts are coiled in a pinwheel. He begins alone, he ends alone. The circle is the mystery and the answer."

"That's a nice game," I said. "See if I know how to play. The bottom of this glass is round."

"That's right," he said. "It holds one form of consolation open to us in this round life. A woman's womb is a circle. Even the word sounds round."

"A man's head is round," I said.

"Yes," he said. "And filled with puzzles. So you see how it goes. When mystified, look for the circle. Now I want to look ahead on the curving line and prevent the next catastrophe."

"What catastrophe?"

"The next one," he said. "The one involving you."

"Nothing's going to happen to me."

"Is that right? Son, you're a walking catastrophe. Interesting you can't see it. I suppose if you could, there wouldn't be such a thing as destiny. But we're going to move ahead on the curving line and change things. And when we do, we'll be changing things not only for you, but for those who come after you. Do you understand?"

"Not exactly."

"That's all right. You're not that smart yet. Maybe in time you'll understand. You see that gun over there, under glass, like some damned museum piece?"

"Yes."

"I'm a fool for ever having kept that. Why in God's name did I ever keep as a memento the instrument of my own bad luck?"

"You're getting carried away, Henry. That's just a gun over there."

"No, it isn't. It's the instrument of my family's destruction. But I tell you what. As soon as you're well enough, you and I are going to put on a little fishing trip. And the first thing we're going to feed to the fishes is that pistol. Is that a deal?"

"Sure, if you want to."

"You ever do any fishing?"

"No, I can't say as I ever have."

"You've never been fishing?" He was dumbfounded.

"No. Except that time Dale pushed me off the wharf. I was the fishbait that day. If you call that fishing."

"What a damn shame. Here you are, practically grown, and you've never really been fishing. Where you been all your life, besides in trouble?"

"Trouble's kept me awful busy. You don't know how much time and care it takes."

"Oh, yes I do," he said.

"Where we going on this fishing trip?"

"There's a lake," he said. "Deep in the woods. Not far from here. I'll take you."

"Good," I said.

It sounded good to me.

That afternoon, as the Judge said she would, Kathleen came to see me. She was wearing a navy blue sleeveless blouse and a full khaki skirt and leather sandals and gold bracelets on her tanned wrists. She looked absolutely lovely and fresh and it was wonderful to see her again.

"Hello," she smiled and bent to kiss me.

When she went to draw back, I held her and tried to kiss her again.

"Easy," she said. "Subtlety is a wonderful quality."

"You don't want to keep me around if you're going to do that," I said.

"I like you," she smiled. "But don't rush me. Hello, doggy."

She gave Cat a good scratch behind the ears which he seemed to appreciate very much. She bent to him, her skirt tucked around her knees, smiling at the silly dog as he rolled his head around in an effort to keep in touch with her gratifying hand. That dog and I have a lot in common, I thought.

"What are you looking at?"

"Just admiring you."

"You're sweet." She sat back in her chair. "Okay if I smoke?"

"Only if you have to."

"My, how inhospitable. I really don't see what's wrong with it. Lots of people smoke. Are you one of these people who are out to reform the world?"

"Why don't you have a smoke," I said. "Then we can talk about something else."

"Good idea," she said, lighting up.

"Daddy tells me that you've agreed with his plan to send you to school."

The idea seemed to make her happy, which I thought was very generous of her.

"Well, not yet."

"I think it's a wonderful idea. I hope you'll do it."

"Did he tell you what he wants me to do?"

"What do you mean?"

The question froze her for a second.

"He wants me to lie. He wants me to say Summers killed Mr. Michaelsmith in self-defense."

"Didn't he?"

"No, he didn't."

"That horrible man," she said. "I still have nightmares. Sometimes I shake all over for no reason. I dream about him at nights."

"It was rough for you," I said.

"But it's over now," she said, brightening. "In a little while the dreams will go away too."

"Do you think I ought to lie?"

"Of course not. But you want to be sure you tell the truth, not just what you want to believe. I know you don't like Summers. He's horrible. I don't know why Daddy keeps him around. But he was doing his job that day. That's part of the truth too."

"You think your father's an honest man?"

"What kind of a question is that? Of course he's honest. He's good. He's tough. He gets his way. But he's honest. And he wants to be your friend, Joe."

With a troubled look, she ground her cigarette into the ashtray.

"Some people don't like Daddy because he's been so . . . successful. Some people hate people who are rich. There are people in this town like that. It's one of the disadvantages. You become a target. You've always got to be on guard. My father has worked very hard to get where he is. He's good to people. He's uncanny. He knows what's good for people better than they do. He can just look at people and tell what they're good at. And he finds a way to use their abilities."

She looked at me, very open and candid.

"Now he's offered to help you. I think you ought to take him up on it. He sees something special in you."

"How about you? You see anything special?"

She smiled.

"Yes, even if you are a little pushy."

"Sorry," I said.

"Joe, Daddy's just wonderful. He'll be such a good friend, if you let him."

"I guess you go to college, don't you."

"Yes, I'm going to Boston University. But I might switch to the Rhode Island School of Design. I like to paint so much."

"Is that right?"

I just wanted to keep her talking so she'd stay with me for a while, giving me the chance to warm myself in her looks and voice. She was so damned beautiful and nice.

"I thought at first I'd like to be a poet," she said. "But I don't have the talent. I love to read. I thought I'd major in English literature, maybe teach somewhere. Only now I spend more and more time painting. That's practically all I've done this summer."

"I don't have any talent like that," I said. "I've never been able to figure out how people do it."

She laughed, pushing her hair back, a beautiful gesture. Everything she did was graceful and without complication and cut into me like a knife.

"You just do it," she said. "I can't explain it. Did you see my tower when you were at the house?"

"Pardon?"

"The stone tower in the woods. I guess you probably didn't. You were pretty busy." She smiled at the joke. "There used to be an old hotel on the property called the Paradise Inn and Resort, back in the twenties. It burned down. The only thing that was left was the stone tower. Daddy's made a studio out of it for me. I'll show it to you when you come out to visit."

"That'll be nice."

"Do you like to swim?"

"Not particularly."

"Bring your suit anyway. We can get some sun."

She looked around the room admiringly.

"Your grandfather has so many wonderful books."

"Yes, he has a lot."

"I used to borrow from him when I was in high school. He has better books than the public library. I told you that in the hospital, didn't I?"

"If you did, I forget. I was sort of woozy. Didn't your father object to you coming here?"

"Daddy never minded. It's your grandfather who has the problem, not Daddy. Daddy got over it a long time ago."

"What happened anyway? I've asked Henry but he puts me off."

"Oh I don't know. Lots of things. My mother was one of Henry's patients before she died a long, long time ago. My father thought that Henry should have done more for her. Or at least recommend that she see a specialist. After she died, Daddy told him so. Did you know that Henry's father killed himself?"

"No, I don't know anything about anything. Doreen never told me a thing."

"Doreen?"

"My mother."

It was true. I guess she wanted to put it all behind her, pretend she'd never lived in this house or this town, or belonged to this family at all.

"Daddy says Henry always held Daddy's father responsible

for his father's death. They were in some kind of business deal together. It went sour or something. And Henry's father killed himself over it. Daddy—Daddy thought that maybe Henry didn't do more for Mother because . . ."

"To get even," I finished for her. "Henry would never do that."

"No, of course not," she said. "But it shows you how deep feelings ran. But Daddy's over it now."

"Yes," I said. "They certainly ran deep."

"And for too many years," she said.

"I bet Henry always liked you. You seem like Henry's kind of girl."

"Yes," she laughed. "Because I was always a reader. All us readers belong to the same secret society. He said I reminded him of my mother. I think he was kind of sweet on my mother. That's why I know he'd never have done anything that might have brought harm to her."

I thought admiration was a curious basis for judging whether or not a doctor would do his job, but I didn't say anything.

"So here we are," she said. "The children of two feuding families. How romantic."

"Let's solve their problems for them," I said. This time she let me kiss her, long and hard. I touched her breast. I began to pull her blouse out of her skirt.

"Wait a minute," she said. "Easy. You really come on in a rush, you know that?"

"Sorry again," I said. "It must be my lack of breeding."

A girl like that wore expensive perfume and pretty lingerie and when you undressed her it would be like stripping the petals off a flower. Even the thought of pushing aside the straps of her slip made me hard.

"We were talking about books," she said. "You ought to

read a few. It'll dampen down your fantasy life."

"I could use a little dampening down. Henry's always telling me I ought to read."

"You're not much of a reader?"

"I've never had much time."

She laughed.

"You always make time for the things you like."

What do I like? I wondered. It seemed things had gone by in a rush for me. I still had no idea what I liked or wanted in life. I'd really never stopped to consider the matter, a fact in itself that puzzled me. What have you been doing all your life? I asked myself. I didn't have a good answer.

"I'll make a list for you, if you like."

"Don't make it too tough."

She laughed again, a sound which surprised and gladdened me each time.

"Don't worry. I'll go easy on you."

She found a tablet and a pencil stub on the table by Henry's chair—he'd discreetly vanished upstairs on Kathleen's arrival—and she went right to making me a list, frowning a little, and going back and forth to the bookcases to make sure of her selections. I lay there on the couch, watching her silently. She was wonderful to look at.

"There," she said. "That ought to get you started."

I looked at the list: *Civilization and Its Discontents; The Uses of the Past; The Magic Mountain; Middlemarch.* Even the titles looked boring.

I think she was anxious to get going then, but I wanted her to stay. I wanted to look at her some more and touch her some more if she'd let me. So I asked her, did she like to ride very much and she said yes, she did, till this recent business.

She was twelve, she told me, when the Judge bought her her

first horse. His name was Trouble Jake. He was a gelding, a quarter horse, with a flat crupper but a fine head and fine legs. He was a strawberry roan with a white patch on his rump, only a little more than fifteen hands tall. Behind her father's house were two miles of fields. I could see it gave her great pleasure to recollect riding those fields, especially in winter, with the hard-packed snow flying up from Jake's hooves. She clipped his mane because it was heavy and pulled the flesh to one side at the base of his neck revealing the big ugly bone there. She clipped it back to four inches in length and he looked just lovely, she said.

She learned to ride on Jake and he never threw her. He threw others but he never threw her. He threw the Judge, for instance, dumped him right against a board fence and banged him up pretty good too, and the Judge never offered to ride that horse again, leaving Trouble Jake strictly to Kathleen. That horse seemed to know who his owner was, I said. She smiled in agreement.

Of course she took care of Jake. Those were the only terms on which the Judge would agree to let her have the horse in the first place. He had begun to purchase other horses and he had people around to care for them, but it was Kathleen's job to take care of Trouble Jake. She shoveled out his stall, fed him three times a day, and curried him nearly every day except when it got too cold in the winter and then she would let it go for about a week unless the weather broke before that. The winters used to be colder, she smiled. She thought they were milder now. Didn't I?

She carded Trouble Jake's tail and it grew long and beautiful. She made sure that old Mr. Waterhouse, the blacksmith, who carried his tools around in a secondhand hearse and refused to work unless she supplied him with a six-pack of beer, came round regularly and trimmed Jake's hooves with the big horse clippers that looked like tinsnips.

Jake came with an English saddle, she said. He had been trained to be ridden English and had never had a bit in his mouth. She learned to ride English, gripping the horse between her knees, keeping her back perfectly straight and lifting her backside before the front hooves struck the ground. She was glad she learned to ride him English, she said, because the small almost delicate saddle didn't break the flowing line of his back. Her girlfriend had a horse too and they rode in the local shows together.

She bagged Jake's tail and dyed the white spot on his rump, sprayed on the stuff to make him shine, and put black shoe polish on his hooves. In the shows, she wore boots which came almost to her knees, and black jodhpurs and a white blouse with a bow at the throat and a white duck jacket, with a pleat at the back, which fit tightly across her shoulders and the small of her back. She wore a visored round black cap with an inner sheath of steel to protect her head in case she fell.

"It was a beautiful time," she said. "I had a wonderful childhood."

"Whatever happened to ol' Jake?"

"He died when I was away at school. I cried so when I heard that."

"How did it happen?"

"We never really found out. He was out in the pasture. He must have eaten something poisonous. We don't know for sure. The vet couldn't tell us, but he thought that's what happened. Horses are funny animals, you know."

"Maybe he died of a broken heart."

She shook her head sadly, as if I shouldn't make fun of her.

"Horses don't die of broken hearts."

By the time she finished her story, I was feeling sick. I don't know what it was. Maybe I'd studied her face too long and listened too carefully to her story. I don't know why. I suppose I could have told her about the time the orange chow dog ripped the seat out of my snowpants, or how I used to bang Pepper on her off nights, or how I caught Doreen in the kitchen that time with Dale. But I didn't think any of those stories could match hers for elegance. No, I just felt used up and half sick like a kid who's had too much party cake. When she got up to leave this time I didn't try to find excuses for her to stay longer.

"I'll call you," she said. As she leaned down to kiss me I could smell her perfume again and it made me ache all over. "You come out to the farm, okay? We'll get better acquainted."

"Yes," I said. "I'd like that."

"So would I," she said.

Henry came in almost simultaneously with the sound of the front door closing. He was grinning like a fox.

"Well, you had a long visit with her. What did you talk about?"

"We talked about her horse."

"Oh yes?"

I told him I was worn out and did he mind saving his funny remarks for later. He said he didn't mind, not at all, and he went out, and I fell asleep almost before he reached the door.

I slept all the rest of the afternoon. I hadn't slept so heavily since Summers had beaten the tar out of me. That evening when I woke I still felt bad. Henry and I didn't have our usual chat after supper although he came in and sat with me, tending pretty much to his book. I was asleep again by nine o'clock. I didn't wake till nine the next morning. But even then, after all that rest, I didn't feel so good.

Fourteen

THE next day we went into training for our
fishing trip. We were both a little wobbly and needed to
toughen our legs. Henry said it was a good long walk through
the woods to the lake. He said he'd been going there regularly
through the years and had all his camp gear stored in a big box
he and his son Donald had built many years ago right on the
water's edge. He'd given up going there about five years ago,
he said, when it hadn't seemed so much fun anymore.

"I used to go to get away from people. About five years ago
I discovered I didn't have to go to the woods anymore to be
alone. I finally got old enough so that it happened naturally."

He said unless the animals had gotten into things, probably
everything was just as he'd left it.

We decided to walk the length of the green, moving slowly
together through the blue and gold, alternately cool and hot
patches of shadow and sunlight.

"What say we get an ice cream cone at Trafton's?"

"Sounds good to me."

"I haven't had an ice cream cone since . . . I don't know when.

Probably before the Spanish-American War. Let's rest on this bench here."

Henry stuck his bony ass out, slowly lowering himself onto the bench like a load of breakable cargo into a freighter bay.

"Yes sir," he said absently.

He hooked his thumbs in the vest pockets of his shiny black suit. His gold watch chain glittered in the sunlight.

"My, yes. Beautiful day."

He breathed deeply and exhaled with satisfaction. He turned to me. I studied the lettering on the windows of the dry cleaning establishment across the street. I felt his gaze on me. I frowned a little, warning off questions. But Henry liked to play dumb at times.

"You don't seem like your old spunky self today."

"I'm not my old spunky self."

"Anything particular bothering you?"

"Just you at the moment."

"Oh yes? My friendly inquiries annoying you, is that it?"

"A little. But I'm used to it. You're just naturally nosy."

"Yes, I guess I am. For example, right now I'm wondering what particularly is eating at your gizzard."

"If somebody kicked in your doors, you wouldn't sit there all puffed out like a turkey yourself."

"I imagine you're right about that," he said. "But that's not what's eating you. You're young and strong. The young come back fast. You've had a couple of weeks to recuperate. Granted you took a hell of a beating. You're bound to be a little tender in spots. But that's not why you're green around the gills."

"That's nice, Henry. I'm glad you got it all doped out."

"You been thinking about that girl, haven't you?"

"Maybe I have, maybe I haven't."

"You like her real well."

"I like lots of people."

"That's a joke," he said. "You like hardly anybody."

"Come on," I stood up. "Are we going to walk or sit here all day?"

"Sit down for a minute."

"I thought you wanted an ice cream."

"Sit down."

I sat down.

"Kathleen's a pretty girl. Intelligent. I don't like her father much, but her mother was a lovely person."

"Kathleen's not my type," I said.

"She's not? Now that surprises me. I thought you found her powerfully interesting."

"I don't go for college girls."

"Why not?"

"They talk too much. Most of them would puke if they ever had to deal with a real problem."

"Just how many college girls have you known?"

"I don't need to know a lot to know how they are. The rich ones are the worst kind."

"I thought Kathleen proved out pretty well at the farm a few weeks ago. She's a courageous young lady."

"She talks too much," I said. "She's as bad as you are. She made me a book list. She writes poetry and paints pictures. She wants me to come out to her place and go swimming."

"What's wrong with that?"

"I don't have a swimsuit."

"I'll buy you one."

"I can't swim, damn it."

"Well, that's nothing to be ashamed of."

"It's Dale's fault. He threw me in once. I damn near drowned. I've never been near the water since."

"Just tell her you don't swim."

"I'm not telling her that."

"Why not?"

"I'm not, that's all."

"It's a minor weakness, Joe. All of us have a few."

"I don't go around talking about mine," I said. "I hate the whole idea of this stuff. Why is everybody trying to change me? What is this crap? You and the Judge and Kathleen all trying to make me read books and go to school and all this horseshit. Trying to get me to lie at the hearing and save that fat cop's ass, when he ought to burn for what he did. Why don't the whole bunch of you leave me alone? I swear to Christ I wish I'd never seen any of you."

I must have been shouting at him. Because afterwards I found I was breathing hard as if I'd just run a mile in a hurry. He sat there, studying me sadly, that little bug on his lip blacker than ever. His carelessly shaved peppery-looking whiskers seemed to darken, as if what I'd said had turned him pale. I thought: damn it, don't take it out on him. It's not his fault.

"The pressure's on, isn't it, Joe?"

I didn't know exactly what he meant but it made me feel uneasy, his voice sudden and quiet, as if he had something on me.

"The pressure's on. Now you have all these people wanting to help you. Urging you to make something of yourself. Some even meaning it."

He widened his milky blue eyes at me, which made him look like some crazy wino geek.

"It makes you mad, doesn't it?"

"I don't know. Maybe."

"Probably scares you a little too."

"It doesn't scare me. I just wish everybody'd lay off. Including you."

"I don't blame you," he said. "Let's get that ice cream."

We crossed Maine Street and walked up the pavement to
Trafton's. Henry bought us each a teetering double-dip, the girl
passing the cones gingerly out to us through the little sliding
screen panel they used for sidewalk service. It was the biggest
damned ice cream cone you ever saw. It was good, wonderful
ice cream too, wonderfully cold and creamy in the throat, just
the thing for a summer day. He ordered coffee flavor and I went
for the pistachio. We walked across the street into the park again
and sat on a bench under the trees. We both tended to our ice
cream, eating fast so it wouldn't run down all over our fingers.
We both pretended that this took our full attention so as to be
left alone to think our own thoughts.

You old son of a bitch, I thought. You're probably right. I'm
scared. I'm scared. I've never been scared before. I've taken a gun
away from Dale Bigler and never been scared. A man's put a
rifle on me. I've looked him in the eyes, knowing I could hold
on if I just kept looking in his eyes and talking to him. I've stood
up to a beating or two. I've knocked some people around and
had the shit kicked out of me once or twice, and it was all right,
not pleasant, but I could take it. But I don't like this. I don't
like this. I thought: maybe I ought to just get on the bike and
ride away. Get away from here while there's still time. Before
I mess everything up.

Summers drove by slowly in his cop car. He had his sunglasses on as usual. He looked in our direction. I think he saw
us but he looked away as if he hadn't.

"There's that creep now," I said.

"So it is," said Henry.

Slowly Summers drove up the street. He turned beyond the
band shell and started down Washington on the other side of
the Commons. I watched him coming. When he glanced in our
direction, I gave him the finger.

"Jesus," Henry said. "Don't do that."

Summers looked away again as if he hadn't seen us. Summers' official black and white Ford with the big silver badge on the front door crept down the street like a bead on a string, turned right on Lincoln at the end of the Commons, and disappeared behind an olive haze of tall shrubbery and trees.

"I don't like that guy."

"I doubt if that guy likes you," Henry said. "Come on. I want to show you something."

We walked back to the house and down the driveway, last winter's cinders crunching under our shoes like burnt popcorn kernels. We went on into the thick coarse grass still wet and webby in spots with the spittle-like residue of the heavy dew we'd had that morning.

Henry led the way across the rotted little footbridge, the boards underfoot spongy and blackly wet and slippery with moss. I made a mental note that we ought to fix it before one of us put a foot through a board and busted a leg. It was a broken-backed bridge to nowhere these days, jumping the little brook at the base of the hill which rose through the twisted apple trees to the crumbling stone wall that marked the end of the dying orchard and the beginning of the pine woods.

"This used to be a fine orchard in my grandfather's day," Henry staggered up the slanting hill. The earth was dead as ashes underneath our feet. The sparse stubbly grass, dry as a broom.

"Now all these trees are barren and mostly dead. Damn shame."

We found a break in the wall and went through into the woods beyond and here we found an old narrow path like a badly healed scar in the flank of the forested hill. The angle was steeper here. I felt the sweat break through my shirt between my shoulder blades. Henry was moving right along like he was a man with a purpose and hadn't noticed the difficulty of the path. I found I had a few midges to slap at too; the insects didn't seem to bother with him. Probably they found him too old and dried up to be of much interest.

We huffed to the top of the hill where another path wove off to the left and we took it till it sank without a trace in a wide floor of pine needles. We were walking comfortably now on a level carpet between the tall straight black columns of the pines, breathing in the pine-winey gloom of the woods with such pleasure. We walked like that for half a mile, in file, like a couple of Indians, without speaking, and then broke into the open sunshine.

"You want to meet your relatives?"

Henry showed me his yellow horse teeth, snagging his lip on his dry gums so that his smile froze for a second. His sunken cheeks looked feverish, the sallow skin bruised with pink spots, but other than that he showed no signs of exertion or excitement.

What he'd led me to was an old overgrown cemetery: tall wafer-thin slabs of marble, blotched with lichens, reeled in the high, blond grass. An old washed-out road, whose ruts had turned into minor gullies, led up to it through the trees but was plainly impassable. The rusty iron fence was down in places, allowing us to wander freely in and out amongst our kinfolk. A big obelisk of polished granite, looking as new as the day it was installed, rose out of the middle of this decay. Carved on its base was the single word, "Weatherfield."

"When I die, see that I'm buried here among my people the way I'm supposed to be," he whispered. "Will you do it?"

"What am I supposed to do? Carry you up here on my back?"

He straightened, glowering at me.

"I'm serious. You see to it."

"I'll cash it before you do," I said.

"You could be right."

The thought seemed to cheer him considerably.

"You're pretty careless of life and limb, like most young fools. Aren't you?"

"I don't carry myself like an egg if that's what you mean."

"Nobody'd ever accuse you of that," he said. "Nobody'd accuse you of being cautious or even simply careless. Foolhardy might be the word. Might have been invented for you, in fact."

He lowered his bushy eyebrows at me.

"I'm not joking about this. I want to be buried up here where I belong. I'd like for you to have the house when I'm gone. But I'm so deep in debt, you'll probably have to sell it to square it with the bank. Unless you get rich suddenly."

"Don't talk dumb," I said. "You're going to live forever."

"I know. That's my destiny: Wandering Jew, New England style. But still the thought of you in the house after I'm gone comforts me. Maybe raising a family there, under your own roof at last. No other family's ever lived in that house. My great-great-grandfather built it. It's been ours on land that has always belonged to us in a country where we've always lived. The thought of somebody else living in it makes me cringe. I'd rather burn it down first, I hate the idea of it that much."

"You can come back and haunt them."

"Hell, I haunt the place now."

He looked around the graveyard gloomily. The wind soughed the trees, sighing peacefully in the trembling leaves. We stood there stock-still, he and I, among the blistered tombstones of our ancestors, that old man in his black suit, his thin white hair whipping in the breeze, and me with my hands in my pockets watching him cautiously out of the sides of my eyes like I would a crazy man.

It was peaceful and lovely in that clearing in the woods and I could understand why he wanted to be buried there in among the several generations of his own kind. And I knew just how it made his pride smart to think of anybody except a Weatherfield living in that house that had always belonged to them, that always would belong to them, no matter what the deed at the courthouse said, because nobody else had a right to it because nobody else could know what it had meant to him and all the others before him, right back to the first one.

"There's my father, bless him."

Henry pointed to a particular stone. He looked at the stone all the while he was telling me about his dad whether I wanted to hear about him or not, as we stood together in the tall, burned-out grass of the cemetery, the shadows of the trees slowly stretching across the rutted road.

His old man had been president of the local bank. But he seemed to enjoy the Latin and Greek poets more than he did poring over his account books. He was a generous man when it came to making loans to the local folks, always willing to help a neighbor and not too particular when a man paid the money back. He thought a certain amount of laxity created goodwill, Henry said.

In the twenties, Lattimore Fiske and his family began summering in Dunnocks Head. They rented the old Longfellow place just down the street from Henry's house. This fellow was rumored to be a bootlegger. He and his wife and college kid son strolled around the village accompanied always by one or two of Mr. Fiske's business associates. Mrs. Fiske usually had a frankfurter dog with her, straining at the end of a red leather leash, apparently more anxious to get the walk over with than anybody else in the party. Mr. Fiske smoked crooked black cigars, wore white suits, and as they strolled along the street doffed his panama to the ladies. They created quite a sensation in town, Henry said.

One day, Mr. Fiske and his friends stopped at the bank to see Henry's father. Fiske offered to buy what was known locally as Jewett's castle, an old hotel with three hundred acres of land located at Roaring Beach on the back road to Bath.

"My father was tickled pink to sell it to him," said Henry. "I told him, 'You don't want to sell that gangster anything,' but he said, 'Why not? He's going to restore the Paradise Inn. Make it a tourist attraction again. Create a lot of jobs.' "

Henry shook his head.

"My poor father. He truly thought he knew how to handle men like Lattimore Fiske."

Henry said his father even lent Mr. Fiske his old collection of sepia-tinted postcards which showed how the place looked when it was built in the nineties, so Fiske and his architect could get the restoration just right. A lot of local carpenters got work out of it. When it was finished it was beautiful, Henry said, just like the original.

Folks from town used to drive out there for dinner sometimes. From the beach road you could see the stone tower, the freshly painted turrets of the main building, and the American flag snapping in the wind on the flagpole on the roof. You drove up a winding gravel drive through pine woods to reach the main entrance, where some lackey parked your car for you. Henry said the whole thing burned down in 1934, leaving just the tower.

He said whenever he was out there the big dark-paneled dining room was almost always deserted. Except for Mr. Fiske and a few friends at their customary table among the potted palms near the service bar.

"My father was invited out there regularly. He didn't like to go alone, so I sometimes went with him. Sometimes we all went out with him—Lilian and Donald, who was just a little boy, and I. Your mother wasn't even born when all this was going on. So all of us were on hand from time to time to supply him with a little moral support to carry through what he, for business reasons, regarded as an obligation. Although an unpleasant one.

"Mr. Fiske always greeted us warmly. He always asked how I was coming along with the practice. He even sent me a few of his friends when they developed one minor medical problem or another. Once he came to me himself with a bulbous growth on his scalp. At first I thought he was trying to grow an auxiliary head in which to house his supplemental schemes. But it turned out to be a matter of minor surgery. Afterwards, he thanked me profusely, told me what a fine job I'd done. He sent me a check for five hundred dollars. That represented about a quarter of my income that year."

Despite the apparent lack of business, Henry said Mr. Fiske started making large deposits at the bank. Mr. Fiske, always accompanied by two or more of his ever-changing cadre of business associates, would show up at the bank every Monday morning with paper sacks filled with bills of small denomination. It got to be such a regular practice that his father didn't even bother to begin his morning translations of Catullus or Juvenal or whoever he was working on that week till he had counted up Mr. Fiske's bags of money and given him his receipt.

"I asked my father where he thought all that money was coming from. He said Mr. Fiske claimed he was doing a big restaurant business during the week, mostly people just passing through. But I doubt if even my father believed that story.

"The old crocodile usually joined us for dessert and for some brandy served in coffee cups. He would sit there making small talk with me while keeping his eyes on Father, who usually studied the tablecloth.

"But normally he let us eat our dinner unmolested. I was in my thirties, but still naive. I had no idea how things were going to turn out. I enjoyed eating a good dinner and being waited on by waiters in white jackets. I enjoyed dining like a rich person in this privileged atmosphere of silence and peace. No doubt my father sat there and suffered the pangs of the damned.

"This one night, I remember, my father seemed particularly disturbed by the presence of the bartender. I remember he wore his hair slicked back, Valentino fashion. He stood behind the service bar at the far end of the room, quietly polishing glass after glass. My father kept glancing at the man nervously. The man kept polishing glasses, never letting on that he was aware of my father at all. I finally asked my father what was wrong. 'Nothing,' he said. He said, 'I am just not feeling well tonight.' "

The next spring, during the annual visit of the federal auditors, Henry's father came home to lunch one day complaining that he was ill. Henry took him in the examining room to see what the matter was.

In the course of things his father expressed an interest in knowing the exact location of his heart. He'd always been curious about scientific matters, Henry said. So Henry accommodated him by drawing his heart in ink on his chest. Having been supplied the appropriate map, his father went upstairs and carefully shot himself in the exact middle of this drawing. The man had been a scholar. People said it was only vanity that kept him from shooting himself in the head.

"You know what gun he used?"

"Don't tell me."

"The same one," he said. "Why the hell did I keep it around all these years? We got to get that thing out of the house fast. Don't go near it."

"I won't."

"Please, for Godsakes, don't go near it. Let's start back. If I get too weak, you don't mind carrying me down the hill, do you?"

"Course not," I said. "You're no heavier than a dandelion puffball anyway."

He laughed and pointed into the woods above the cemetery.

"That lake I was telling you about is right up there."

"How far?"

"About fifteen miles."

"We're going to walk that?"

"We're going to get in shape first. Then we're going to walk it. Some great fishing in there. That's because nobody ever goes there. You know, at one time, we owned all these woods and that lake too."

"Is that right?"

"Yes. We owned all this country once, by deed from the English king."

"Think of that," I said.

"Yes," he said. "You think of that."

Every day after that we took the dog and walked through town and up into the woods, walking farther and farther each day. I was very pleased to see how much stronger Henry was getting. Damned if he didn't have plenty of spring left in his old bones after all. At the end of a week we started carrying packs because Henry said we'd want to pack in some food and other stuff when we went.

I was back cooking again. I made sure Henry got plenty of

vegetables and fruit, although I wasn't crazy about them myself. I figured he wanted to be good and strong for our trip.

Every time we went into the woods Henry showed me something new. He showed me how to find dry tinder after a rain on the lower inside branches of little evergreen trees. He told me that a polar bear's liver is so rich in vitamin A that it'd kill me if I ever took even a little bit of it, and he made me promise not to try it, ever. I said it wasn't likely I'd get the chance. You never know, he said.

He told me about the lake. He said it was the clearest, most beautiful lake I'd ever see. He had a boat up there and a glass-bottom bucket. He said the lake was so clear you could put that bucket in the water and see clean to the bottom except in the deepest part. He said you could watch the fish swimming around, minding their own business, unaware they were being observed by fierce predators.

He demonstrated the fine art of making birchbark stew. He cut the inner bark into spaghetti-like strips and boiled the whole mess in water.

"How do you like it?"

"It's awful," I said.

"It's good for you."

He dipped his cup in the pot for another sample, took another swallow, and smacked his lips, as if I had to be shown how to appreciate this concoction.

"You're just a kid," he said. "You don't know what's good and what isn't."

He showed me how to use his gold pocket watch for a makeshift compass; how to lay the watch on a rock and point the hour hand directly at the sun, checking with a pine needle held directly at the edge of the watchcase to make sure the needle's shadow fell directly along the hour hand. South, Henry explained, lay midway along the smaller arc between the hour hand and twelve o'clock. If you knew where south was, he said, you weren't lost, were you? I allowed how that was probably true.

The night we were packing to get ready to walk into the lake, I had a telephone call from Kathleen.

"Why don't you come out and visit us tomorrow, Joe? We'll have a cookout."

"I can't tomorrow, Kathleen. Henry and I are going on a fishing trip."

"Oh that sounds wonderful, Joe. How long will you be gone?"

"I don't know. Maybe a week."

"Well, then, maybe next weekend. I'm having some friends up from school. I'd like to meet them."

I didn't like the sound of that.

"I don't know if I'll be back for sure."

"If you can make it, I'd love to have you come out. If not, we'll arrange for another time."

"Okay."

When I came back out in the kitchen, Henry asked, "Who was that?"

"Kathleen. She wanted me to come out to the farm tomorrow."

"Oh? You going?"

"I'm going fishing. With you. Remember?"

I noticed he was putting an orange life jacket into one of our backpacks.

"What's that for?"

"That's for you."

"I'm not going to catch these fish by hand, am I?"

"No, but you'll be in a boat in water too deep for you to walk to shore if you fall out."

"I'm not wearing that rig."

"Yes you are," he said.

He didn't even bother to look up, certain that he'd already won the argument.

We started early in the morning and it took us all one day to walk in. We stopped just once, at noon, to eat the peanut butter sandwiches which Henry had fixed and packed for our lunch. His idea of a peanut butter sandwich was just peanut butter and dry bread, no jelly or butter. The damned thing stuck to the roof of my mouth like a ball of putty. I had to use my finger to dig it loose. I cleared my throat with a little tepid black coffee from Henry's thermos, which didn't keep anything very hot or cold.

We wolfed down this miserable meal while crouching together in the loamy darkness under the trees. I had no idea where the hell I was. Other than a little chafing under the arms from my light backpack and a feeling that my sore feet were commencing to balloon inside my shoes, I was all right. Where Henry found his reserve strength for this trip, I couldn't say, but he seemed just fine. All those fruits and vegetables I'd crammed into him had paid off, I guess.

Our lunch break lasted not long, as Henry was eager to get to the lake in time to set up camp before dark. So we lurched on through the shadowy woods. Every once in a while I had the sensation that the trees were slowly revolving around me—more evidence, I supposed, in support of Henry's theory about the circular nature of all human experience. We didn't talk much. That seemed to be part of Henry's code in the woods: no unnecessary bullshit. He'd pause, get his bearings, and we'd go on.

As the day wore on, it got hot. We were picking our way through the dead lower branches of a stand of close-set pines, the points of the branches sharp as claws tearing at our clothes.

I noticed the air seemed to lighten. The sweat on my forehead began to dry. With the suddenness of a minor miracle, we burst out of the slant and shadow of the endless trees onto the hot sand of the lakeshore and there of course was the lake, streaked with dark blue wind trails, cupped among the green hills as if a giant had suddenly opened its palm to show a big gleaming gem to the sky.

Henry and I grinned at each other. A steady breeze blew off the lake, drying the sweat on our faces and miraculously healing our itching bug bites.

"Look at that gorgeous lake!" Henry shouted. "Isn't she something?"

Yes, indeed she was. Henry had told me the Indians had regarded the place as holy, and it was no wonder if you considered how bewildered and dazzled they must have been, coming on this mammoth emerald after crashing around for days in those dark, lonesome woods. I was so giddy from the walk in, I could hardly stand up. My knee joints snapped like rubberbands, sitting me down hard on a piece of driftwood. My sight clouded over for a moment, I was that fatigued. Henry, however, seemed to have plenty of energy left.

We found the wooden box, spattered with bird droppings and pine needles, but pretty much as he'd left it. The padlocks were in good repair if a little stubborn about taking the keys. He'd thought to bring some 3-in-1 oil along, and he got the locks to work without much trouble. This box was big as a feedbox. It had two separate compartments with wide double doors on each side, and it was full of stuff he'd either lugged in at one time or another or had built right there on the spot. We began to unload the stuff.

"Isn't it beautiful?" he beamed, signifying the lake.

It was. I nodded, too numb to trust to words. The steady

breeze from the lake was starting to revive me a little.

We got the boat out, a beautiful lightweight thing studded with copper nails, the natural wood beautifully varnished.

"This is a Rangely Lake boat," he said. "Isn't this nice?"

He and Donald had built it right there on the spot, he told me, some twenty-five years ago, making it light enough so that one man could take it in and out of the water by himself.

We set up the tent and the cots and the camp chairs. We set up the two-burner cookstove that used the canned heat we'd packed in. We drove the stakes to secure the lines for the tarpaulin and set in the side curtains of mosquito netting for our open-air dining parlor. When we finished, we had a darned nice camp.

"Now can we quit?" I said. "I'm so tired I could sleep on a sack of rocks."

"We can't sleep now." Henry was shocked by my suggestion. "We got to have dinner first. Aren't you hungry?"

"I'm dead," I said. "Not hungry."

The first night in camp it rained hard. It didn't really start in earnest till we'd eaten the supper that Henry had insisted on preparing, and we'd gone to bed. Henry had warmed up a can of beef stew while I sat by worthlessly, too tired to move. We'd brought some bread in our packs, and we used the bread to sop up the gravy in the bottom of our tin plates. Henry made some coffee which he served very hot and strong in big white mugs. Everything was surprisingly delicious.

"This is living," said Henry.

I agreed. Apart from this one remark, we ate in silence, very peaceful together, the rain pattering on the stretched tarpaulin overhead. It grew dark suddenly. The lake faded in the gathering mist. The black trees quickly bled into the surrounding darkness. It was the kind of rainy, black night you don't argue with. We went to bed. I slept like a dead man, and woke at dawn. The dog came and put his cold nose on my face, then with a sigh of resignation went away. And the quiet steady rain put me to sleep again. When I woke for the second time the roof of the tent had turned orange under the sunlight. Henry's cot was empty. I could smell bacon and eggs on the air.

"Come on," he said after breakfast. He did not intend for us to sit around. We went through the trees the few hundred yards to the lake where it was almost windless that morning. Henry loosened the painter which he'd tied to a tree. He told the dog to jump in, and the dog jumped in. Then he and I shoved the boat into a few inches of water.

"Put this on."

He handed me a life jacket from the bottom of the boat. Even the orange color bothered me, marking me out as a pantywaist from five miles away.

"I don't need that thing."

"We're not going anywhere till you put it on."

He was serious, I could see. I hadn't come this far to be left behind on shore. So I put it on. He told me to get in and get the oars ready and he pushed off since he had his waders on, coming in over the bows with surprising agility. He told me to turn the thing around and row into the middle of the lake. I had never rowed much, but that boat didn't seem to require much experience. When we got out where he wanted us to be, we dropped the drag anchor, nothing more than an old pail tied to a rope, over the side. He had a nice little Danforth to use closer in, but he used the drag out here in the middle. Then he showed me what was on his mind. He took the pistol out of his creel and said, "Now get your bucket ready."

I put the bucket over the side.

"All right," he said. "Goodbye, bad luck. And be god-damned."

The pistol dropped into the water with a discreet little plop. Through the glass-bottomed bucket I followed the pistol, wavering and sparkling in the clear sun-shot water, in its trembling descent toward the distant gray weedbed at the bottom of the lake.

"I see it," I said.

"Goodbye, dishonor," said Henry. "Goodbye all the crap of years past and sundry disappointments."

The pistol disappeared into the weeds at the bottom of the lake. A second later a little cloud of mud slowly writhed over the spot like a poison mushroom.

"Now let's fish," Henry said.

And we did. We caught a lot of fish, bringing the trout cold and firm out of the lake. We cleaned them off the end of the boat, slitting their ghost-white bellies with Henry's sharp fileting knife and dribbling the slick burgundy innards into the water. Each night, we cooked the day's catch over wood coals for our dinner, and it was some of the best eating I've ever had in my life. Or probably ever will have.

We had a good time.

Henry looked a sight, dressed in his old fishing cap with all the hooks in it and the little green plastic window in the turned-down brim so he could look up without looking up, as he put it. Every day he wore the same damned old khaki shirt with eight million pockets in it and his waders over the same old pair of gray herringbone pants in case we wanted to drift into shore and fish the edges. In this outfit he smelled just like a fish himself, which he told me was part of the plan.

Of course he was full of himself. He had to tell me a different lie each day to keep himself amused. He told me the lake was

sacred to the Indians, a magical place. Seen from the air, he said,
the lake was star-shaped, like a little silver scar in the tremen-
dous green flank of the endless forest.

"This is not technically a lake anyway, you know."

"Oh? What is it technically?"

"Well, I suspect it might be the belly button of the universe."

"Is that right?"

"Yes. Right over there it's never been plumbed by man. I
suspect if you dove deep enough, you'd come out the other side
of the world and float right up into the clouds and join the
constellations in the evening sky. But that's just a guess of
course."

He told me an old hermit had once lived on the shores of
the lake, about a hundred years ago. One day, some trapper
who'd come in after something or other was out in his canoe
and he saw the old hermit, who was just an immaterial rumor
up till then, never having been seen by anyone, appear out of
the density of trees and step onto the shingle beach and just stand
there as if he were waiting patiently for the next thing to
happen. The trapper stared across at him. But the old hermit
didn't seem to notice him. Then, Henry said, a fishing line with
a giant hook on the end of it was lowered down out of the
single cloud in the sky that day. Without hesitating, the hermit
stepped on the fishhook and gave the line a firm tug. And he'd
been hoisted right up into that cloud and vanished, in full view
of the astonished woodsman.

"You believe that story?"

"Why not?"

"You got to be kidding."

"Well, you never know. An occasional man jack among us
might be hauled to heaven that way. We might be fished for,
who knows? I suspect the fisherman throws back most of the

smallfry. He only wants the real catches, the trophies who've lived at the bottom for years and who've waxed wise with experience . . ."

"People hear you talking that way," I said, "they'll lock you up."

He wheezed asthmatically, going heh-heh soundlessly, looking goony as hell sitting there in that silly hat with all the hooks and feathers in it.

"I suppose you're right."

You can see we had a good time. Henry grew ten years younger on that trip. I myself came back feeling rested and just fine.

Fifteen

⌐ "WOULD you like some iced tea?"

Ice tea. I never drink ice tea.

I said, "I'll take a beer if you have it."

I wasn't going to change my drinking habits just because I'd been invited out to the farm.

When I walked in on them the Judge, just coming from the pool, grabbed a towel from the back of his chair and scuttled across the flagstones in his bare feet to welcome me.

"Ah, here you are, Joe," he said, smiling. "Good to see you."

He gave me a clammy hand to shake, asking me to excuse him for shaking hands when he was all wet. No big deal, I said.

As he talked, the Judge rapidly patted away the water streaming down his temples from his wet, ropy white hair with his towel. Water from his sodden swim trunks spattered on the flagstones at his feet.

"Where's your grandfather?"

"He's catching up on a few things."

"Pity. I hoped he would decide to come with you."

Cut the bullshit, I thought. You didn't invite him in the first place. And in the second, he wouldn't have come anyway. Who you trying to kid? I guess my nerves were raw that day. But I couldn't understand the Judge's classy form of hypocrisy. I wondered how anybody could think it passed for good manners. Just be cool, I said to myself. What are you getting so excited for? You just got here.

Kathleen came over to say hello. She just knocked me out, she looked so great in her black tank suit and white terry-cloth beach jacket.

"Hello, Joe." She leaned forward to whisper, "The next time it'll be just you and me. I promise."

She pressed my hand, smiling frankly into my eyes. I couldn't breathe, she looked so lovely. Her whispered remark deserved an answer but the sight of her, even prettier than I remembered, blotted all the proper words from my brain. I wanted to say, get rid of these jerks and we'll do it, right now, on the flagstones. But I couldn't say that, and nothing stupid, noncommittal, polite, and socially acceptable would come into my head. So I stood there, working my jaws, acting like a feeb.

For public consumption, Kathleen said it was so nice to see me again. Her hand was warm and supple and soothed my nerves. Holding her hand had such a wonderful effect on me that I held it too long.

Turning to Kathleen's friends who'd been watching quietly, the Judge introduced me by saying, "This is the young man who saved Kathleen's life."

It made me wince inside. Maybe he thought he was doing me a favor by explaining my presence at poolside like that. But I was thinking: Yes, that's right. Goddamn you. You wouldn't have a fellow like me around unless you had a good reason, would you? I almost walked out right then.

Kathleen's pals grinned like the animal act had just come on.

What's up? I wanted to say to the skinny guy. You see something funny? But I caught myself. Don't start any trouble, I thought. This won't last long. You'll be out of here pretty soon. Then it'll be over.

We settled the question of what I wanted to drink.

"Come sit down," said the Judge.

The skinny guy, whose name was Dennis Macleod, stood up.

"It's nice to meet a real hero," he said pleasantly. "Kathleen's told us all about your exploits."

He gave me a limp handshake and we all sat down.

"Weren't you scared?" said the fat girl to Kathleen. Her name was Adrienne Murphy. "Honestly, the man held a gun to your head? I would have died."

This fatso peered at me over the tops of her granny glasses. Her curly hairdo stood out in all directions like an explosion. Unlike the others, she was completely dressed. No swimming for her. Her fat knees were blotchy red with sunburn and boneless as a couple of inner tubes. I'd seen old ladies in support hose with knees like that but never anybody under a hundred.

Dennis Macleod looked at me carefully. He sprawled in his chair, dressed in just bathing trunks and loafers and a white shirt which he wore unbuttoned. I noticed his belly button was inside out. Instead of the usual notch, a hard little bubble of flesh protruded in the middle of his flat stomach.

"How does it feel to have a gun pointed at you?"

"Not good."

"But how did you feel?"

"Dennis wants to be a writer," Adrienne explained. "He wants to get all the feelings right."

Dennis smiled at Adrienne.

"She's right. I do want to get the feelings right. I hope you don't mind."

The Judge had gone up to the house to get me a beer so it was just the four of us sitting around the table. Kathleen seemed a little anxious for me as if she were afraid Dennis's questions might annoy or embarrass me. As I didn't say anything, Dennis repeated his question.

"Really, how does it feel when somebody points a gun at you?"

Kathleen said, "Perhaps Joe doesn't want to talk about it."

"Right," I said. "I don't want to talk about it."

Dennis smiled.

"Oh? May I ask why not?"

"Because it's over. I don't know how I felt or what I thought. I just did whatever I did when it happened. I didn't think about it. I'd have to make something up to try to explain it to you. Whatever I told you would be a lie. See, the thing is: I didn't feel anything. I didn't think anything either."

Dennis seemed impressed by this little speech, which made me sorry for it right away. You can't talk about stuff like that without ruining it for yourself. Maybe he knew that better than I did.

"You weren't afraid when he pointed the gun at you?"

"No, I wasn't afraid. I wasn't anything."

He smiled.

"Weren't you afraid he'd kill you?"

"I wasn't afraid."

Everybody went quiet. I guess they thought I was bragging. But I wasn't bragging. I was telling the truth, and ruining it for myself, realizing too late that this dink had probably set me up.

"Joe says what he thinks," said Kathleen. "No false modesty."

"That's refreshing," said Dennis. "There are too many phonies around."

"What do you mean by that?"

He seemed surprised by my reaction, but I never liked the word phony and I wanted to find out fast what he meant by it. If he was calling me a phony I was going to punch his ass.

"Only what I said. Too many people like to brag about things—"

"I'm not bragging," I said. "You asked me a question."

"I know you're not," he looked nervously at Kathleen for support. He would need all the help he could get if I started after him. "I'm just saying sometimes people talk too much," he explained. "There's a difference between candor and braggadocio. Take Hemingway for example—"

"What's he got to do with it?"

"He wants to be heroic all the time. He wants to prove it to you all the time."

"I still don't get it," I said. I think I'd rattled him, and he'd lost the string himself and had retreated into book talk where he felt safe and secure.

Kathleen lit up a cigarette.

"Well, we're certainly off and running, aren't we?"

"I heard he's sick," said Adrienne.

We looked at her.

"Who's sick?"

"Hemingway. I hear he's really very sick."

"He's been sick a long time," said Dennis.

I was looking at him hard, to see if he wanted to be a wiseguy. I wondered whether he was sort of Kathleen's boyfriend. If he was, I didn't think he was so great. If I kept after him much longer, it was altogether likely that he'd pee in his pants. I could feel Kathleen looking at me, signaling me to be nice, but I pretended not to notice. I was feeling mean that day.

"He hasn't written anything good since the forties."

"What about *The Old Man and the Sea?*"

"Bosh. Sentimental drivel. He's finished. He was never as good as they said anyway."

"I think it's popular not to like Hemingway these days," said Kathleen. "We're all tired of him. We've had too much of him. Someday we'll feel differently again."

"What do you think, Joe?" asked Adrienne.

"I never thought about it."

"Where do you go to school?"

"Joe doesn't like school," Kathleen put in. "But Daddy's been talking to him about it and Joe is reconsidering. Aren't you, Joe?"

"School's a bunch a bullshit."

I looked at Dennis.

"What are you going to do when you get out of school?"

"Me?" He sat up in his chair. "Well, I suppose I'll teach somewhere. Get an advanced degree and teach till my ship comes in."

"What will be on your ship when it unloads at dockside? Bananas? Old dirty socks?"

"Joe," said Kathleen. "Aren't you being—?"

"I'm just saying college doesn't teach you anything you can use. You won't know how to grease a car when you're through."

"Yes, but," he said, "I'll be able to use my mind. The imagination—"

"We got cockroaches back home," I said.

They all looked at me.

"They were two inches long some of them. Doreen called the exterminators, but we couldn't get rid of them. Those cockroaches used to eat square holes in my socks. Did you know that cockroaches will eat a square hole in your sock, just as neat and precise as if you'd taken the scissors and very carefully cut a little box in the sock yourself?"

"No," said Dennis quietly. "I didn't know that."

"You want to be a writer," I said. "You ought to know stuff like that."

The Judge came back with the drinks at that point to everyone's relief, I guess. I suppose I was coming on a little strong, but I was wound up, determined not to take any crap from a bunch of fancy college kids. Maybe I overdid it a little.

They started talking about school, a subject they felt comfortable with.

"Are you really going to the Sorbonne this fall?" Dennis asked Adrienne.

"Yes. I'm trying to get Kathleen to go with me."

"Oh?" I said, suddenly interested. "What's that?"

"The Sorbonne is a school in Paris," Kathleen explained, leaning forward in her chair. She was very pleasant about it. But I was not grateful to her for this information even though I had asked for it, it seems. It made me mad to have her openly assist me in conversation with her snobby friends. She'd chopped regular English into baby food for my benefit, as if I were some kind of idiot. While I sat and smouldered about this, the people of normal intelligence around the table kept on talking.

"Come on, Kathleen. We'd have such a good time."

"I don't think I'm ready for Paris. I'm not even sure I'm ready for Boston."

"Are you going to transfer to Brown?"

"I was thinking of the Rhode Island School of Design."

"I knew it was something Providential. Are you going to do it?"

"I don't know. It means starting over again. I feel sorry for poor Daddy. He shouldn't have to pay for my mistakes."

"Don't be silly, my dear. If you want to change your course of study, do it. You'll regret it if you don't. Besides, I would just as soon you stay in school for ten years as do anything else. The more education you have the better. And the broader. So you see, dear. You'll have no trouble convincing me."

"I know. I have trouble convincing myself. I really do love English literature."

"And English literature loves you," put in Dennis.

"But I love to paint too. I love to, more and more. I worry about throwing away two years. Maybe I should get my degree at Boston and keep painting on the side. I could take courses at the museum after I get my degree. Then if I really liked it, I could, I suppose, take another degree, this time in art. Although it seems like I'm wasting time."

Kathleen smiled at me.

"What do you think?"

"I don't know. Whatever blows your skirt up."

Everybody laughed. I guess it sort of eased the tension that had been building ever since I'd started in on Dennis. Dennis said, "I'll never forget your story about cockroaches."

"Where'd you find this guy?" said Adrienne.

Kathleen smiled. "He just rode up one day."

"Well you're not crazy about school," said Adrienne. "If you don't go back, what will you do?"

"I don't know. I was thinking about going to Quebec."

"Have you been to Quebec before?"

"No."

"You'll like it. It's lovely. You ought to stay at the Chateau Frontenac in the old city. That's the place to get a feeling for things."

I was not sure what the Chateau Frontenac was. A hotel, I guessed, but I was not about to ask.

"You ought to go to Europe. You'd probably like that. Have you thought about Europe?"

"No, I never have."

"Well, you ought to think about it."

"It's an interesting idea, Joe," said the Judge.

"Go to Holland," said Dennis. "Count the tulips. You know what's better than tulips on a piano?"

"Dennis," said Adrienne.

I wondered how much they'd discussed me before I showed up and whether the Judge had told them about the generous offer he'd made me, leaving out the bribery part, of course.

"How about a swim?" said Dennis to everyone. "How about you, Joe? Did you bring a suit?"

"No."

"I have one I can lend you," said the Judge.

"No thanks. I'm not much for swimming."

"I'll go in with you," said Kathleen to Dennis.

Everybody pushed their chairs back.

"I'm going out to the car for some zinc cream," said Adrienne.

"Want another beer, Joe?" asked the Judge.

"No thanks."

Dennis, skinny and white-legged, pigeon-toed toward the pool.

When I looked up, Kathleen was standing right over me. I had to squint to see her against the sun.

"There's no reason to be so defensive," she said in a quiet voice.

"I think your friends are assholes," I said. "Don't you know any real people?"

She walked away without another word. I watched her say something to Dennis as she put aside her jacket and tucked her hair inside her bathing cap. He inclined his head in her direction and smiled reassuringly. Maybe she was apologizing for the barbarian in their midst, I don't know. I began to wonder if I hadn't been too much of a hardass. But it was too late to do much about it.

The Judge came back from wherever he'd gone and sat down next to me.

"Well, Joe. Enjoying yourself?"

"Having a ball."

Kathleen walked in quick, rhythmic steps to the end of the diving board and sprang into the air, rapidly folding, then opening her lean body into a rigid line as she cut cleanly into the water. She swam nearly the length of the pool underwater rapidly as a seal. When her head reappeared, Dennis, who was standing on the end of the diving board, applauded her gravely before crumpling into his own unspectacular dive.

Adrienne returned from the car, rubbing cream on her nose, just in time to see Kathleen's dive.

"She's such an athlete. She can do everything. All I can do is eat and read books."

The Judge laughed.

"Well, that's not so bad. Both are indispensable to your happiness."

"Is it true, Judge Fiske?"

Adrienne pushed her glasses up her nose.

"Is what true, my dear?"

"Is Bobby Kennedy really coming here next week to meet with you and the governor?"

"Well he's supposed to. It's not certain yet."

"I think he's so cute, with those buck teeth and everything."

The Judge laughed.

"Well, I don't know about that. But they better start to take us seriously if they want Maine. Ed Muskie and I can't do it alone."

"People won't vote for Nixon, will they?"

"Oh yes. He's very strong."

"What kind of a judge are you anyway?" I asked.

He looked a little surprised at the sudden question, but it had been on my mind.

"Well I used to be a judge. The title is merely honorific."

"I see."

I wondered whether I ought to think myself up an honorific title. Something like, Duke McCabe, or, Joseph, Earl of East Jesus.

The Judge rumbled politely.

"Will you excuse us, Adrienne? I'd like to show Joe the house."

Adrienne of course said she didn't mind. I followed the Judge along the flagstone path to the back door of the house. Mrs. Pennell, the Judge's housekeeper, was busy laying chunks of thick, red meat on a tray covered with aluminum foil for the Judge to broil on the grill by the pool. While we'd been talking out in the sun, I'd seen an old guy in a ball cap and green coveralls come out the back door with a bag of charcoal, lay a bed of it in the grill, and set a match to it.

So when the Judge invited me to admire the steaks we were going to have for dinner, I told him, "I can't stay for dinner. I promised Henry I'd be back in time to get his supper. He's not too handy around the kitchen."

"Oh? That's too bad. I was counting on your staying. Let's go in here."

We went into his study. He had almost as many books as Henry except they were more neatly arranged and new-looking. He went to the built-in bar at the far end of the room.

"Let's have a real drink," he said. "Would you like a real drink?"

"I ought to get going."

"Spend a few minutes with me before you leave. I won't keep you long."

"All right."

"How about a real drink?"

"A beer is fine."

He fixed himself a martini and handed me a cold can of beer as he came around the bar.

"Want a glass?"

"No, this is fine."

"Here, let's sit over here."

We sat on the couch in front of the fireplace. The fireplace had been swept clean for the summer. A big brass peacock fan decorated the opening.

"What do you think of Kathleen's friends?"

He studied me carefully.

"They're all right."

"You really think so?"

"Sure," I said.

"Dennis's father owns a printing house," the Judge said. "If he ever becomes a writer, he should be able to get his publisher a great price."

"Good for him."

"Adrienne's father is an attorney in New York. Wall Street."

"That's nice," I said.

He chuckled and took a sip of his drink.

"A couple of rich kids. Very nice kids, really. Dennis is a little supercilious at times. But he's bright and very decent in his way."

"That's good. I wasn't sure I liked him."

"He's always gone to private schools," said the Judge. "You may be the first person without a similar background that he's ever met socially."

If he's such a rich kid, I thought, why doesn't he get his belly button fixed?

The Judge studied me for a moment. I thought he was talking strangely, almost as if trying to bait me to see what I'd do. He was always trying to get a line on me. I guessed he did that with everybody. So I thought I'd give him something else to work with.

"Kathleen go with him?"

"No, they're just friends. So far as I know. Of course, you don't know everything your children think."

I looked at my beer. I could feel the Judge looking at me.

"Are you ordinary, Joe?" he asked me quietly, his drink stopped midway to his lips.

"No, I'm not ordinary," I said. "Neither is any other ordinary person."

He smiled and took a sip of his martini.

"You know what makes for class distinction in this country?"

I was not sure what he meant or why it had come up just now.

"It isn't money. It's education. It's so simple, yet it eludes so many people. The Negroes, for instance. They're still trying to get ahead by playing basketball. But the only way up the ladder is education. The Jews and the Asians know this, have always known it. They're never long on the bottom, no matter what country they find themselves in. But the Negroes can't seem to learn the lesson."

"What's this got to do with me?"

"I don't understand your attitude," he said. "Most young men would jump at the opportunity I've offered you. You're a smart boy. Don't you have any ambition?"

"I don't know. I haven't had time to think about it."

"What do you want out of life? Have you thought about that?"

"No."

"Well, think about it. How about something fun? Like a car. Would you like a car? A convertible. All young men like convertibles, don't they?"

"I don't want anything, thanks."

"You make me feel bad, Joe. I'd like to show my appreciation."

"You have," I said.

"Do me one favor, will you?"

"Sure."

"Think things over carefully. This is your future we're talking about: the rest of your life."

"I will." I stood up.

"Good."

He seemed to want to shake my hand, so I gave it to him. He stood there pumping it, smiling into my face, his eyes very thoughtful and searching as if he was looking for something and was puzzled he hadn't found it yet.

"It's always a pleasure talking to you, Joe. You're always honest and to the point. It's refreshing. If you knew the kind of people I had to deal with in politics and business. Well."

He laughed and shook his head, wagging his big nose. His nose, although big, lent a certain dignity to his face.

"I'll get Ambrose to run you back to town in the car."

"That's all right. I've got my bike."

"Are you sure?"

"Yes, I'll be fine."

"The hearing is in three weeks, Joe."

"Oh?"

"Yes, I expect you'll receive something in the mail to that effect in the next day or so. I might be able to arrange for you to make a sworn statement rather than go to court."

"Is that so?"

"It's a possibility. Would you like to have me look into it for you?"

"If you want."

"I'll ask Preble to look into it."

"Okay."

"There's no sense in going to court if you don't have to, is there? Joe, I've been thinking. Maybe you don't want to go away to school right away. This little high school we have here in town is pretty good. It'd give you a chance to get used to the idea of continuing in school and let you stay on with your grandfather."

"Yes," I said. "I been thinking too. If I decide to go back, I'd probably stick around here. I don't want to leave Henry on his own again in that big house."

"I can understand that," said the Judge. "Your grandfather is all alone. Besides, this is a nice little town in which to get your bearings. It doesn't hurt to start off the way you did either, doing something wonderful that everyone will hear about eventually. Incidentally, I appreciate you and your grandfather not going to the papers about Michaelsmith."

"That's okay. Hell, I never even thought about it."

"A lot of people would, Joe," the Judge wagged his nose at me again. "You know, get their names in the paper. Draw a lot of attention to themselves. But you handled it the right way. And I won't forget it."

"Thanks," I said. "I got to be going."

"We have to get beyond this hearing, Joe. You really have

to begin to look out for yourself, you know."

He patted me on the back.

"Look to the future, Joe."

I had looked to the future the last three nights while lying in bed. I hadn't been able see anything but a blank.

We said goodbye in the hall, he shaking my hand again, but he followed me to the door anyway and asked if I wouldn't reconsider staying for dinner.

"No," I said. "I really want to get back."

"Kathleen will be disappointed. The others will be too. They liked you."

Holding the screen door open, the Judge watched me mount my bike.

"Come back again," he said.

He let the door close quietly, subsiding into a shadow behind the screen. But he did not move away from the door.

I glided down the long winding driveway to the road with the distinct impression that the Judge's eyes were still following me.

The surf breaking on the beach across the road from the Judge's farm made for a pretty sight. It must be nice to be rich and live in sight of such views all the time, I thought. The sound of the surf soothed me as I pointed the bicycle in the direction of town.

I suppose I shouldn't have run out like that. But by that time I realized I'd made a fool of myself in front of Kathleen and I was in no mood to hang around. Besides the Judge, with his honorific titles and political connections and modest innuendos, was beginning to put on the pressure again. I just wanted to get out of there before I did something else foolish.

The whole episode left me feeling sad and helpless. I was definitely out of my league out there, what with the Sorbonne and the Chateau Frontenac and the other junk they'd thrown at me. And I was damned unhappy about the interview I'd had with the Judge. Maybe he was telling me stuff for my own good. Maybe the truth wasn't good enough; maybe Sam Summers ought to get by with killing a man so I could get on with the rest of my life. It was hard to know what to do.

I reached town just before dark. The light was on in Henry's study. I wondered if he'd thought to fix himself anything to eat. If not, I would take care of it. Maybe we'd have steaks and fries and a couple of beers together.

When I gripped the doorknob of Henry's house in my hand, hard and cool in my palm, I actually felt a second's worth of relief and pleasure. It was the first time I realized that the house itself could soothe me, just as the sound of the surf had when I'd started for home.

Sixteen

TOUCHING a doorknob was not enough to banish all my confusion. Henry was in the library reading. He'd left the door to the hallway open so he'd hear me when I came in. But when I opened the door and stood there in the hall I discovered I didn't want to talk. I wanted to nourish what little comfort the ride home had given me. I wanted to go upstairs and in the silence of my room figure out why Kathleen always made me feel so bad. I wanted to get away from people for a while. The need was urgent. There was no time for drinks and dinner first.

"Hi there."

Henry put down his book, making as if to rise.

I mumbled hello and started up the stairs.

"Where you going?"

"I'm going to bed."

I turned on the stairs and looked at him.

"Is that all right?"

"Why, sure, if you want to. Did you have anything to eat out there?"

"No."

"Don't you want some supper?"

"No."

"You sure?"

"Goddamnit, Henry . . ."

"All right. All right."

He put up his hands in surrender, subsiding back into his chair. I stood for a moment on the stairs looking down into the room at him. He picked up his book, opened it, and with a sigh affected to be immediately engrossed in it.

I hesitated, thinking maybe I ought to attempt a few pleasantries before disappearing up the rope of my own self-confounding anger. But I couldn't bring myself to do it. I was afraid if I did, it would encourage him to lay down his book again, and really start to talk. The last thing I wanted from Henry or anybody was conversation.

I couldn't have told you why I was suddenly so mad. Maybe it was the shock of returning to the bright circle of human habitation after being out in the darkness. Still I hesitated on the stairs, glaring at Henry's brow wrinkled against the light of the floor lamp beside his couch, the raised book blocking the rest of his face from view.

He looked like a man laboring over a difficult stool. Is the getting of knowledge so tough, even for an old practitioner of the art like you? I wondered.

He said reading was wonderful, a time machine in which you could travel safely, backward and forward. The long-dead, the good and the famous were alive and well again in the pages of books. They always had time for you. They talked in familiar voices. They whispered good advice in your ear in the middle of the night. They would walk with you to the river and back. Reading was fun, he said. But looking at him sitting there, straining after the page in the dim lamplight, you wouldn't have thought so. He looked tired. I wanted to say, why don't you turn out the light, old man? Why don't you give up and go to bed? Give your tired brain a rest and lay your head down on the pillow. Instead of trying to understand everything all the time.

But I couldn't say anything. It all died in the back of my throat. I turned and went up the stairs.

It was for the best. I was like a loaded gun anyway. I wished to hell I'd never met Kathleen, or anybody like her. I wanted to be alone, upstairs in the dark, till I'd figured it out. So I skulked upstairs, leaving Henry posing for animal crackers under his reading lamp.

I didn't sleep much that night. I'm not a sleeper, never was. Which is okay. It gives me that much more time to think. I lay on my bed in the dark room studying the cool distant fog of the white ceiling. I could hear the Judge's smooth voice in my head, telling me things for my own good. I heard again Adrienne's prissy dissertation on the value of travel, and that skinny dink's porkchop talk on literature.

And, of course, I saw Kathleen, her long dark hair parted in the middle, falling away from her forehead in two dark wings, and her large eyes, beautiful and honest, and heard her quiet, straightforward voice. She seemed to like me. You don't know me, I thought. From your safe place, you can't have any idea of who I am or what I feel. I got more in common with Michaelsmith than I do with you and your fancy friends.

Goddamn you. You rich kid, with your big choice between art and literature, Paris and Boston. You're not doing this to me. You're not going to make a damn fool out of me. Nobody's going to make me feel this bad about myself. Not you, hot stuff. Not anybody.

That night I made up my mind to do something about it.

The next morning I said to Henry: "How'd you like to do me a real favor?"

Henry looked doubtful.

"What would that be?"

"Lend me some money so I can get out of here for a while."

"Why? Did something happen out at the Judge's to upset you?"

"I just got to get away. I don't like the way I feel. If I don't get out of here fast, I'm liable to do something stupid."

"Like what?"

"I don't know. Something stupid. Like punch somebody. I just have to get off by myself for a while. Too much is happening all at once."

"Where do you want to go?"

"Anywhere. Someplace out of here."

"How much do you need?"

"I don't know. I thought maybe a couple of hundred dollars. Can you lend me that much? When I get back, I'll get a job and pay you back."

Henry looked at me.

"You're planning on coming back, are you?"

I guess he thought I was getting ready to run out on him.

"I'm coming back," I said. "Hell, if you want me to, I'll stay right here in this house with you forever."

Henry looked away. I guess he didn't expect me to say something like that. He looked back at me, scowling fiercely, giving me his famous old eagle look, blinking his eyes rapidly.

"It is all right if you want to live here with me," he said. Said it in such a humble voice, I wanted to say cut it out, Henry. You don't have to talk to me or anybody like that. Show me some pride, for Godsakes.

"That would be fine with me," he was saying, looking

weepy. "I like having you around. Even though you're more trouble than a skunk under the garage."

"Careful," I said. "Don't offer me too good a deal. You'll never get rid of me."

"That's right. A bad penny like you. So you're going to get a job when you get back, is that it?"

"I guess. Maybe part-time. Maybe I'll go back to school."

"Is that so?"

"I'm thinking about it. I haven't made up my mind yet."

"Well don't rush. I wouldn't want you to make a hasty decision. You really think you're coming back in this direction?"

"Sure," I said. "You ever hear of a place called the Sore-bone?"

"The Sorbonne. Yes, I have. What of it?"

"You think most folks know what it is?"

His fingers made a rasping sound as he scratched his whiskers.

"Most quasi-educated people probably have heard of it. Why?"

"I made a fool out of myself yesterday. Kathleen's friend Adrienne said she was going to the Sore-bone and I asked what it was and gave everybody a good laugh."

"Such is life," said Henry. "We're all the butt of somebody's jokes."

"Well, I'm not going to be. I could have punched that Dennis guy in the mouth."

"What Dennis guy?"

"Kathleen's friend, Dennis Macleod. Long skinny smartass. Goes to Harvard down there in Boston. I guess Kathleen thinks he's wonderful. He knows all about books. But he looked like a dink to me."

"You got to learn the rules," said Henry.

"What rules?"

"Well, first you have to make up your mind. Do you want to go to Harvard? You want to know all about foreign travel?"

"And turn out like him? No thanks."

"That's a good answer," said Henry. "You're a tough guy and pretty smart. But you don't know anything. Now if you knew something and you were tough and smart, why that'd be a pretty good combination."

I thought about it.

"You don't have to turn out like Dennis Macleod," he said. "In fact there is no way in hell that you would. Actually it makes me laugh. Here we are, talking like you'd be taking a risk if you got a little education."

"Well, wouldn't I be?"

Probably it didn't deserve a serious answer but he gave me one.

"An education would only make a young man like you better. Some it might turn into fools and posers. But not you."

"I got to think about it."

"I'd like you to go to the university," he said.

"What university?"

"Harvard. What other university is there? I'd like you to bring home one of these."

He clasped the Phi Beta Kappa key, dangling from his watch chain, in his hand.

"This town thinks the Weatherfields are finished. You could prove they're wrong."

"Wait a minute. I'm only talking about going back to high school. I haven't said anything about college."

"Well, start thinking about it. High school isn't going to teach you what a Sore-bone is. In fact, no school is going to teach you anything, actually. You know that, don't you?"

"What do you mean?"

I saw too late I'd given him an opening to make one of his favorite speeches.

"I mean schools only put you on to things. They assist and guide. You've got to do the learning. Books are the great repositories of knowledge. They're like time machines, son. You open a book like Plato's Dialogues and men who've been dust for twenty-five hundred years spring to life. You hear them talking in their own voices again; they're up and walking around again. They're acting foolish or wise, as the case may be. You get to meet the great man, Socrates. You cry each time he says goodbye to you at the end. Books are miracles, son. I feel sorry for people who haven't discovered it."

"You make it sound pretty good."

"It is pretty good. You don't like people. You'd make a perfect book reader."

I laughed.

"Thanks a lot. Will you lend me the money?"

"Of course. I thought we settled that. Why don't you go down to Boston and look the town over as a prospective tenant?"

"A prospective tenant?"

"Yes. For when you go to Harvard."

"I've been to Boston," I said. "Maybe it ought to be Quebec."

"That's a good idea too. Have you ever stayed in a hotel in Boston?"

"No."

"Ever eat dinner in a fine restaurant?"

"I went to a Red Sox game once."

"Ever go to the Museum of Art or to the Boston Pops or the Public Library or walk along the river?"

"I've been to the Public Gardens."

"You see? You been to Boston, but you haven't been there."

"Maybe I'll give it a try."

"You ought to get to know that town," he said. "It's the only town we've got up here. It's a fine one."

I told him I wanted to get on a train or a bus as soon as I could and get out of Dunnocks Head. In fact, the longer we sat there with our elbows on the kitchen table talking, the more I felt the need to get out.

"What's your hurry?"

"I just want to get out of here. I've got to get away and do some thinking."

Henry seemed to understand. Say one thing for him, he didn't need a lot of explanations. The next morning we went down to the bank and he drew out three hundred dollars and gave it to me.

"There's a bus that leaves out in front of Caldwell's Variety Store at eleven o'clock."

"I'm going home and pack," I said. "I want to be on that bus when it leaves. I want to get the hell out of here."

"Okay, you do that. That's fine with me. You coming back in time for the hearing?"

"I guess so."

"You do what you think is right," he said. "If you want to come back, come back."

"Okay."

"You're always welcome here."

"Thanks."

"It's that girl, isn't it?" he said. "It's Kathleen."

Which made me red.

"It isn't anybody. It's all of you. I got all of you hanging around my neck. I just got to get away."

"All right. I'm sorry for asking. Just come back when you're through doing what you have to do."

I said I would.

"You think I'd miss the chance of hanging out with a mean old guy like you?"

He gave me one of those sudden demented smiles of his, a sudden flash of horse teeth somewhere between Teddy Roosevelt and outright senility.

"You come back. I'll take you fishing again. I'll buy you your own goddamned fishing rod. What do you say to that?"

"I'll come back. Didn't you tell me all time was circular? All you have to do is wait on this street corner and catch me next time I swing past. You couldn't bribe me with a fishing pole anyway."

"You don't remind me of anybody," he said suddenly, glaring at me fiercely. "You don't act like your mother. You sure as hell don't act like that tomcat who passed for your father. You don't remind me of my father or your mother's mother or my grandfather or anybody. Who the hell are you, and how did you get into this family anyway?"

I didn't answer him. Right there, on Maine Street, with his eyes watering like a baby, Henry gave me a sudden violent hug, pushing my face down into his bony shoulder, clutching on to me as if he'd have crushed me into powder if he'd only had the strength. Then, just as violently and abruptly, he shoved me away.

"You damned skunk. You're nothing but a skunk. Why the hell do I like you so much?"

"Christ, don't act like a baby. It's embarrassing to hang around with an old man who cries in public."

"Goddamn it," he said. "I'm not crying."

He wiped his cheek angrily.

"My eyes are watering, that's all. It's this wind blew something into my fucking eye."

"Don't talk nasty."

"I picked it up from you. See how it sounds? Don't like it, do you?"

"Not from an old man."

"Sounds horrible in the mouths of babes, too," he said. "I can assure you."

We went home. I packed a few things. It was only ten o'clock in the morning but we decided to have a beer together. He wanted to do that since I wouldn't be there in the afternoon when we usually had one.

"Want me to walk along to the bus stop?"

"Not really."

"Thought so. Be careful down there. Don't do anything foolish. If you get into trouble, call me."

"Stop worrying."

"I'm not worrying. I'm just planning for contingencies, as any prudent man would. You better get going. You'll miss your bus."

"Well, I'll see you, Henry."

"Maybe you will," he grinned. "Take care of yourself."

"Sure. Stop worrying."

It was good to be going somewhere again, soothing to be among strangers. I felt that good feeling the minute I started down the dark narrow aisle of the bus, past the fat black driver in his sunglasses and blue uniform. I passed a white-haired couple who looked dazed and numbed sitting hunched in their seats like a pair of zombies, a big dark jar of pickles wedged between their battered suitcases in the overhead rack.

In the seat in back of them, a mousy woman in an ugly brown

coat gazed fixedly out her window as if her whole life was spread out on the sidewalk. An old gent had his feet in the aisle. He had his rubbers on; the day was overcast and chilly. This old guy was ready for the weather to turn on him, even if the rest of us weren't.

I found a seat I liked and laid my head back on the prickly, closely shaved upholstery of the headrest, searching for the lever so I could lean back, barber-chair fashion. I liked riding in a bus, high up like that, looking down like a god on the swiftly moving countryside. The world always looked better from the window of a bus, less cluttered with people and their garbage.

As we rushed headlong, it began to rain. I watched the silver streaks of the raindrops jitter down the glass and thought about nothing. The trees, the gas stations, the rise and fall of the telephone wires, they all cranked by. Nothing particularly interested me except the sweet motion of the bus itself. It was damned restful.

When we got to Boston, I took the MTA over to Kenmore Square and rented a room in a hotel. I liked that part of town, near the ball park. My idea was to hole up for a few days starting right when the door swung shut behind me. But, hell, I was itchy in ten minutes. The damn room started closing in on me. The quiet plugged my ears and nose. I felt like I was going to smother to death in a blanket of invisible cotton. I stood it for as long as I could, then practically exploded into the hallway.

Now what, I thought. So I walked around to Fenway Park, bought myself a bleacher ticket, and enjoyed a game of baseball. Some fat guy spilled his beer on me when Runnels tied up the game with a double off the Wall.

"Watch what you're doing!"

He had those jiggly tits that fat guys get. I didn't like the looks of him anyway. I thought he might give me some shit and I'd get to punch his fat face and get the value out of my ticket right away.

But this fellow surprised me.

"Cheez, I'm sorry," he said. "Lemme buy you one."

What could I do after that? So I bought him one back, and we ended up good buddies. He knew all about the Red Sox, all the sad stories and little interesting facts, being one of those fat dinks who make a career of committing every sports detail to memory and then retail them around the bleachers on summer evenings. We even walked out of the park together. With a wave of his hand, he waddled west and I went back to my hotel.

That night I slept like a baby. I never had trouble falling asleep in hotel rooms. It was always familiar places that brought on my insomnia.

Henry had recommended that I go to Locke Ober's, off Park Street, for dinner. He said I ought to add a fancy restaurant to my repertoire of memories. I'd stuffed one of his old black suit jackets into my gym bag in order to meet the restaurant's dress code.

How he talked me into it, I don't know. Maybe I was still smarting from my Sorbonne gaff. Anyway, the next night, off I went to Locke Ober's, armed with a newspaper in case things got dull.

Henry had recommended the beef Wellington, so I ordered it and a bottle of beer. Spaced along the bar globular lights, big as basketballs, sat on the tops of gilded pillars. The noisy crowd, the white dining cloths draping the clutter of tables, the fogbank of blue smoke hanging over the heads of the customers, all multiplied in the fancy gilt mirrors on the walls.

The food was okay but the place itself was a little boring.

So I read the sports section, studying the box score of the game I'd seen the night before.

I wondered if Kathleen had ever eaten here. She probably had. But this dump wouldn't be her first choice. This would be the kind of place some jerk like me would take her on a first date. What she really wanted was quiet elegance. I looked around the smoky, noisy room. No. This was definitely not her style. The thought depressed me, much as if Kathleen had actually been sitting there and had just expressed disappointment in my selection of a restaurant.

It's Henry's fault, damn him. He put me on to the wrong thing. This is like a men's club, not a place you'd take a girl like her. I put another forkful of beef Wellington into my mouth. It tasted like cardboard. Hell, I thought. You can't offer a girl like that anything. You can't show her anything she hasn't seen, except dirty stuff. Who you kidding?

Even if I got an education, I'd never catch up. People like Kathleen would always be ahead of me. Face it, I told myself. You're Doreen's kid; they put you into business in the back of an auto parts truck.

I pushed my plate back and paid the bill, leaving the waiter in the baggy tailcoat who'd served me a big tip. I didn't want him to think I was a piker. So there you are, I thought. Now you've been to a fancy restaurant.

I decided to have a few cold ones in the bar at the hotel before going upstairs. I wanted to stop thinking about everything and just sleep all right, the way I deserved to, in a strange hotel room.

It took me three beers to notice a well-tailored woman of about twenty-five, across the bar from me. Maybe she hadn't been there when I started, I don't know. She was pretty, sort of, with short red hair. She was sitting there alone minding her own business. I decided to send her a drink.

"You want to buy her a drink?"

The bartender raised an eyebrow and rolled out his lower lip. "Right. You got a problem?"

I looked at him hard, wondering why he was making a point of it. Isn't that what you did in places like this? He sighed and moved away. Eventually he got around to it, indicating with a nod that she had me to thank. She smiled at me briefly, then went back to minding her business.

I thought to myself: see how easy it is? You just go to Boston, meet a woman, and forget your problems. You forget that Harvard malarkey. You find a girl, if the hotel room doesn't work. You find someone who doesn't know what a Sorbonne is, so you can be yourself.

I gave her a few minutes and then I decided to go over and sit next to her.

"This your first time in here?"

She answered in a foreign accent, which I liked. Up close, she wasn't especially pretty but she had nice eyes and that nicely cut thick red hair.

"Where you from?"

"Denmark. Are you from Boston?"

"Just passing through. I'm staying here at the hotel for a few days."

"You're young," she smiled. "Are you old enough to be in here?"

"That's nice, I like it when people say I look young. Actually I'm forty-five."

She sipped her drink thoughtfully. So much for humor.

"How come you're so far from home?"

"I'm on vacation."

"All the way from Denmark?"

"Yes. I like the United States."

"Can I buy you another drink?"

"No, thank you. I'd like to go someplace else."

I didn't get it.

"Oh? Where would you like to go?"

"Your room?"

I wasn't sure what I had here: a very impulsive young woman or a real prostitute. She must be a prostitute, I thought. You're not that good-looking. But she didn't fit the picture. So what? I thought. What do you want? References?

"Why not?" I said, thinking this will make me feel better after that bum meal at Locke Ober's.

I paid the bill, the bartender giving me a deadpan look as I did. I gave him a big tip.

"Here you go, Dad. Cheer up."

But he didn't thank me.

I walked with her on my arm to the elevator and we rode up to the room silently. Nobody ever says anything in elevators.

When we got in the room, she pressed against me and gave me a kiss soaked in bar whiskey.

"How much is this going to cost?"

"Fifty dollars."

"Fifty dollars! I could buy a secondhand TV for that."

"Not one that will fuck you, darling."

It sounded kind of funny said in a Scandinavian accent.

"Make it thirty-five."

"All right."

She was an agreeable girl. We stood across the bed from each other taking off our clothes, and talking like a couple of buddies in a locker room. She said she was going to the Berkshires the next day. There was some kind of music festival out there she wanted to catch. She said she was going from there down to New York to hear some real jazz.

I thought, this is nice, being with a stranger like this. No phony baloney. We just get into bed and do it and I pay for it like a gentleman and that's that. No regrets. I stripped fast and climbed into bed.

She had her blouse and brassiere off. Cupping her small breasts in her hands, she said, "No tits."

Later, when she took off her half-slip, she patted her hips. "Big hips, good for babies."

"Forget the babies," I said. "Get in here."

She laughed, a surprisingly rich, throaty laugh. I pulled her into bed with me.

"Is this your first time?" she whispered.

"No," I whispered back. "Is it yours?"

After some preliminaries, we brought our sudden friendship to a conclusion of sorts. When she came out of the bathroom, I gave her the money.

"Would you like me to stay the night?"

It was about two o'clock in the morning. I was tired from all the beer I'd drunk. The last thing I wanted was a business partner in bed with me in the morning.

"I don't think so. I'm tired as hell."

She didn't say another word. She dressed quickly, and I let her out the door.

"Goodnight," I said. "Have a good trip."

"Goodnight."

What impressed me was how empty and forlorn the hallway looked as I held the door open for her. After I let her out, I stood by the edge of the bed, staring at the crumpled pillows, wondering how she must have felt wobbling down that hall in her high heels at two o'clock in the morning. Maybe the hotel dick would nab her. Only then did it occur to me that she might have offered to stay because she didn't have any place to go. It was late for a lone woman to be checking in anywhere. Maybe that thirty-five bucks I'd given her was all the money she had.

I put my clothes on and went out after her. But by the time I reached the lobby, she was gone. I looked out on Commonwealth Avenue; it was dark and empty. I thought: my, aren't you a nice fellow.

The next morning I walked over to Boston University to see where Kathleen went to school. Walking up and down outside the tall cold buildings, I decided I didn't like the place.

How can she go here? I asked myself. I expected her to go to a school with ivy-covered buildings and the hour tolling from a high white belfry.

After that I walked rapidly up Commonwealth till I found a likely bridge that might lead me to Cambridge so I could see what Harvard looked like. It was a good walk but, what the hell, what else did I have to do? I liked the look of Harvard better than I did Boston University.

But I sure didn't like it well enough to want to go there. I don't want to go anywhere, I thought. I just want to be left the hell alone. I was so damned depressed by the whole thing, I walked around in circles for the next two days, mainly hanging out in the park watching old folks and kids feed the pigeons. This one old guy fed them cashews.

I didn't speak fifty words in two days. Just enough to order breakfast and dinner in this little joint I found on Boyleston Street. I thought of going out to Revere Beach to see Doreen and Dale, but I was depressed enough already.

I didn't know what to do. I felt so bad. I'd never felt that bad before in a strange place. It always felt good before. What's wrong with you, I asked myself. Why aren't you having a good time?

I thought of Henry, fumbling around his house like a zombie. Probably not taking care of himself or eating properly. Sleeping

on the couch downstairs again. Probably worrying about me.
I remembered I hadn't even called him. I'd been gone four days,
and I hadn't even bothered to tell him where I was or whether
I was alive or dead. I thought: well, aren't you a thoughtful guy.

Christ, you know how Henry worries over nothing. If I
know him, he's probably making himself sick over it. He just
loves to worry anyway.

I'd been feeling so sorry for myself I'd never even stopped
to think about him.

I wolfed down my supper and went back to the hotel and
gave him a call.

"Where you been?" he said. "Are you all right?"

"Sure, I'm all right."

"You having a good time?"

"I'm having a hell of a time."

"Well, that's wonderful. I'm glad to hear it's doing you some
good."

"It's doing me wonders. I guess I'll catch a bus home tomorrow."

He said that sounded like a good idea to him.

So the next day I caught a bus and went home.

Seventeen

 S o o n as I could, I went out to the farm to see Kathleen. I told her on the phone, "Look, I have to talk to you."

"What is it? What's wrong?"

"I can't talk on the phone. Can I come out?"

"My, you're a strange boy. Full of urgency and mystery."

"Look, can I come out or not?"

"Yes, of course you can."

Kathleen was out by the pool enjoying the last of the sunlight when I got there. She'd pulled on an old pair of shorts and a cotton shirt over her bathing suit and was curled up on the chaise longue.

She watched as I leaned the bike against the hedge. Her hair lay in thick wet tangles against her brown neck. She looked faintly amused, her chin cupped in one hand.

I suppose she found me slightly ridiculous riding out there immediately on my bicycle like a delivery boy, after sounding tongue-tied and half sick on the phone. Look at her, I thought. She knows she's beautiful. She can read my mind. She knows I begin to ache like a bad tooth at the sight of her.

It made me mad to think how funny she must find it, to have a delivery boy like me crazy about her. You bitch, I thought. You're not doing this to me. You can make those college boys lovesick. But you're not making a fool out of me.

I bent over, taking the bicycle clip off my pant leg. I stood up again so suddenly it made me dizzy.

"I got to talk to you," I croaked. The whole world dimmed and swam before me.

"Go ahead," I heard her say. Then, "Are you all right?"

"I'm okay."

My knees had turned to mush.

"You better sit down."

She was sitting up now and patted the cushion beside her. I just wanted to push her down and climb right on top of her. But damned if I would sit next to her where I could breathe in the scent of her hair or study the fine satin of her skin. I wasn't that much of a jackass. So I picked a folding chair several yards across the flagstones from her, sitting with my back to the pool, and waited for the spell to pass.

"Be careful. You're close to the edge."

"I know where I am."

The truth is, I'd probably have moved if I hadn't been so woozy. The water slurped greedily in the gutter behind me. The smell of chlorine didn't help either.

"I don't like the way I'm feeling. Ever since I got mixed up with you and your father."

"Is that why you've been staying away from us?"

"I've been out of town. I went down to Boston to get away from it all for a while."

"What have we done to hurt your feelings? Whatever it was, we didn't mean it."

"Isn't that nice. You don't mean any harm. People like you never do."

She looked surprised at that, but I couldn't help it. Rich people like to pretend they come by it at nobody's expense. You're supposed to believe that they were elected rich by popular demand. She expected me to admire her because she was so pretty and had everything she wanted. Well I didn't find anything adorable about that. Except she had some kind of hold on me, had had from the first minute I saw her, and I was mad at myself because I couldn't shake it.

"I saw where you go to school."

"You did?"

"Yes, I went over there and looked at the place. It looks like a damned insurance company."

"Sorry you don't approve."

"I took a look at Harvard too."

"How did that measure up?"

"That was better. It looked more like a school. But if it turns out people like Dennis, I wouldn't want to go there."

"You ought to keep an open mind," she said. "Dennis is just Dennis. He has nothing to do with how Harvard is."

"I imagine a lot of them are like Dennis. I wouldn't last two minutes in a place like that."

"Don't sell yourself short, Joe. Daddy says you're very intelligent."

"That's a real compliment. An important man like your father thinks I'm intelligent."

"Why are you so angry? What have we ever done except be nice to you?"

"Maybe I don't want to be treated nice. I'm not one of your hired hands."

"What's that got to do with it?"

"Shit," I said.

She started to reach for her cigarettes on the table.

"Don't do that."

"Don't do what?"

"Don't smoke. Don't start that sophisticated shit again."

"I like to smoke."

"Well, it's not sophisticated. It stains your teeth. It's bad for your health. You could get bad lungs."

"Hey, you're not my boss."

I just looked at her. I wanted to get up and go over there and give her a smack alongside the head.

She screwed a cigarette into the corner of her mouth, scratched a match on the flagstones, and lighted the thing, squinting against the smoke. She crossed her legs Indian fashion and tossed her head back, blowing a long faint stream of smoke against the darkening sky. I just sat there, watching her show off.

"You're a strange boy."

"I'm not a boy."

"What are you—a man?"

"Better than some you'll find."

"You disappoint me, Joe."

She stubbed out her cigarette in one of the quahog shells they used for ashtrays around the pool. She'd made her point, I guess, and now was ready to put the weed aside.

"Why is that?"

She looked at me a little sadly.

"I didn't think you were a braggart."

The theatricality of that sad look got to me.

"You like to fuck people around, don't you?"

When she stood up, I noticed the pockets of her shorts hung down in half-moons below the hem. Somehow those pockets dangling at half-mast made me like her better.

"If you're going to talk like that—"

"Sit down. There's nobody here to show off for."

Kathleen hesitated, looking toward the house, then sat again on the longue. She studied her hands.

"Say what you have to say. Then kindly go."

"I apologize for the language. You and your father give me the jitters. Why is that?"

She shrugged her shoulders.

"Don't ask me. I don't know what your problem is. We're grateful to you for what you did. Daddy and I—"

"You act like you're married to him. You're not actually married to him, are you? What's this 'Daddy and I' stuff all the time?"

"If you're going to be rude—"

"Don't give me that stuff. I had all the phony talk I could take the other day when your friends were here."

"You take a lot of liberties," she said.

She sat forward stiffly, staring at the flagstones. Her wet dark hair was pulled back from her small ears. She looked sleek as a sea otter. Behind her, the sky had gone pink and the tall pines on the hillside looked black against it. She had little scallop shell earrings on, which glowed like molten gold, as if some smithy god had taken them directly from his forge and fastened them to her small perfect ears. The half-moons of the pockets below the hemline of her shorts glowed against her smooth tan legs. Her pink blouse with its round collar and narrow blue stripe was unbuttoned. As she leaned forward, creasing her forehead in distaste at my behavior, I saw the dark pear of her breast sculptured against the bodice of her bathing suit—the same black tank suit she'd worn the other day which had made me feel so weak and sad that I could hardly stand it. It was that careless way she had of using her looks against me that I resented most, I think.

"You better go home," she said. "Come back another day when you're not so grouchy."

It was getting darker by the minute. Her outline was beginning to soften, losing some of its fine detail. The fire went out of her earrings. The lights in the pool turned the water into smoky phosphorus. I began to ache even worse.

I would have to ride home in total darkness if I didn't get going. But I was too lovesick to make any move to get up. I hated feeling this way. It left you too weak to go anywhere. So you couldn't get away. You couldn't tell the person to go to hell even if you wanted to. It was all a trap and I knew it. I wanted to die.

Suddenly she began to talk in a soft, wondering voice—not to me so much as to the darkness.

"Ever since we lost Mother, Daddy and I have been very close. It's been almost nineteen years but Daddy never got over it. He'd be lost without me. I'm everything he has."

"So you're his girl. His good little girl."

"Is that so bad?"

"What happened to your mother?"

She looked away.

"I don't want to talk about it."

"You don't have to. I know how you feel."

I was going to say something smart about Doreen, but she didn't give me the chance.

"She killed herself," Kathleen said. She'd made a steeple of her fingers in front of her mouth, whispering these words through them.

I thought I'd misunderstood.

"Pardon?"

"Killed herself," she whispered again.

"I'm sorry."

She looked at me, smiling.

"You thought I was just a little rich girl who'd had it soft all her life, didn't you?"

She was right.

"I don't know what to say."

"Don't say anything."

We sat there, half hidden from each other in the dark.

"She was sick. She'd been sick for a long while. Daddy said he guessed she'd got sick of being sick and she killed herself."

"Don't talk about it."

"I want to talk about it. I never talk about it, but now I've started. Don't you want to know how she killed herself?"

"No."

"Are you sure? Aren't you curious to know how the rich kill themselves?"

"You're trying to be tough," I said. "But it's not working."

"You want to know," she said. "You don't like us, but you're fascinated by us. You nearly got yourself killed by Mr. Michaelsmith so you could hang around and look at me some more, didn't you? Well now you ought to know how we kill ourselves. That's the least I can do for you. You probably think we inject ourselves with expensive perfume or something."

"Tell me, if it'll make you happy."

"She used a shotgun. She drove down to Daddy's office one night and parked outside. She put the end of one of his shotguns in her mouth and touched off both triggers with her toes."

"Jesus."

"She was a pretty woman. I was a little baby when it happened. But I've seen her pictures."

After a minute, she added, "I hope I never do anything like that."

"You won't."

"What do you know about it?"

I didn't say anything.

"They say it runs in families," she said.

We sat there in the darkness, thinking about it.

Kathleen reached for another cigarette. I stood up and took it out of her hand.

"Forget that stuff. It's bad for you."

I threw the cigarette into the nighttime.

When I sat down again, my chair slid off the edge, sending me ass over backwards into the swimming pool. It was like plunging into a tank charged with electricity. Every hair, every follicle, stood on end as my body took the full shock on impact.

I sank like an anchor, my arms outstretched and fists clenched, bubbles seething in my ears. I opened my eyes. I was trapped in a giant lozenge of cloudy green light. The light began to shut down from the edges inward. I was going to die, I knew it.

Then Kathleen was in the pool with me and had me by the shirt. In a panic, I clawed at her. It seemed I was not dead after all. We went around in a circle underwater, the sound roaring in my ears. She kneed me in the face. But I wouldn't let go. Then she kicked me again. I let go. When I grabbed again, she was gone.

Bitch! Bitch! I thought.

I was on my knees at the bottom of the pool. She grabbed me by the neck from behind and kicked off the wall, dragging me up the incline of the pool floor. I clutched onto her again. I must have flipped her over my shoulder because suddenly she was in front of me again. She put her foot in my throat and kicked off, damn near breaking my neck. Then she was back and this time I didn't fight and she grabbed me under the arms and stood me up and we were in five feet of water and I gagging and coughing and blind and clawing at her still and she fought me into shallow water where I puked my guts out and tried to bite off chunks of the unyielding air. God, didn't it hurt to breathe.

Kathleen pounded me on the back.

"You crazy. You nearly drowned us both."

I grabbed her by the shirt, tearing it right off her back, and swiveled her around.

"You bitch!"

I swung at her, catching her a glancing blow on the chest. Kathleen staggered back in the shallow water.

"You tried to drown me, you bitch."

I was leaning over, gagging and spitting up water.

"No, no," she said. "Don't act crazy. It's all right now."

"You tried to kill me."

"No, no."

"Yes," I whispered to the water, exhausted. "Yes you did."

"No, I didn't. I tried to help you."

I stood there in the shallow water, my hands on my knees.

"I can't breathe."

"It's all right. You'll be all right."

I buried my face against her, digging my fingers hard into her back.

"Kathleen."

"It's all right," she whispered. "Nobody'll ever know."

Her fingertips slid along my spine till they touched the back of my sodden head. I lowered the strap of her bathing suit, cupping the smooth cold fruit of her breast in my hand. The dark bruise of her nipple was already hard by the time my fingers reached it. She pressed against me tightly, her arms icy cold around me, textured like an orange by the cold air. I kissed her. I held her, kissing her long, drawing her toward the stairs

at the end of the pool. As I kissed her, I pulled her suit down
to her waist.

"Don't," she said, sounding drugged.

"Yes."

"Nooo."

I made her sit down on the edge of the pool and stripped her
swimsuit clear of her legs. Her skin in the untanned places made
a glowing white duplicate of her suit in the dark.

"No more, Joe."

"Why not?"

I tossed her suit over my shoulder into the deep end. It landed
with a splat. Turning, I saw it dangling off the diving board.

"You fool," she said. "You couldn't do that again in a
million years."

I pushed in as she sat on the edge of the pool, standing in my
six-ton khakis in water almost to my knees. She scissored her
legs around my waist. She drew my head toward her face.

"Please," she whispered.

I was sorry I'd started because I knew once we'd made love
I'd never get over her. You sap, I thought. You're really in for
it now.

We rocked together on the edge of the pool. Slowly we
worked our way out of the water onto the flagstones, where we
fell asleep. Kathleen was on top. I had my arms and legs
wrapped around her, clinging to her like a newborn possum
clings to its momma. The chill air woke us almost right away.

Kathleen seemed dazed, if not embarrassed.

"We shouldn't have done that."

"Probably not."

When she asked me to fetch her swimsuit from the diving
board, she saw me hesitate.

"Never mind," she said, and got it herself.

"Goodnight, Joe."

"Goodnight."

She ran naked toward the house holding the suit in one hand, and seemed to fade on the dark air itself. I waited for the sound of a door, but I never heard a thing.

When I got home Henry was in the study, the door to the hall ajar, pretending he wasn't waiting up for me.

"Well," he put down his book. "You and Kathleen get everything settled between you, did you?"

"No. We didn't settle anything. Things are worse than ever."

"That's too bad. That must mean you like her even more than you thought you did. Holy Sam, boy. What happened to you?"

I looked down. At my feet a puddle was forming on the linoleum.

"Fell in the pool."

"You fell in the swimming pool? What you do that for?"

"Fell ass over backwards out of a chair."

He started to laugh.

"It wasn't funny," I said. "I nearly drowned."

"Really, you ought to learn how to swim," he said. "Did you fall into the deep end?"

"I did. Swallowed about half the pool before Kathleen fished me out."

"Kathleen pulled you out?"

"She came right in after me. I fought her like hell, I was so damned scared. I tried to use her as a ladder to climb out. It was probably the worst thing I ever did in my life. I just panicked. I thought for sure I was going to die. I damned near killed her. I punched her around and everything."

"What did she do?"

"She fought me. She fought right back. She dragged me into the shallow part."

"Picture that," he said. "She's something, is that girl. Go upstairs and get out of those wet clothes, then come back and tell me some more about this."

"I don't think so. I want to go to bed."

"Wait a minute. Don't run off. Tell me some more."

Henry always picked a fine time to be a pain in the ass. Here I was feeling miserable and hopeless, so naturally he wanted to talk.

"So you go out there, all set to tell her off," he settled in his chair as before a warm and hospitable fire. "Then you, always the fool, manage to fall in the pool. And she drags you out like a puppy. What else happened?"

"That's enough, isn't it?"

"Was the Judge around?"

"You're just dying for the details."

"Frankly, yes. You fascinate me. You unfold like a natural disaster. Everywhere you go, something fantastic happens. What else happened? You didn't get struck by lightning on the way home, did you? Or are you saving that for tomorrow?"

"I'm going to bed, funny man. I'm tired as hell."

"Wait a minute. Didn't you two talk about anything?"

"Yes, we talked. She told me about her mother."

"My, that's a sad story."

"She killed herself, she said. Shot herself in front of the Judge's office late one night. Is that true?"

"Yes, sadly true enough."

"Why did she do that?"

"Plenty of reasons, I guess. None of them good enough."

"Well tell me."

"Poor Lois Fiske. I know more about her than I ever wanted to."

"Get on with it, Henry. I want to get out of these wet clothes sometime."

"I heard the blast the night she killed herself," he said.

"You did?"

"Yes," he paused to rub the back of his knobby hand against his whiskers.

"I was sitting here, reading as usual. I heard the shots go off. I ran out the door. It was pitch black. The streets were empty. I had no idea where the noise came from. Then through the trees I saw a dim light from inside a car across the Commons and what looked like somebody flung back against the seat. I went across and found her. On the passenger side in the front seat. The car an absolute mess. I remember her purse. It was white. She'd placed it on the floor against the pedals on the driver's side. It stood there neat as a daisy without a spot on it."

"You found her?"

Henry unwrapped the spidery-thin steel-rimmed glasses from his soft, rubbery ears, closed his eyes, and squeezed the bridge of his nose between his forefinger and thumb.

"Not quite," he sighed, squinting up at me. His milky-blue eyes were blind and naked as a baby's.

"Summers was there before me. He was the town watchman in those days."

Henry shook his head.

"Jesus. I remember it all so clearly. The door was open. The dome light was on. One of her shoes was in the gutter. The air was loaded with the hot smell of blood and gunpowder. 'She killed herself,' Summers said, like a man in a daze. 'Who is it?' I asked. Because I didn't recognize the car right off and I sure as hell didn't recognize the person. I was used to seeing her drive around town in the Judge's white Cadillac. 'It's his wife,' he said. 'Whose wife?' I said. 'The Judge's,' he said."

We didn't say anything—either of us, for a minute.

"That's a bad story," I said.

"Yes it is. Only that's not the half of it. If you promise to keep it to yourself, I'll tell you the rest. I'm probably the only one who knows certain parts of this. But promise to keep it to yourself. I don't want Kathleen getting hurt over this."

"Who am I going to tell?"

"Sit down and I'll tell you. Don't you want to go upstairs and change out of those wet clothes first?"

"I'm all right."

"Sit down on the floor so you don't ruin the furniture."

"Are you going to tell me or worry about the furniture?"

"All right, all right. Just keep this to yourself, will you?"

"I said I would. Who would I tell anyway?"

"Good," he said. "Because this goes to the Hippocratic Oath. One day, the Judge came to me with an eye problem. It turned out to be a detached retina. I sent him down to Massachusetts General. They put him to bed and sandbagged his head to keep him still, to give it a chance to heal. He had just the ceiling to keep him company. One of the nurses who took care of him was a young woman. When he got out of the hospital he married her, brought her back here with him. That was Kathleen's mother, Lois. She was young enough to be his daughter."

"Was she pretty?"

"She was pretty all right."

"Was she as pretty as Kathleen?"

"Well, I'd call it a toss-up."

"Sorry," I said. "Go on with it."

"If you'll shut up for a minute."

I shut up and he went on.

"They seemed happy at first," he said. "They had a baby right away."

"Kathleen."

"Yes. The Judge seemed very proud of himself. Things went along well, so far as anybody knew. Then she started coming to see me regularly. Vague complaints. I checked her over. Nothing wrong physically. I suggested a change of scene. One day I remember she began to cry in my office. I looked up and there she was sitting across from me, the tears streaking her face, crying soundlessly. I asked her what was wrong. 'Nothing, Doctor,' she said. I said, 'Then why are you crying?' She said, 'I'm not crying.' 'Yes, you are,' I said. 'No,' she said. 'You are mistaken.' Maybe it was the differences in their ages. Who knows?"

"What happened?"

"What usually happens. She sought her solace elsewhere."

"How do you know?"

Henry looked at me, smiling sadly.

"Because I was a damned fool. She came to me for help. Told me she was pregnant. 'Why that's wonderful,' I said. 'No, it isn't,' she said. 'It isn't his. We haven't slept together for months.' I was shocked. Funny, isn't it?"

He looked at me, shaking his head.

"I'd been a doctor for twenty-five years. But I had no idea what people will do if they think it will bring them happiness. Or temporary surcease from its bitter absence, at least. I examined her. She was right, she was pregnant all right. 'Will you help me?' she asked."

Henry smiled, only it wasn't pleasant memories he was remembering.

"Naturally, I refused."

"You turned her down?"

"What she wanted was against the law. I didn't believe in

abortion anyway. I doubt if she found much consolation in my high-toned principles."

"Probably not. What did she say when you turned her down?"

"She said she'd find some other way. 'Maybe you ought to go home and talk it over with your husband,' I said. She looked at me like I was crazy."

"What happened?"

"That was all. At least I thought that was all. Weeks went by. Then one night, I had a telephone call from a frightened young man who wanted me to come out to somebody's farm and take care of Mrs. Fiske, who was awful sick, he said. Mrs. Fiske, he called her. He was her lover and he referred to her as Mrs. Fiske. 'Please, Dad,' he said to me. 'Will you help us?' "

Henry smiled, shaking his head.

I didn't know what to say. I sat there, puddling on the linoleum, waiting for him to club me with the rest of it.

"Yes," he said. "It was my boy who'd become her special friend. I found out later she'd been going down to Boston to visit him at Harvard. Where they'd met I don't know. He'd been sneaking home to see her some weekends, only I didn't know that either. So they called me. After some quack had made a mess of things. I rushed out there. She was bad off, bleeding badly. I had to cut the fetus out of her—"

In a slow quavery voice, as I grew toad-cold on the linoleum, Henry told me how he almost lost Kathleen's mother that night under the dim light of a kerosene lantern, the shadows big on the bedroom wall.

Why didn't you call me earlier, Donald? he asked his boy. His boy answered, We did. But you wouldn't do anything.

Henry told me his kid insisted he was going to stay in the room all the time, stay right there and comfort Mrs. Fiske, but he broke down almost at once and began sobbing, "Don't die. Please don't die." Kathleen's mother held his head between her hands and told him to shush. It was all right, she said, because she was feeling better now. But he was such a mess Henry kicked him out of the room anyway.

Afterwards Henry and Donald took the fetus, still in the white-enamel basin, out in the back to bury it. Donald shambled after his father, making subhuman noises as if he'd been kicked in the chest.

It was almost sunrise, plenty of light to see by. Henry had his sleeves rolled to the elbows. His vest was open, blowing in the dawn breeze. He was moving toward the barn, he said, trying not to get anything on his pants. That's when Donald got a good look at what was in the basin. Standing there in the barnyard, Donald started barking like a fox.

Henry told him to shut up, shut up and keep walking. Donald calmed himself and went along with Henry to the barn. Henry sent him inside. Finally, he thought he'd have to put the basin down and go in after Donald. But just then, Donald came out with the stuff.

Together they started for the pasture, stopping just beyond a line of old apple trees. Donald started digging. Henry had been carrying a towel over his arm like a waiter. He spread it on the ground and laid the mess in the basin on it. Donald was digging fast, not looking up. Henry kneeled in the grass. He folded the four corners of the towel and fitted the bundle into the mouth of the empty nail keg which Donald had found in the barn. Henry tapped the cover into place with the bone handle of his pocketknife.

They put the keg in the hole Donald had dug. But Donald couldn't fill in the hole. Here give me that, you fool, Henry said, and he took the shovel from him. He filled in the hole in a hurry, tamping it down good as Donald stood by shaking with grief and biting his fist. Henry threw the shovel aside and began slapping Donald, coldly and methodically. Donald didn't even put up his hands. Finally Donald came to himself and Henry led him back into the house.

In those days, Henry said, he had a cottage on the Belgrade Lakes. He drove Kathleen's mother and Donald up there so she could rest. Kathleen's mother was supposed to be shopping in Boston and wasn't expected back for a few days. So Henry took them up there to give her a chance to recover.

That was when Donald dropped out of medical school and joined the army. And eventually got himself killed at Monte Casino.

Kathleen's mother dropped from view for a few weeks. She was away, the Judge told people. She was not well and was staying in the White Mountains.

"When she came back," Henry said, "she was thin and sickly looking. I heard she was doctoring. But she no longer came to me. She went to somebody up to Bath. Within six months, she killed herself. I never wrote to Donald about it. But somebody else must have, because he wrote wanting to know why I hadn't told him."

Henry ran his hand through his cloud of white hair.

"I could have stopped the whole thing if I hadn't been a horse's ass."

"It wasn't your fault, Henry."

"No, it wasn't. But I could have stopped it."

"You think you could have?"

"Probably not. But I should have tried."

"Why don't you go to bed? Put aside the books for one night."

He didn't argue. I led him up the stairs to his room.

"Goodnight," I said. But I guess he was too tired to answer.

That night I slept long and hard and dreamless.

In the morning, I woke thinking about Kathleen. But I didn't lie there for long. I borrowed Henry's car and drove up to the YMCA at Bath.

I asked the fellow behind the counter, "Do you give swimming lessons here?"

"Sure we do. Go right through that door there. It'll take you right into the natatorium."

"The what?"

He cackled.

"They call it the natatorium around here. But between us chickens it's a swimming pool."

"Oh."

"Just right in there and talk to Mr. Hicky. He's giving a swim lesson right now."

So I went in there. The room was completely tiled, tan and shiny, with a green trim line three-quarters up the wall. The smell of chlorine was sharp as a finger jabbed up your nose.

At one end of the pool, holding a clipboard, stood a man dressed in a yellow T-shirt and dark gray shorts with a silver whistle around his neck.

In the pool, holding a paddleboard, thrashed a long narrow-backed Negro in a swimsuit no bigger than a jockstrap. His head, wet and shiny like a black rubber ball, was half submerged. His pink feet churned the water furiously.

Mr. Hicky studied the man in the pool.

"He's doing real well," said this guy, Mr. Hicky. "Only ten lessons. Most of them are sinkers."

"Sinkers?"

"Yeah, they sink."

I looked at the fellow struggling conscientiously in the pool.

His cocoa-brown back was long and thin and muscular. The water ran down the sluice made by his spine. He held the board rigidly, his head still submerged, and threshed his feet like a paddlewheeler.

"Why would that be?"

Mr. Hicky shrugged his shoulders.

"Beats me. They just are."

The Negro reached the end of the pool and stood up, tall and skinny, in the shallow water, wiping the water from his eyes. His big dingus pressed like a crooked finger against the canary yellow fabric of his tiny swimsuit.

"What can I do for you?" asked Mr. Hicky.

"Nothing, just looking the place over."

"Sure, look around. If you have any questions, I'll be here."

"Thanks," I said and walked out.

There was no point in swimming lessons, I decided. Likely I was just a natural sinker, like that fellow in the pool.

Eighteen

⌐⌐ LIFE knocks you off a molecule at a time. You go along thinking you're okay, but it wears you down, you just don't know it. Then you wake up some morning and find you're weak beyond words.

That's the way I felt the next day. I wanted to lie there and die because Kathleen wasn't right there with me. I felt like a sick man—sick and aching inside. I wanted to migrate right up into her belly, curl up in the warm darkness, and go to sleep forever.

You pathetic dink, I thought. She's got you now.

I got dressed, took the dog, and went for a walk in the woods.

"Why don't you go for a long walk," said Henry at breakfast. "Go out in the woods and get the stink blowed off you."

I wasn't very pleasant company, I guess. So I got the dog and went out the door.

We walked deep into the woods. I began to feel better. I thought about the lake, like a silver scar on the big green flank of the forest. Far from the hand of man. I was hoping we'd get back in there again before winter set in. Damn, I thought. Don't I need that place now. Get away from here and forget all this stuff.

We were coming back. We'd just reached the clearing where the cemetery was when Summers suddenly stepped from behind an obelisk as if from the granite itself. I must have jumped a foot.

"Where you been, little man?"

"What the hell do you want?"

It shook me, him suddenly appearing out of nowhere.

He just chuckled, one meaty hand hooked in his gunbelt. The sun reflected off the beetle-backed badge pinned to the black pocketflap of his gray shirt.

"You a little jumpy, ain't you?"

He had his sunglasses on, and was picking at his teeth with the corner of a matchbook cover.

"I didn't scare you, did I? No, course not. I couldn't scare a tough kid like you. Could I?"

I didn't say anything.

"What are you doing out here anyway? City boy like you liable to get lost in these woods."

To hell with him, I thought, I'm not saying anything. I'll just get into trouble if I do.

"You could have an accident out here," he said. "Some hunter might take you for a bobcat and shoot you right in the middle of the back. Hell, you liable to lay out in these woods till spring 'fore anybody'd find you."

I didn't say anything.

"You ever think of that?"

"No, I never did."

"You think about it. These woods are dangerous. Lot of bums drifting in and out of the woods these days."

Summers put his hand on his gun. From behind his no-see-um sunglasses, he looked around the cemetery. He looked just like a pig up on its hind legs, trussed up in a uniform and sunglasses.

He's trying to scare me, I thought. Or am I in a worse fix?

I wondered if I should wait to find out. I considered kicking him in the balls and making for the woods. All kinds of things burned in my head. But I decided to wait it out.

"Don't keep this place up very good, do you?"

He pretended to study the grounds carefully. The bastard was enjoying himself.

"Grass all growed up to your ass. Just like your grandpa's backyard used to be."

He turned back to me, his teeth white and grinning below the twin black circles of his sunglasses.

"You ought to take a scythe and clean this place up. Show a little respect for your dead ones. You related to these people, ain't you? Or are you just your mother's bastard?"

I should have kept quiet. But I never did know when to shut up.

"Don't push me," I said. "I don't care if you are a cop."

I never even saw it coming. Next thing I knew I was on my back in the grass, my head against the cold granite of a tombstone. He reached down and picked me up by the front of my shirt. The dog started barking and carrying on. Summers turned on it, cussing, and put a boot in the dog's ribs, knocking him end over end. The dog let out a yelp, gathered itself, and skittered across the clearing for the underbrush. That was my chance, when he kicked the dog. But that suckerpunch he'd laid on me still had me stupid.

He pulled me close.

"Someday you'll learn not to threaten folks."

In the lenses of his sunglasses, I saw a funhouse version of my face.

"Turn around and put your hands on that stone."

"What the hell you doing—"

He slapped me alongside the jaw with the butt end of his gun.

"Turn, Shitbrain. Move quick when I say so. Now take those pants down."

"Goddamn you, Summers—"

He kneed me in the thigh—hard—damn near taking me to the ground. My whole leg went numb.

"Drop those pants like I said."

"You don't have the right to hassle me."

"I ain't hassling you, Shitbrain. I'm conducting a weapons search on an accused felon. Now you kick those pants off to the side."

"I'm not—"

He hit me in the back of the head.

"I ain't arguing with you, motherfucker."

He jammed my pants down over my head, pulled down my underwear, and pressed his gun against my ass.

"Want me to pull the trigger, Shitbrain?"

I didn't answer.

"How'd you like it if I put you out of your misery, you little prick? Just blow you to hell where you belong. I'd be saving people a lot of trouble, wouldn't I? Turn around."

He swung me around, jerking one pant leg down tightly over my head, and kneed me in the balls all in the same motion. I went down. He cocked the gun against my head.

"You been causing me a lot of embarrassment. But I'm going to give you a second chance. You don't deserve a second chance. But I'm giving you one. When you're at that hearing next week, you just remember what it's like to have a gun up your ass. You just be nice at that hearing. We'll forget past differences. I bet the Judge will fix everything for you back home too. You can keep on enjoying the good life. How's that? You like the sound of that?"

I didn't say anything.

"You suddenly very quiet, Shitbrain," he pressed the pistol against the side of my head. "I thought you'd like that deal."

He jerked me to my feet, pulled my pants off my head, and threw them down the hill. I blinked against the sudden light.

"You got a bright future," he said. "The Judge likes you. The Judge's little girl likes you. You got it made. Just don't fuck it up."

He paused to see if I was going to say anything, but I didn't.

He prodded me with the pistol.

"Now get home," he said. "Think over what I told you real good."

I started down the hill, found my pants, and stopped to put them on. Summers watched me from the cemetery. I zipped my fly and started down the hill again.

"You remember what I told you!"

I kept walking.

"Don't fuck with me, Shitbrain!"

When I got to the house I went to the barn and found the hatchet. I started back up the lawn for the woods.

Henry caught me at the footbridge. He must have seen me out the kitchen window.

"Where you going with that hatchet, son?"

"Get out of my way."

"No, I want to know what's going on."

He grabbed my hand.

"Give me that."

"Get away from me. Goddamn it, if you don't get away—"

"What's wrong with your eye? What happened out there?"

"Nothing. Just let me go. Go back in the house."

He shook me, as if trying to snap me out of a trance.

"Tell me, damn it. What happened to you?"

"Summers," I said. "He caught me in the woods. I'm going to kill the son of a bitch."

"No you're not."

"Yes, I'm going to kill him. I should have killed him the last time. You're not going to stop me either. Get the hell out of the way."

"Come back to the house. We'll call the state police."

"They won't do anything. They're in with him. I'm doing this myself. That son of a bitch is never going to hit me again."

"No." Henry started wrestling with me feebly, trying to get the hatchet away from me.

"Goddamn it, Henry."

He slipped and went down. But he got right up again.

"You're not going anywhere. You're not throwing your life away on that idiot. Give me that hatchet."

"Get out of my way. I'm warning you, old man."

"Oh yes? What you going to do? Kill me too? Well, go ahead. I'm old enough to die. But you're not."

He looked down at his hand, shaking it gingerly. I saw he'd slashed it when he'd fallen. He must have caught it on a loose nail on the rotten old footbridge.

"Doesn't that hurt," he said, suddenly conversational.

And in just that split second of distraction, he twisted the hatchet right out of my fingers. He was across the footbridge in a second, moving rapidly through the old orchard.

"Henry!"

He didn't answer but kept climbing rapidly up the slope through the gnarled trees.

I went after him. He was moving surprisingly fast for an old man. I had to run to catch up to him.

I blocked his path. He was wheezing badly, his eyes wild and crazy-looking.

"What do you think you're doing?" I reached for the hatchet but he held it away.

"You want death and destruction, is that it? I'll kill him for

you. Will that make you happy, you fool? Because I'm not
letting you throw your life away."

Suddenly he sat down, hard.

"This running up hillsides. I can't do that anymore."

He looked at me, his eyes haggard and watery.

"Are we through with this foolishness now?" he asked quietly, his breath still whistling through his teeth. He was all
sweaty, bright with sweat, as if he'd contracted a sudden fever
as he'd hastened up the hill.

"All right," I said.

"Good. Help me up. Let's go back to the house. You want
me to call the state cops?"

"No."

"He's been hanging around," Henry said. "He drove past the
house a couple of times this morning. I knew it was trouble."

He looked at me again, studying me carefully.

"You sure you're all right now?"

"Yes, I'm all right now."

"No, you're not. Help me back to the house and I'll fix us
lunch."

I helped him up.

"Promise me something."

I looked at him.

"Promise you'll forget it this time, whatever it was. That
asshole isn't worth it."

"If he comes near me again, I'll kill him."

"Over my dead body," he said. "You're not throwing your
life away. Goddamned if I'll let you do it."

He flung the hatchet as far as he could into the woods.

That night the phone rang. It was the Judge.

"Listen, son," he said in that deep smooth voice of his. "I'd like very much to talk with you tonight. Can you come out to the house? I'll send Ambrose in with the car."

"What do you want to see me for?"

"I'd like very much to talk with you, Joe. I can't explain over the telephone very well."

"All right, send Ambrose."

What does he want from me, I wondered. Summers had "talked" to me, now he wanted to talk to me. I had an idea the two conversations might turn out to be related. I wanted to know the tie-in.

So Ambrose, the old guy the Judge kept around to work in the garden and drive his car, came in for me and I got in the front seat alongside him and we drove in silence in the big car out to the Judge's house, past the surf at Roaring Beach, the wet beach looking like a silver mirror in the bright moonlight.

"You never say much, do you Ambrose?"

"No," answered the old guy, his eye still on the road.

That was our conversation.

When we got there, Mrs. Pennell took me into the study. The Judge greeted me warmly, as if I were the most wonderful person on earth.

"Joe, it's good to see you. Can I fix you a drink?"

Sure, I told him. Fix me a drink.

So he did. After he'd settled in his chair and we'd taken a couple of pulls on our scotch, he set his glass down, leaning forward in his chair. He made a little steeple of his hands.

"Joe, I'm awfully embarrassed."

"Is that right? Why is that?"

He shook his head darkly, in repudiation.

"I heard Summers visited you today."

He showed me a side view of his big-nosed face, all profile

like an actor's, his small ears pressed against his close-cropped white hair. The line of his neck ran straight out of his collar to the top of his head, like Dick Tracy in the funny papers.

"He visited me all right."

I asked him straight-out.

"Did you send him?"

"What? No, of course not. God, no."

"How do you know about it then?"

"I know everything that goes on in this town. It's my business to know."

"That's nice. You know everything. Does he check in with you daily?"

The Judge pointed his nose at me, narrowing his eyes.

"He keeps in touch fairly often. When I heard what he'd done today, I was very angry. He's a stupid man, Joe. I apologize for him. I was very harsh with him. I told him to leave you alone, not to make trouble for you."

"That's good."

"Yes, I don't want you to have any more trouble. You've had enough for one lifetime already."

"They don't divide it up evenly, do they?"

He laughed.

"No, I guess not."

"Well then maybe I'm not finished with it yet."

"There are things you can do," he said. "You know it and I know it. I won't go into it anymore. It's up to you, Joe. You can make things easy on yourself. Give me a chance to help you. You know how much I appreciate what you did for Kathleen."

"Where is she, anyway?"

"She went down to Boston."

"She did?"

"Don't look so crestfallen," he smiled. "She'll be back tomorrow. She's taking some things down to the apartment. Getting ready for school."

"Oh."

We didn't say anything for a minute.

"Maybe you'd like a car," he said. "Maybe a little Ford convertible. Then sometimes you could run down and see Kathleen at school, take her out to dinner. How does that sound?"

"No thanks. You don't owe me anything."

"Come on, Joe. Let me do something for you. Show my appreciation."

"If I think of anything, I'll let you know."

He sighed, studying the ice cubes in his drink. He looked up, smiling.

"I hope you're getting ready for school too."

I didn't say anything.

"Give me a chance, Joe. Don't you trust anyone?"

"Why should I? I've never been wrong yet."

"Joe, don't make a fool of yourself next week."

"I figured that's what this was about," I said. "What's between you and Summers anyway? You queer for each other?"

"You don't understand. This is my town. I'm responsible for making it work well. I'm trying to do the best I can for everybody concerned."

"I bet you are. What did he do? Did he do you some big favor? Is that it? That's the way you run this town, isn't it?"

I was just blabbing mad, the words didn't mean anything to me.

"Don't talk like a fool," he said.

"Why not? I'm the biggest fool around."

"Well don't be."

"I like it that way," I said. "You squat and Summers shits. That's right, isn't it? He's always around, isn't he? He was even around when your wife died, wasn't he?"

"Shut up," he said. "Don't ever mention her again."

"Why not? I thought you were in charge of everything. Weren't you in charge then?"

I was just busting off because I was mad, tired of being pushed around. I don't even know why it came to my mind, except I wanted something to hit him with. But when I said that, the room changed. It was like the temperature dropped ten degrees instantly.

The Judge's face was white and trembling.

"Get out of my house. How dare you talk to me about my wife's death."

"That's right. It's none of my business. My life is none of your business either. You pull that fat bastard's string. Keep him off my back."

"Get out, Joe. Before you say something you'll be sorry for."

"I'm not finished. You run everything. But you don't run me. I never liked you anyway. I never thought you were as good as you pretended."

"You're a damn fool," he said. "I wanted to help you."

"I don't want your help. You got this town buffaloed. But you don't fool me."

He looked at me. His eyes were dead, his face absolutely bloodless.

"Stay away from my house. You understand? You're not welcome here anymore. Stay away from Kathleen too. Do you understand me? You come around again and I'll have you arrested for trespassing."

"You're not taking anything away," I said. "I always knew where I stood with you."

"No, you didn't. I thought you were smart. But you're not. You're stupid."

"Did you really think I'd lie for that bastard?"

"I never asked you to."

"You probably believe that. You been lying to yourself for so long you couldn't tell the truth if you had to."

He just looked at me. He was gripping the arms of his leather chair. He looked rich but unhappy.

"I'm going to tell them what happened," I said. "You or nobody else is going to stop me."

"It won't make any difference."

"Maybe not. But I'm going to tell them. How that fat bastard killed that man in cold blood."

"You do that."

"I been feeling bad ever since I met you. Maybe after that I'll feel good again."

"Goodbye, Joe."

"Tell you something else. It's not up to you whether I see Kathleen again. It'll be up to her."

When I turned, Ambrose was in the doorway. His sudden, unsummoned appearance made the hair stand up on my neck. It was like the Judge really did control everything, without even lifting a finger.

"One last thing."

"Get out."

"It was my uncle who was plugging your wife. Did you know that?"

"Get out! Get out!"

"I wondered whether you knew."

"GET OUT!"

Ambrose had shuffled forward, agitated but made helpless by the Judge's shouting. I brushed past him as I went out. He didn't

offer me any trouble. I was glad. It wouldn't have done a thing
for me to lay out that old guy.

I went down the drive quickly. By the porch light I saw
Ambrose come out of the house and get in the big car. Then
the car started down the drive.

I don't know why I did it, but I got off the road. I didn't
want any ride back to town from him or anybody who might
be with him. He was harmless enough. But I got off the road
anyway and lay behind the stone fence in among the birch trees
till the car slid by.

I couldn't explain it. It was just a feeling I had. The room
had changed. Now even the night had changed. There was
something dangerous in the air.

I walked home, careful to stay out of the moonlight and back
in the shadows under the trees. Every time I heard a car coming
I slipped into the woods. The Judge's big car, coughing softly,
glided past my various hiding places half a dozen times that
night. It made me think that Ambrose wasn't alone. Yet I hadn't
seen anybody come out of the house with him. Maybe it's my
imagination, I thought. Maybe nobody's looking for me. But
I wasn't taking any chances.

When I reached Washington Street, I cut through the back-
yards to reach our house. Henry always kept the back door
locked so I didn't even try it. I shimmied up the porch post to
the balcony and slipped through Henry's room to my room.

I didn't sleep well that night. The next day I didn't feel like
leaving the house. Then I thought: they're getting to you. Next
thing you know, you'll be lying for them, convinced you're just
telling the truth. So I went out in the evening and walked
around town just to keep in practice.

Really, I was jittery. I even considered getting on the bike
and heading for Quebec. But I couldn't do that. At least, not
yet.

I went back to the house and called Kathleen.

The housekeeper answered in her singsong voice.

"Hello, Mrs. Pennell. Is Kathleen at home?"

"Who is this please?"

"It's Joe Weatherfield, ma'am."

"I'm sorry."

"So am I. Will you tell the Judge I'm sorry about a couple of things? I never meant to say anything about his wife."

Mrs. Pennell hung up on me gently.

About an hour later the telephone rang. It was Kathleen.

"What did you do to Daddy?"

"I lost my temper. I said things I'm sorry for."

"He wouldn't tell me what you said."

"That's all right. You really don't want to know."

"Oh, Joe."

"Well—"

"He says we can't see each other anymore."

"What do you say?"

"I don't know."

"Come down here."

"I couldn't do that."

"Yes you can. Come down here. I want you so bad."

"If Daddy catches me—"

"He won't catch you. What are you—his prisoner?"

I told her to keep Henry out of it by coming around the back. I'd let down a clothesline, I told her, with a loop in it and she could put it under her shoulders and shimmy up the porch post and I'd help by pulling in the rope.

"Are you crazy?"

"Yes," I said. "Are you?"

"I must be."

So she came down and I lowered the rope which I'd gone out and found in the barn and I helped her up just as I said I would and it was no trouble at all. And then I had her in my room in the dark and it was wonderful.

She made me sit on the bed.

"Don't do that. I'll come all over you. You'll get it in your hair."

"Go ahead."

"Come up here," I took her by the elbows.

When I made love to Kathleen it was different. I reached deep inside her and it was sweet. I wasn't outside myself, watching us do it, like I was with other girls, thinking to myself: there now, babe. Don't you like that? No, I was with her completely, lost in her, and when I came the explosion shuddered through my blood and bones like a fit of epilepsy. At first, I felt myself going out of myself like a tide into the darkness of my room and then coming back with a mindless shuddering sweet crash, holding on to Kathleen so I wouldn't die in the crash, my face buried in her hair, then coming back to myself, settling down heavily on her, holding her close.

We lay there for a long time saying nothing. I stroked her soft hair and thought my heart would break with love for her. I wasn't mad about it anymore. It was too late for that.

She lifted her head to whisper in my ear.

"Promise me something."

"Anything."

"No matter what happens, go to school. Will you do it?"

"All right."

"Promise?"

"Yes."

"You're so bad," she said. "But you're so good too. Please, please. Give yourself a chance. Okay?"

"Sure."

She was quiet then. We were lying on our sides now. She

snuggled her face against my chest.

"Can't you do as Daddy says, just this once, so he won't be mad at you anymore?"

"No," I said. "I can't do that."

She didn't ask again.

Nineteen

So I went to court.

I told them exactly what happened that day outside Michaelsmith's shack. How Michaelsmith stepped outside his door waving his arms as if trying to quiet a crowd. And how Summers shot him for no good reason and Michaelsmith, without even looking surprised, spun around when the first one hit him and fell into his garden, pulling down his bean poles as he went.

Gorman had finished with his questions and now the little bald-headed judge had a few of his own.

"Mr. Michaelsmith was still holding his rifle when he came out the door?"

"Yes sir, he was," I said. "But he didn't raise it to his shoulder or offer to shoot anyone."

"You're saying he did not brandish the weapon in a threatening manner?"

"No sir. He did not brandish anything in my opinion."

"Thank you, Mr. Bigler."

"That's 'Mr. Weatherfield,' Judge. If you don't mind."

"Mr. Weatherfield. I beg your pardon. Counsel, any questions for the witness?"

So then Summers' lawyer—this Barnsworth fellow from Portland—came over to me and leaned in confidentially, smiling, and asked, "You do realize you're under oath, don't you, Mr. Bigler?"

"Yes, I do. And it's Weatherfield."

He pretended surprise.

"Oh—your name is Weatherfield? I thought Weatherfield was your grandfather's name. Has your grandfather adopted you?"

"No."

"And your mother is married to a Mr. Bigler, is she not? And did this Mr. Bigler officially adopt you some years ago? Is that not so?"

"That's just paper," I said. "Nobody can adopt you if you don't want it."

"That's an interesting legal theory, Mr. Bigler. Tell me, why were you on the scene of the Michaelsmith incident?"

"Because I drove him home."

"You drove him home. He'd abducted Judge Fiske's daughter. And you drove him home. Didn't the police have to disarm you at the scene?"

"What is this—"

"Please answer counsel's question."

"Yes," I said. "They disarmed me. They beat the shit out of me too."

"Watch your language, young man," said the skinny bald-headed little judge from his bench. "One more remark like that and I'll hold you in contempt of this court. Continue, counsel."

"What sort of a weapon were you carrying that day, Mr. Bigler?"

"A pistol."

"A thirty-eight-caliber pistol, wasn't it? Where did you get this pistol?"

"It was around the house."

"Whose house?"

"My mother's house."

"You mean it was your stepfather's pistol, don't you?"

"Yes, it was his."

"And did you not steal it?"

"I took it. I didn't steal it."

"Your stepfather reported it stolen. How was it that you were armed and allegedly Mr. Michaelsmith's hostage?"

"Because he was cracked. He didn't know what he was doing."

"Why were you carrying a weapon in the first place?"

"What's this have to do with Summers' shooting Mr. Michaelsmith?"

"Just answer the question, young man," said the judge.

"I don't know."

"You don't know why you were carrying a gun?" asked Barnsworth, looking significantly at the little judge.

"No," I said.

I wasn't going to tell these yo-yos my personal problems.

"Had you met officer Summers before your encounter with him at Mr. Michaelsmith's house?"

"Yes."

"When and where, please."

"Earlier in the day at Henry's."

" 'Henry' is your grandfather, Henry Weatherfield?"

"Yes, my grandfather."

"And what happened?"

"Nothing much."

"Did you knock him down?"

"Yes."

"Why?"

"He was in my way."

"How do you feel about authority, Mr. Bigler?"

"Weatherfield."

"Please answer the question."

"It's a dumb question."

"Young man," said the judge. "I will not warn you again. One more remark like that and I'll hold you in contempt of this court. Now answer the question."

I looked at Barnsworth.

"I don't let anybody push me around, if that's what you mean."

"No further questions, your honor."

Gorman, dressed in his tight blue suit, was clutching the edge of his table. He did not look happy.

So that was the way that went. The judge brought the gavel down. Gorman rapidly packed his papers in his briefcase and turned without looking in my direction and left the courtroom. I never saw or heard from the man again.

I went over to Kathleen afterwards. She looked absolutely beautiful, her dark hair pulled back from her face.

I said, "I did a swell job up there, didn't I?"

She smiled, holding her purse against her blouse almost as if she were shielding herself against me.

"You did what you thought was right. That counts for something. Well, goodbye, Joe."

"Goodbye—what do you mean?"

"School starts on Tuesday. I'm going down tonight."

"Maybe we can get together sometime. Boston's not so far away."

"Remember what you promised me," she smiled.

"I will."

The Judge was over in a corner talking to Summers and Barnsworth. Summers had shown up in a green suit with stitching on the lapels, his hair slicked down, doing his best to look meek and respectable. The Judge looked up and saw me talking to his daughter. He excused himself and came right over to us.

"Joe," he nodded, formal as a post.

He took Kathleen by the elbow.

"Kathleen—"

"Goodbye," she said again. I watched her walk out of the courtroom on her father's arm.

"Congratulations," Henry said as we went down the courthouse steps. "You made a few more enemies today. Very successful day, you'd have to call it."

"I'm going back to school."

That stopped him in his tracks.

"You are?"

"Yes, fix it up for me, will you? I'm going back. Then I'm going to college. I want to get the hell out of high school as fast as I can and get into college—Harvard. Is that where I should go?"

"How did you come to all this so suddenly?"

"I just did, that's all."

"I like hanging around with you. Damned if I don't," Henry said. "I never know which way you'll blow next."

So Kathleen went back to Boston and I started to school at the little high school in Dunnocks Head. It was about as bad as I expected. I didn't mind, really. I just wanted to get on with it.

I wrote Kathleen letters, she didn't write back. I kept writing. I never suggested in my letters that she was less than the ideal correspondent. I figured she probably knew that already. Besides, I wasn't going to rag her about it. She had the right not to write to me if she didn't want to. I suppose if she'd written and told me to cut it out I would have. Because she had that right too. But she didn't even write to tell me to stop. My letters didn't come back, so I knew she was getting them.

A few weeks following the hearing, we heard that the judge in Bath had found Summers innocent of any wrongdoing, based mainly on the testimony of the state police.

Shortly after that Doreen wrote Henry a note saying that someone had been around to the house asking Dale if he would like to prosecute the case against me. But Dale was tired of the whole thing. If he got his gun back and I just stayed away, that was enough for him.

This fellow seemed anxious for Dale to take up the case again, explaining that he represented a citizens' law and order group. He said Dale owed it to the community to see this case through. No costs would be involved so far as Dale was concerned, he said. Nothing for Dale to worry about at all. But even the prospect of a free ride didn't interest Dale. Doreen said in her letter that she believed it was because football season was coming on and Dale didn't want anything to interfere with his tube time. Anyway, for whatever reason, he wouldn't go along with it. The man left the house feeling very disappointed. "What kind of trouble is Joe in now?" she wanted to know.

"You made a powerful enemy," said Henry.

"I know it. Maybe I better move on. Keep you out of it."

"No, no. What would the dog and I do for excitement if you left now? I wouldn't know what to do without you. You're better for me than a pacemaker."

"I don't know. It might even be dangerous."

"Dangerous? How so?"

"Remember the night the Judge called me out to the house after Summers jumped me in the woods?"

"Yes. What about it?"

"Well, I blurted out a bunch of bad things that night, Henry. Even some things you told me in confidence."

"What things?"

"I was mad, Henry. I didn't stop to think what I was saying. I suggested that maybe the reason he wanted to get Summers off so bad was because he owed him a big favor. I even made remarks about his wife."

"Jesus."

"I know. I'm a damned fool to slap a man in the face with memories of his dead wife. But I did it. I did worse too."

"Oh my God. What else did you do?"

"I told him it was my uncle she was fooling around with."

"Jesus, Joe. No wonder he's angry with you."

"Do you suppose he knew before I told him?"

"That's hardly the point. But I don't know. I suppose so. This is a small town and it's an old story. But I don't know."

"The thing was he turned white when I said maybe Summers owed him a favor. Something in the room changed after that."

"What the hell are you talking about now?"

"You said he didn't even come out of his office that night she shot herself."

"That's right."

"Why didn't he?"

"I don't know. I suppose he didn't want to see her. I wish to God I'd never seen her like that."

"Wouldn't a man rush out before anybody could stop him? Wouldn't he rush out before he said to himself, 'Wait a minute. I don't want to see her all messed up?' "

"I don't know what I would do in that situation," said

Henry. "Nobody does. What are you inventing anyway?"

"Didn't you say, you heard two shots?"

"No, I didn't say that."

"I thought you said you heard shots."

"No, she'd used both barrels, that I know. But the shots were simultaneous so far as I remember. Don't try to make a murder out of this, for Godsakes."

"Why not?"

"Because it wasn't, that's why." Henry ran his hand through his hair agitatedly. "The poor woman was distraught. She killed herself. If he had her killed, why would he have it done right out in front of his office?"

"I don't know."

"Yes, that's right. You bet you don't know. You're a danger-ous lad. You've got too vivid an imagination. I'll tell you why," he said. "Because she couldn't have picked a better way to mortify him than committing suicide right in the middle of town in front of his office. That was a fine piece of revenge on her part."

"I suppose you're right. But why did he act weird when I mentioned Summers and his wife's suicide in the same breath?"

"Because, you heartless whelp, you'd brought up the sorest subject of his life. How would you expect him to act?"

"But why didn't he even come out of his office that night?"

"Maybe Summers advised him not to. Maybe he was too smart to give the poor woman her full measure of revenge."

I just stared at the wall of books behind Henry's head.

"Close your mouth," he said. "You look stupid with it hanging open."

"I might be in bigger trouble than I thought," I said.

I stood up and stretched.

"Joe."

"What?"

"You give me the creeps. You know that?"

"I don't like the way I feel about this," I said. "You should have seen the way the man acted that night. Something's wrong. I ought to get out of here before something else happens."

"Put those thoughts out of your mind and tend to school," said Henry. "For Godsakes, don't tell anyone else what you've been thinking."

"Who else am I going to talk to? Besides I already blabbed to the wrong person."

He looked at me keenly.

"You worry me," he said.

I went up to bed and thought about it. I thought about those phone calls we were getting, with nobody on the other end of the line. I thought about how I'd come out of school a couple of times and found Summers sitting across the street in his patrol car. I thought about getting on the bike and heading for Quebec, something I should have done weeks ago. I couldn't do that now. Because I couldn't leave Henry alone to face whatever came next.

You're really in a fix now, I thought. You stuck your finger in that man's eye. It doesn't matter that Summers got off. He can't let you get away with it. He might've let you get away with it, if you hadn't raked up that old story about his wife. He might still let you get away with it if you got on your bike and got out of here, now, tonight.

Maybe if I just leave. Maybe that'd be the end of it. Likely they'd leave Henry alone.

I didn't know what to do—or if I should do anything at all. Or if it wasn't just my overheated imagination, as Henry said.

I was getting damn restless. I had my troubles, but I couldn't stop thinking about Kathleen. I kept writing but she wouldn't

answer. So I decided to go down and see her. She could shut
the door in my face, if she wanted. But I had to see her. So one
Saturday morning I jumped on a bus. If I can just see her, I
thought, we can work something out.

"Joe," she said when she opened the door.

"Hello, Kathleen."

She looked beautiful. She didn't look like any college girl.
She was wearing a silky pearl-colored blouse and a white nub-
bly skirt. She looked absolutely great.

"Joe," she drew me through the doorway into her arms. I
kissed her hard. Her gold bracelet dug into the back of my neck
as she held me tightly.

"I missed you."

"I missed you too."

Her warm breath struck my lips as she whispered to me. The
mixture of her flowery perfume and the warm scent of her skin
made me dizzy.

"You write nice letters, Joe. Do you mean all the things you
say?"

"Yes, I mean them. I mean everything I say."

"I'm sorry I didn't write back."

"That's okay. Don't talk about it."

"I've been awfully busy."

"I know."

"Oh, Joe. I've missed you."

She was against the sink in the kitchen. I was feeling her
through her clothes. She opened my shirt and nibbled me deli-
cately as a goldfish.

I reached under her skirt and with my thumbs stripped her
panties down her thighs. She kissed my arms. She mumbled into
my skin, speaking to my bones and blood, but didn't say a word
I could—or needed to—understand.

I turned her around. I wanted to give her something she wouldn't forget. And we made love that way, standing at the sink together, she with her arms braced against the counter, her head thrown back and the long black tangle of her beautiful hair lying in the hollow made by her thrust-back shoulders.

My hands under her blouse, I pressed her close to me. At times I laid my head against her back, holding her tightly about the hips, exhausted by the burden of my love for her.

"You ought to wear stockings sometimes."

"You want me to?" she turned her head, whispering to the ceiling.

"Yes."

"If you really want me to. I'll do anything you want."

It made me feel good when she answered that way, even though I knew it was just the mood she was in and not the way she'd feel tomorrow or next week. But I wanted to think there would be another time, that she didn't want it to end any more than I did.

Kathleen made tuna fish salad sandwiches that night. We had them with some cold, dry white wine, sitting at the little table in her kitchen. Hardly a word passed between us.

After dinner we piled the dishes in the sink and made love again.

She said, why don't you stay the night?

I said, I'd like to.

In bed, she asked me if I was religious.

"No, I don't think so. Are you?"

"No, but I think about it. Don't you ever?"

"No, not much."

"You're so bad," she said. "And yet you're good in so many ways. You make my heart hurt. Do you know that?"

"Why is that?"

"I don't know. You make me feel sad sometimes. You remind me of what Origen said about the souls in Purgatory. Do you know who Origen was?"

"Not something you put in spaghetti sauce."

"Don't be a wise guy," she said. "He was a saint of the early church. He said the souls in Purgatory aren't really being punished by God but are undergoing purification by trouble. What he called, 'salutary troubles.' Do you understand that?"

"No."

"I think you're undergoing salutary troubles," she said. "I hope to God it's salutary. Do you ever pray?"

"No."

She hugged me.

"Well, I'll pray for you."

"Purgatory," I said. "Is that where your mother is?"

"No, she's in hell. In the Wood of Suicides."

"The Wood of Suicides. What's that?"

"There's a special forest in hell. The souls of people who kill themselves are sent there and sprout into trees and bushes. They're torn and ravaged by animals. When a branch or limb is broken off, they can speak through the sap that dribbles out. It's called the Wood of Suicides."

Well, I thought. Maybe she's not there after all. Maybe she's in Purgatory, undergoing some of those salutary troubles.

Before dawn, we made love again.

"Don't stop," she said in my ear. "Please, please."

When I woke again she'd gone to the library to do some work. She left me a note propped against the cereal box. She thanked me for a wonderful night. That official thank you made me uneasy for some reason. I hung around till noon thinking maybe she'd stop by for lunch. When she didn't show, I hopped on a bus and went home.

It was another week before her letter came. Henry handed it to me when I came in the door from school.

"Here," he smiled. "I believe you've been waiting for this."

I had been, but not in the way he meant. In the letter Kathleen said she'd decided to study in Europe after all.

By the time I got this, she wrote, she'd already be in Amsterdam. Fortunately, she had some friends who wanted to sublease the apartment and so she was able to leave without delay.

She had finally made up her mind, she said. She was going to study art. It was foolish to think of everything that had come before as simply a waste of time and money. Particularly since her father didn't mind the cost of her mistakes. So now she would study art as she'd secretly always wanted to do.

She told me that she'd never forget me. She wrote, "I hope I've been as good for you as you have been for me."

She said other things too. She was quite a letter writer. I had a lot of good in me, she said. I should work to bring it out. She still was holding me to my promise, she said. Just because she was out of the country I wasn't to think that it didn't count. One day we will see each other again. I just know we will, she wrote.

That night I lay in the darkness and thought about it. I watched the curtains flutter like ghostly flags in the night breeze at the open window. It took a lot of talking to myself.

This is not going to kill you, I told myself. You're sure as hell going to live through this. This is no worse than the time Henry and I bored through that boy's skull. Only this time it's me that's being operated on. The thought made me growl aloud, impatient and involuntary, as if the dark room and the endless night were a permanent curse.

You're not going to die. You'll be all right. Pretty soon you'll be through the worst of it. Then you can get back to business.

I must have looked pretty bad at the breakfast table because Henry said, "How was the news?"

"Not good."

"I been thinking," said Henry. "How would you like to go fishing this weekend? Before the cold weather sets in."

"Fine, let's do it."

He looked at me, giving me that fierce old eagle glare of his.

"Goddamn people," he said. "Why do they act the way they do?"

Twenty

⌐⌐⌐ WE rinsed the breakfast dishes in the brook and toted the gear down to the lake.

The boat looked just lovely, the wood warmly blond in the coppery morning light. It was a fine morning, the slightly chill air supercharged with enough Canadian oxygen to make anyone feel good.

The cool nights had already smudged the hills around the lake with patches of gold and Indian red. In six more weeks likely we'd have snow. Time was moving on. I wondered if this was it, or if Henry would be up to coming into camp after the snow started. But I didn't ask. I was afraid to hear the answer.

I needed the woods, needed them bad. They soothed my nerves like nothing else. I'd always thought being alone in a hotel room was the best medicine. Now I'd found out it was even better to be in a pine wood.

In the woods I could forget about Kathleen and Summers and the Judge and all the other associated shit. I could forget about school too, which was beginning to feel like another one of my mistakes.

This fellow, Mr. Libby, was my homeroom teacher. I had him for math and science too. I couldn't get away from the idiot. He was a veteran of the Korean War, and had only one arm. He kept the empty sleeve tucked in the side pocket of his suit jacket. I didn't mind about the arm, except he seemed to have to make up for it by being a tough guy. He had a buzz haircut, a high voice, and wore thick glasses. Behind the thick lenses, his pupils darted like little tadpoles.

On the first day of school, he got acquainted by calling out, "Which one's Bigler?"

I raised my hand.

"You're the troublemaker," he said. "I heard about you."

That's a nice beginning, I thought. I told him there was a mistake about the name.

"You're not Bigler?"

"No, I've never been a Bigler."

He studied the paper he held in his hand, practically touching it to his nose. Behind his thick lenses, his eyes wriggled like flatworms under a microscope.

"You transferred from Revere Beach, didn't you?"

"That's right."

"Then you're Bigler. Unless we got two kids from Revere Beach. Are you trying to be a wise guy?"

"No," I said. "Bigler's not my name. It never was."

"Uh-huh," he said. "You go down to the office and talk it over with Mr. Harrington, smart guy. Save your jokes for him."

So that's the way it began, with me taking orders from that idiot.

After Henry saw Harrington we almost had the name business fixed. The other teachers didn't care what I called myself. Weatherfield would do as well as any other name. But Libby had some need to keep on calling me Bigler. He said that was

my name, like it or not. He couldn't have people in his class-
room changing names at will. Next thing you knew, he said,
everybody'd be calling themselves something different. Why is
it any of your business, I wondered.

I wouldn't answer when he called me Bigler. He'd halt class
and insist I answer to the name but I never would. On days
when he wearied of his game and called me by my first name,
I would answer him. But normally he called everybody by their
last names, including the girls, as if he were still in the army and
we were all in his platoon. He was a complete horse's ass, really
not smart enough to leave me alone. I didn't want trouble, but
he was going to get some if he kept it up. I thought he ought
to know that.

One day, after he'd wasted half the class time trying to get
me to answer to Bigler, I went up to him afterwards.

"Why don't you cut it out?"

"What?" his little worm eyes registered surprise.

"I said, leave me alone. I don't want trouble. Don't keep
pushing me."

He did a little dance, his face turning red.

"You arrogant . . . Don't threaten me, you . . ."

"Get your finger out of my face."

I walked away.

"Come back here, Bigler. I'm not through with you."

I kept on walking.

Of course he reported me to Harrington who said he'd
suspend me if I kept it up.

"Keep what up?"

"Don't get fresh with me," he said. "I'm trying to help you."

You see it was hopeless. Without a trip to the lake every few
weeks I didn't see how I was going to make it through the
winter. But I was studying for the first time and making the

grades, and that was a nice way of sticking it in Mr. Libby's ear. Except if I didn't get away every few weeks I was liable to flatten one of them, and it looked like it was going to be Libby.

The cold air on my face that morning in the woods was like a splash of brookwater waking me from a bad dream. Only fall, I thought. All winter with Libby. All winter to go, and maybe not even a camp to come into at that.

I needed this year to be over quick, and the next one, so I could get on to college and begin to catch up in earnest. I hated going to school with a bunch of kids. They were all shorter and soft-minded and daffy as hell and I didn't want anything to do with any of them. They knew it and left me alone. I couldn't wait to get out of there.

That asshole Mr. Libby and those little screaming meemies. Kathleen: the word itself was like a knife. Summers across the street in his car. In the woods, none of that mattered. Isn't that nice? Look at the hills again and drink your coffee. You have all winter to grit your teeth.

We loaded the rods, the bait pail, the creels, and the other stuff into the boat. I picked up Cat before he got too muddy slopping around the edge of the lake and put him in the boat too. No use starting with a wet dog.

I thought I heard something, some stealthy crackling in the undergrowth. I cocked my head, much as the dog might, peering over my shoulder into the green screen of pine trees.

Henry looked up under his famous fishing hat, full of glinting hooks and feathers, its little green celluloid window flashing cheerily in the sunshine.

"Climb in," he said.

"Shut up for a minute."

"What—?"

"Shhh. Listen for a second. You can do that, can't you?"

"I don't know, tough guy. I'm badly out of practice."

"Just shut it for a second."

We listened, tilted like old Indian totems, staring into the trees. We didn't hear anything.

Cat started to bark excitedly. I couldn't tell whether he was just reacting to us or because he'd heard something too.

"Shut up, dog."

Henry closed his fingers over the dog's muzzle, the dog whimpering under his hand.

"Cease," Henry released the dog.

The dog licked his chops and kept still. We listened again. The water rapidly tapped the side of the boat. The breeze off the lake seethed in our ears. That was all.

"What is it?"

"Nothing. I thought I heard something in camp."

"Everything's put away," said Henry. "No animal can get to anything. You want to go back and check?"

"Forget it. Let's get on the lake."

It was beautiful on the water. We had a nice clear sky, light blue at this hour.

Halfway into the middle, the wind died suddenly. Quiet fell on the lake like a pause in the middle of one of those piano works by Beethoven that Henry admired so much. He always said the pauses were as lovely as the music itself. Now, here in the middle of this lake which we both liked to pretend was still haunted by the ghosts of ancient Indian chieftains and half-crazy pioneering hermits, I could understand what he was talking about.

Without a word, Henry took up the oars. For a second the only sound was the eerie lyric of water from the oars striking the glassy surface of the lake. Henry began to row. The oars rattled in the oarlocks, the boat began to move, the breeze started up again—just as if everything were hooked up to a giant rowing machine and Henry had set everything in motion again.

Standing up, under the spell of some self-mesmerizing compulsion, I balanced against the tug of Henry's oars like an acrobat on a wire in the wind. Over the side, I saw a wavering green negative of myself peering back, a skinny beanpole of a kid.

That's not me, I thought. *That's not really me.* Because I never thought of myself as a kid, but as someone a hundred and four at least, trapped in a youthful body. It was always such a shock when I saw myself. *If I look like that,* I thought, *it's no wonder Kathleen fled to Europe.*

"Sit down," said Henry. "Before you fall out of the boat. How many damn times do I have to tell you to put on your life jacket?"

"I was going to." I shrugged into the stiff bulky thing.

"No you weren't. You were going to see what you could get away with. Here, you row for a while. At least it'll keep you in your seat."

We changed places and I began to row.

"Stop for a second," he said. "Bring those oars inboard."

"What the hell is wrong now?"

"I want you to buckle that life jacket." He stuck his jaw out and squinted at me.

"I don't plan to fall out," I said.

"Buckle it."

"What an old lady."

I pulled the white straps through the cinch rings.

"You satisfied now?"

"Yes, now I'm satisfied."

I ran the oars out and began to row again.

Cawing angrily, three big crows exploded out of some trees not far from where we kept the boat tied up. They soared over the lake, circling above our heads. Everything suddenly was quiet again. I heard their wings creaking as their shadows crossed our boat. We were in the middle of the lake. The crows seemed to be using the boat for a halfway marker in some frantic private race they'd decided to have. They wheeled over our heads, shooting back to shore, settling into the same trees they'd just come out of, it looked like to us.

"Something scared those crows."

"You can't go by that," said Henry. "Those big crows like to jump around."

"That's pretty close to camp."

"Concentrate on what you're doing. Row for the point. Let's stand off about fifty yards. Always plenty of fish, right there in that deep hole."

I made for the long sharp spine of gray ledge on the opposite shore which slowly sank into the lake at that point. Cat wriggled past Henry's waders, positioning himself in the bow.

"Get down, dog. Get the hell out of the way."

The dog slipped under Henry's elbow, scrambled over a thwart, and landed right in my working room.

"Get," I told him.

He got all breathy at the unexpected pleasure of my company, pretending to be unaware of the difficulties he was causing. But he'd been around Henry long enough to know what was what in a boat. I pulled in the oars, grabbed him by the collar, and without ceremony dragged him over the seat so he'd be behind me and out of the way.

"Stay back there."

He didn't like being slung from one end of the boat to the other. I think he had the idea he was really the captain and our behavior qualified as mutiny. But he seemed willing not to press the issue till our return to civilization.

I rowed on.

It was a lovely coppery morning. Along this part of the shore the birches grew down to the water's edge. The white trees in the morning light were as brilliant and starchy-looking as the trousers of cadets. A faint breeze dimpled the lake, then died. The lake seemed thicker than mere water, almost like syrup, as if over the summer the hot sun had slowly changed it into a green soup.

"Here's the magic spot," said Henry.

I lifted the oars while he plopped the anchor overboard. The boat pulled up gently against the anchor line. I stored the oars under the seats.

We always caught fish here. I was anxious to get at it and so did a dumb thing. Henry was standing up in the bow. I made to stand up to get my fishing rod and he said, "Sit down, you fool. Do you want to dump us out of the boat?"

It was a dumb thing to do. I sat down again without giving him any lip.

As I did, it thundered suddenly, or I thought it did, and Henry pitched backward out of the bow of the boat.

The thing seemed to take an hour and a half.

I watched it unfold in slow motion, glued to my seat, unable to move: saw the sudden burst of blood at Henry's shoulder like somebody had just hit him with a tomato, saw his back arch and his head go back, falling backward in slow motion in what looked like an impromptu back-flip. Helplessly, I watched the sunlight flash off his steel-rimmed glasses and saw the haggard astonishment on his face. The second shot came before the *crack!* of the first had stopped echoing in the hills. The bullet tickled my ear it passed so close.

I made a grab for Henry as he fell.

No! somebody cried out.

And Henry just pitched over backwards out of the boat like a wooden Indian. When I grabbed for him, I came away with his big pocket watch. It swung at the end of its gold chain in a crazy arc.

Ten minutes of twelve, it said. Dumbfounded, I studied the time as if it might offer some explanation. I was standing up in the boat. I must have glanced at the shore in the direction the shots had come from. A puff of smoke rose lazily out of the trees. I didn't see anyone but I knew who'd fired at us—at me—and missed because Henry had told me to sit down and the bullet hit him instead. Summers had a clear shot at me now. But nothing more came out of the woods. It flashed through my mind that he'd gotten scared and run off. I stood there in the gently rocking boat, staring at Henry's watch, almost hoping Summers would kill me too.

Henry had barely made a splash. His hands, still clutching the expensive fly rod, were high above his head when he hit the water. Goggle-eyed and glued to my seat, I'd reached for him, hollering and not knowing that either, not even raising off my seat an inch, the whole thing unfolding with excruciating slowness, ending with the waffle soles of Henry's boots floating up, eerie as helium dirigibles, right in front of my eyes before they too vanished over the side.

That's when I stood up and found I had his watch in my hand, swinging in a lunatic arc. *Tentill tentill tentill* it insisted crazily.

"No!" I hollered.

The hills answered me back, crying, *no, no, no.*

The boots! I thought. *He he's got those—*

I was standing up now but my joints had turned to stone, my heart full of dread. Maybe he'll bob to the surface, I thought.

But I knew that was a lie, with those boots he had on. I'd have to go in and get him—me, who was scared of a toilet bowl if it had water in it.

I got to, I told myself. *I got to.* But I couldn't make myself do it.

He's going to drown if you don't get him out of there he's dead already no he's not you saw him get it in the shoulder no I yes he's you can't swim anyway. I stared into that suffocating sticky green substance waiting to suck me under, hoping Summers would end my misery. But had that numbnuts fired again, probably he'd have missed anyway.

I tried to move. I couldn't break the seals on my joints. Petrified I stood in the boat, now rocking gently as a cradle. Suddenly the point of Henry's fishing rod broke the surface of the water about six feet away. Cat began to bark. Then Henry himself almost floated to the surface again, he was just under the surface, looking up toward daylight. His eyes were open. I could swear his eyes were open. He seemed to be looking right at me. His expression seemed sad, almost apologetic, as if he found the situation embarrassing for us both.

That's all right, son, his expression seemed to say. *I know you can't swim.*

He wasn't struggling much, he seemed to be hovering resignedly, waiting on the vagaries of the lake, still clutching his expensive flyrod like a buggywhip. Then he began to recede, fade. Still not struggling, he began to drift away.

"No!"

I couldn't stand it anymore. I jumped out of the boat then, certain I couldn't do anything for him but at least I could drown trying. I hit the water awkwardly with a hard slap, bobbing immediately to the surface, coughing water, momentarily blinded. I wiped the water from my eyes. Looking down, I found I was bobbing like a cork in a golden-green web of undulating light.

I was so damned scared, I couldn't catch my breath.

I tried to dive, kicking frantically, but came up water-blinded again, vomiting from my nose and mouth. The dog was in the water now, paddling in a wide circle around me, yipping nervously. Cat held his nose straight up as he swam, as if appealing to heaven for help. He looked damned silly, but at least he could swim.

"Henry!" I guess I expected him to answer me.

Not far away, the boat rocked on the water. Everything was quiet, hushed. Cat continued to dog-paddle industriously in widening circles around me.

I got to got to got to was running through my head like a squirrel on an exercise wheel. But I didn't know what to do. He was gone.

Gone. Goddamn you, God.

I was crying like a baby, thrashing about in the water, tugging on the cinches of my life jacket. I bobbed on the surface of the lake, wimpled now by a softly whispering breeze in the bright morning. My head was down, my nose pratically trailing in the water. No sound was coming out, my jaws were locked open with the ache. I was drooling like a fool into the water. Henry's damned hat drifted within reach. I grabbed it, hiding my face against it, the hat still palpable and warm with his tobaccoey smell.

You chicken bastard, I thought. You let him drown.

I fought the water awkwardly till I reached the boat. I heaved myself over the gunwhale, tumbling hard into the bottom of the boat. *You chicken bastard,* I thought. *You let him drown you, just let him, because you were too scared to help.* The sun burned hot on the back of my neck. I lay face down inhaling the fishy

smell of the warm boards. *You chicken bastard. You let him drown.*
I raised up, hearing the dog whimpering. Cat had paddled near the boat, looking for help. *Pull in the dog,* I told myself. *You can do that much, you chicken bastard.*

I grabbed the dog by the collar, hauling his stiffened, toylike forelegs over the top of the gunwhale, reaching back to give his backside a shove. He came scrabbling into the boat, shaking himself, spraying cold bullets of water in all directions.

I found myself staring at the taut anchor line.

It's still not too late, is it? not even for a dirty coward like me.

I tore the life jacket off and went over the side into the water again. Please, God, I said. I might have even said it aloud. Catching a good breath, I ducked under and started hand over hand down the anchor line.

You'll never know how it felt, how scared I was.

Each hair on my head seemed hollow as a marsh reed. The cold water squeezed my skull, got me in a shocking grip. Each little hysterical brain cell wanted to escape from my head. One by one they squeezed like bubbles through the hollow tubes of my wavering hair, diffusing into the dark open water around me.

It was like that time I fell in the pool, just as if I'd lowered myself into an electrically charged liquid medium. I was dying of electrocution, blindly dying in the cold darkness, the water pressing against me everywhere. I pulled myself down into the deeper dark-green reaches, my legs floating above my head.

I could feel myself going. You're not going to make it, I said. You're not. I could feel myself numbly sloughing off into the cold dark water, losing minute parts of myself as I went down the taut anchor line. You got to breathe, I told myself. You're going to have to let it out now. You'll never make it back to the top in time.

I touched him on the first try.

Twenty-one

⌐╖ I HAD to dive again, this time looping a short line around the anchor line and tying it to my ankle. I took the longest line in the boat and tied it to the life jacket. Come on, come on, I told myself fumbling with the knot. I went over the side, moving down the line more quickly, and found him again.

I tried to get his boots off. I had to wrap my legs around the anchor line and use both hands. The rubber boots stuck to his legs, glued on by the water pressure. Finally I stripped one off. It was taking too much time. I grabbed him around the neck and started up the line with one hand.

I thought my lungs were going to blow out before we reached the top. I just couldn't let go of him and get some air and come back. I'd never find him again if I did. So I hung on, dragging myself up the line, reaching up, letting go, then reaching up as high as fast as I could to keep from slipping back again.

We broke through. It was like dashing my head through a plate-glass window, the water exploding all around us with the noise of breaking glass. I was blowing like a walrus, hanging on to the anchor line, my arm so numb it felt ready to fall off.

Blind, I swung on the line like a monkey on a stick, my ears plugged with lake water, and coughing and spitting, spastically batting the blinding water out of my eyes, sawing at the air. It had never felt so good to see the sky. I held Henry's sodden head out of the water. The water ran out of his nose and mouth. He looked dead all right. I kept talking to him in case he wasn't and maybe could hear me. If he was any place where he could still hear me, I knew he'd come back if he could.

"I got you, Henry. You're going to be all right. I'll get you in the boat. Then you'll be all right for sure."

Cat looked over the side and began barking at us. Using the line, I dragged the life jacket toward us. The steady glare of the sun had turned the lake molten gold, hurting my eyes. The anchor line was cutting the palm of my hand. I held Henry under the chin.

We rested, two dark specks in the molten lake. We dangled for a second, slack and stupid and useless as a pair of windsocks on a windless day. Then I was seized again by the need to get him into the boat. Jesus Christ, I told myself. This is no time to daydream.

"Here," I said to him. "Aren't you going to help at all? Put your arm in this."

The wind had come up a little. The water slapped against the boat. I heard the dog's toenails, hard and nervous, in the bow.

Henry was still gone. But I knew he could still hear me, even if he couldn't even flicker an eyelid to let me know.

Just about the time I got Henry cinched into the life jacket, the dog jumped out of the boat into the water again. I grabbed the gunwhale and made to heave myself into the boat without swamping it. My arms were heavy and dead. Come on, you lazy bastard, I thought. You can be tired later.

On the third try I made it. I didn't stop to celebrate. I pulled

Henry in by the line and hauled him in and laid him in the bottom of the boat and began pumping the water out of him.

Don't be a prick, I said. Give him back. What the hell do you need this old man for? I don't know whether I said it aloud or not. Goddamn you, I said. Take me if you want. But give him back.

I kept on working. I rolled him over and pinched his nose and blew air into his lungs. His blue hands trembled spastically for a second. I blew air into his lungs again, then pressed hard and rapidly on his breastbone, depressing it as far as I could till I thought I'd caved in his chest. What's a few broken bones, I thought, if I can set him to breathing again. I kept it up.

He vomited a glutinous mass of something that looked like paper pulp. I stuck my finger down his throat to make sure his throat was clear. His eyes opened, his lids flickering rapidly as insect wings. The foggy blue color of his irises had drained evenly and uniformly into the whites of his eyes, leaving his stare sightless and astonished as a newborn baby's.

"Henry, listen to me. Goddamn it, listen. Summers shot you out of the boat. But I got you back. You damn near drowned."

He shut his eyes again, denying it all—the blue sky, the steady beat of the water against the boat—and the life seemed to ooze out of him.

"You're going to be all right," I said. "You don't want to run off just when it's getting interesting, do you? Don't you want to see how it's all going to turn out?"

I kept talking to him, telling him any kind of nonsense to keep him in touch with the sound of my voice, pressing hard on his breastbone, turning his head when he coughed, pounding him and pinching him, trying to get him to understand by such reminders that he was back in the misery-making natural world again. He groaned and rolled over on his side, pulling his legs up.

"You're going to be all right."

He looked like a mummified old fetus, curled up in the bottom of the boat.

"You're not going to leave me here alone in this goddamned place, are you? How am I going to get through all this shit without a little help?"

I pulled the foolish dog in the boat for the second time and threw him in the stern out of Henry's way. I rowed for shore, going for the point on the side opposite from camp. Summers was still around somewhere. There was no sense in asking for it by going back to camp.

Another shot came out of the woods when I started for the opposite shore. A spout of water leaped up several yards behind and to the right of the boat. I guess he'd been quiet all this time hoping that, if he laid low, I'd row right back to camp and make it easy for him. Now he registered his disappointment. I pulled hard on the oars, keeping my head crunched down and my eyes on Henry.

"Fix you up," I muttered. "Damned if I won't."

Another shot came out of the woods. This one hit farther astern. A puff of blue smoke drifted lazily out of the treetops where the big crows had vanished. The bottom of the boat scraped the ledge. I jumped out and tugged the boat up on the rocks as far as I could with the painter. I fisted Henry, all loose and boneless, out of the boat, dragging him out of sight into the dry rasping bushes. I ducked back out to the boat, grabbed some things I thought we might need, and kicked the boat loose into the lake. Because I didn't want to mark the spot where we'd entered the woods for Summers.

That night we lay in the thick pine forest with no fire. At

dusk, I'd asked Henry if he wanted one and he shook his head no, still unable to talk. I asked him if he knew what had happened. He shook his head no. I told him I'd tell him sometime when he was feeling better. I'd made a bandage out of one of my pant legs for his shoulder but it was pretty torn up, it was not bleeding much, although the pine needles where he'd lain were dark and sticky with his blood. I couldn't tell whether the bullet was still in him or not.

I used his knife to make a little lean-to of pine boughs for him. Didn't really know what else to do for him. I lay down beside him with the dog between us for warmth and fell asleep instantly.

In the morning he was shivering badly. I took off my shirt and pants and pulled them on over his own clothes, giving him two layers for warmth, and that seemed to help some. I took the belt out of my pants, sliding the leather case of Henry's fishing knife onto it and fastening it around my middle. So as not to lose it, both timepiece and compass now, I tied Henry's watch around my neck with a leftover strip from my pant leg. Now you're a real Abenaki, I thought. At least the ghosts in these woods ought to be on your side.

I went down to the lake and looked across. The sun was sharp as a knife blade on the water. I could see no traces of smoke above the trees on the opposite shore. Where is he? I wondered. I decided we better get out of there. It was dangerous to stay too close to the edge of the lake. Likely that was where Summers would look first. So we had to get back into the woods, I figured, to be safe. I went back to get Henry.

Henry was light as a pinfeather but too weak to hold on. So I carried him over my shoulder, fireman style. We could go a few hundred feet like that. Then I had to rest. He was light. But carrying him like that, he got heavy in a hurry.

"Go, dog."

Damned Cat was always underfoot. We had to be quiet as we could, I decided, since we didn't know where Summers was, and he had the gun. It was slow going. It worried me, going so slow, because Henry was bad off. I had to get him back to town fast and get him some help. But if I went crashing headlong through the woods, likely we wouldn't get back at all.

The woods were dark and shadowy, the ground soft underneath. I lugged Henry as far as I could, rested, then went on till I had to stop again. So far as I could tell we were traveling in a straight line away from the lake.

At noon, I laid Henry on the ground and sprawled out beside him. When I woke up it was dark, pitch-black. I was cold, shivering so hard my teeth were chattering. The dog stuck his nose in my face, scaring me half to death. He was that close and I hadn't even seen him. I grabbed the dog, hugging him for warmth. My arms and legs trembled uncontrollably. Get a hold of yourself, I told myself. You can act like a dink later, once you're clear of this mess.

I thought I heard something in the woods. Something big crashing around clumsily. What is that? Could be a moose. Or a bear. I gripped the handle of the knife in my belt. What if Summers is around? I thought. He'll be able to stick a gun in my ear before I even see him.

Slowly my arms and legs stopped dancing against the ground, leaving me dryly hot and hollow-bellied. I slept fitfully between dreams till daybreak.

When I woke in the green gloom, I began to thrash about on the ground, thinking I was at the bottom of the lake again. Breathing hard, I stared across the little clearing. Propped up against a big tree trunk, as rough and ageless as a rhino's hide, Henry stared back glumly.

You're trembling awful, he said. I been watching you in your sleep.

You're better, I said. Damn, that's something, anyway.

He just looked at me, his arms motionless at his sides, looking silly in two layers of clothes, especially with the one missing pant leg from the left knee on down.

You need some food, he said. You got to eat.

I'm not leaving you, I said. I've got to get you out of here as quick as I can.

Don't be a damned fool, he said. The first thing is survival. You're too weak to carry me out. Next thing you know, you'll get delirious.

Well, how—

Use your damn brains. The first thing is water. Find some water. Boil it before you drink it.

I don't have any matches—

Maybe you don't. You ever know me to go in the woods without matches? Buttoned right here in my shirt in that little watertight container. Unless you tore my pocket off getting me out of that lake.

Shit, they still can't be dry.

They're dry. Don't you worry. Now how you going to find water?

Follow the land downhill, look in the gullies.

That's good. You won't have to look hard. Plenty of water in these woods. Just be patient. Then you find a game trail. Set a trap like I showed you. Build a fire tonight. You're plenty safe.

Summers might be—

Hell, boy, he's not around. These woods run all the way to Canada. It'd be like trying to find a cricket in a wheat field. He just came in here to bushwack us, not to track us. He didn't bring any camping gear, he doesn't know how to live in the woods. Besides he doesn't want to be gone too long. People might wonder where he'd been.

Jesus, I'm so shivery I could use a fire. You think it's all right? Sure it is. Do as I say. You'll be all right.

I found his advice so comforting that it put me right to sleep. I must have been worn out, to sleep like that. When I woke, Henry was asleep at the base of the tree opposite, still and profound as a scarecrow hurled into the dust.

I took the watch off my neck and set our course by it the way Henry had taught me. My idea was to search for water and food on the way back. If Henry was right, we had nothing to be wary about. My hot rush at the woods had got us lost, but now, with the watch, if I was doing it right, maybe we could find our way out. I bent, heaving the old man onto my shoulder. He was dry and light as cornhusks.

By noon I was lost and confused, not sure I was anywhere. I'd climbed down into every gulley we'd come to and found nothing. I'd put Henry down and was staggering around in an aimless circle in a clearing we'd come to, muttering to myself intent on using the last of my strength on cussing everything that stood in my way of getting Henry out of the woods.

But when I stopped babbling at last through sheer exhaustion, I thought I heard a few quiet piano notes of water strike on the hushed, green-gloomed air. The dog and I studied each other. I heard it again and so did he. Together we started off in the direction of the music.

A few yards off, in another of the endless shallow troughs we'd looked into that day, we found a little brook barely trickling over some stones at the bottom of a dried-up little channel which ran in a dark streak from the base of a big boulder till it disappeared twenty yards later into some ferns. I scooped

up the meager water in my hands, pressing it to my sore mouth.
The few drops stung the back of my throat. I dug with my
hands into the wet mud and gravel at the base of the big rock
and cupped to my lips the niggardly little bit of water which
had bled slow and muddy into the earthen bowl I'd scooped out.

Boil it first, I remembered Henry telling me. Hell, not
enough here to be careful about. Nobody but him would worry
about it this deep in the woods anyway.

I went back to where I'd dropped him.

"Henry. We found water."

I didn't recognize my voice.

He didn't look interested. I carried him down into the little
gully.

"I think it's all right. I'll boil it first if you want me to."

He didn't answer.

"No reason to get sore. Just because I don't do everything to
formula."

His head was practically touching his shirt front, his face
entirely in shadows, hidden from me. You eternal rockhead, he
whispered to his shirt front. You never do as I tell you.

"All right, all right. Give me those matches."

I had his shirt pocket unbuttoned and the little round silver
match container in my hand before it even came to me.

"Hell. What do you expect me to boil water in? What are
you talking about?"

The canteen, he whispered. Use my canteen.

"Oh," I said.

I was thinking of pots, you see. I never even thought about
the canteen. A little shiver passed through me like a cold wind:
you're going to die, I thought. You're not thinking straight.
You're lost again. You drank brook water without boiling it.
Your head's not working straight. You're going to die if you

don't pull yourself together. How many mistakes do you think you can make out here?

It took me half an hour to fill the canteen half-full with muddy water. I built a fire within a circle of rocks, using birchbark paper for starter, and propped the canteen against the rocks so I could get it out again once it started boiling. Well, I did, without burning myself, then let it cool off. When it was ready, I held the canteen to Henry's cracked lips but he still wouldn't drink. The spot on his lower lip had faded to a faint blue.

"You still mad?"

I wetted my fingers and moistened his lips, but he still didn't want any. I sat back and watched the fire.

Now food, he whispered.

I looked up. But he lay curled and quiet as a baby against his tree.

I built up the fire and told him I'd be back as soon as I found something for us to eat. Cat wanted to go along, but I told him to stay with Henry.

"You stay, Cat. If I get lost, you'll have to bark me back into camp."

I took my bearings, set my course by Henry's watch, and stepped out of the little clearing into the woods. For this job, I'd borrowed back my shirt and pants from Henry, to keep from getting scratched or bitten up anymore than I was already.

A cold, glutinous sweat pasted the shirt to my spine. I found myself panting like a dog in the close, pine-scented afternoon. How long had I wandered before waking in the grip of this green suffocation? I couldn't say. But it seemed hours before I found what I was looking for—a faint seam in the seemingly trackless woods running against the grain of a thickly wooded hillside. The trail led down to some marshy ground and a little

shallow pool of clear water. There were deer tracks in the soft
black ground around the spring.

Of a sudden, I was weak with hunger. Crouching, I filled the
canteen, then worked my way up the side of the hill on the
game trail. Where it hooked off to the left almost at the top,
I whittled a sharp stake and fastened it to a sapling with some
fishing line. I bent the sapling almost to the ground, tied it off,
set the trigger string across the trail. Any deer coming along this
trail would catch the spike about chest high. I took up a position
downwind on the hill above the trail, out of sight, and waited.

It was easy to wait. I went into a green trance, seeing nothing,
motionless, a part of the forest now. A sound so slight as to be
no sound at all brought me back to myself. I did not move. I
listened. Screened by bushes, I had a safe view of the faint trail
below.

Nothing.

I waited some more. Come on, I said in my head. Come on,
critter. Come to me, for Christsakes, before I faint.

A big buck loomed in the trees. The soft white glow of his
chest first then suddenly his rack materialized out of the air
above his head. I was counting the points when he hit the trigger
line. The sharpened stake plunged into him like a dagger. Almost before it hit him he whirled in his tracks and started to
plummet down the trail.

I had my knife. I jumped up and sprang down the hill after
him, running down the wooded slope as fast as I could, slipping
on the mossy rocks, making no effort to keep quiet now, with
only the aching need to keep that buck from getting away.

I ran on the diagonal several yards ahead of him on the path.
His rack appeared above the bushes just as I reached the trail.
I jumped at the antlers blindly, landing on his back like a bronco
rider. His whole body shuddered on impact in surprise and

shock. He leaped forward, twisting his neck, trying to reach me with the elaborate weaponry of his head, one tine just barely grazing my cheek before I pulled back.

I tucked my head low against his neck, holding tight. I had him around the throat. With my free hand, I stuck the knife into his chest. He was so solid with muscle, it was hard to sink it in. I stuck the point of it in the reddening white fur of his chest but it wasn't slowing him down much. I hit him higher, more in the gully where his neck joined his body. I sawed at the sinews in his throat. I heard his frightened breathing in my ear, saw his scared dark eye roll in my direction as if he were eager to know the identity of his murderer.

His licorice lips began to bubble with a bloody foam. He bucked, kicking the bushes with his sharp hooves. Come on, I thought. Die, you son of a bitch. I was weak and he seemed to know it. He bucked more frantically. My grip around his neck started to slacken. I stuck him with the knife again, wheedling it among the tough ligament and sinew.

It popped out, clear of my hand, repelled by his churning muscles. You're dead, I remember thinking. You're certainly dead now. And then the damned dog, who hadn't stayed at camp after all, the way I'd told him to, with a low growl appeared out of nowhere, throwing himself at the buck's hind-quarters. The big deer buckled when the dog hit. I gave the buck's head a sharp twist. Over it went, threshing the ground with its hooves.

I jumped clear when the buck went down. The crazy dog never let go, fastening his jaws on the deer's back leg, shaking his head from side to side, growling deep in his throat, a sound more like gargling than a regular growl. Feebly, the buck kicked at the dog but the dog stayed clear of those razor-sharp hooves without ever letting go.

The buck held up its antlers like an offering, getting his front legs under him, and tried to rise, but couldn't. He fell back hopelessly. I had an idea his back was broken.

I went back for the knife. It took me some time to find it. It was further back on the trail than I thought it would be. I never would have found it except the blade had stuck in the ground and the handle was sticking straight up, the sun sparkling off the metal. I found it and went back and finished the deer off.

He was a hard dier. I practically had to saw his head off before the light faded in his eye. My legs gave out, sitting me down hard on the trail, completely finished, unable to move.

The dog came over and lapped my face. He made a slow deliberate job of it, then went back to the carcass and sat down and waited patiently for me to recover. How long I sat there I don't know. But when I came to myself and looked up again the forest looked different to me—somehow everything very clear and sharp, every leaf carefully incised as carved ivory on the dark air.

I crawled over to the buck. Using the fishing knife, with difficulty, I cut him down the length of his white belly, rocking his body till his steaming guts slid in a dark mass onto the trail. I cut the liver free and gave it to the dog. I cupped my hands to the buck's throat and drank his warm sticky sweet-tasting blood, hoping it would give me some strength.

I worked fast as I could, which was too slow. I wanted to do my job and get away from there. The woods were going dark. It was getting late. I wanted to get back to Henry, feed him something before he grew any weaker.

But I was so feeble myself I knew I had to eat before I could be of any good to him. I had the matches with me. With birchbark paper and kindling I built a fire right next to the buck.

I cut a chunk of meat out of his side and cooked it on a spit over the fire and when it was charred on the outside I popped it into my mouth and ate it fast and it was strange and delicious-tasting to me, but the sudden lump of juicy thick stinging food after so long made my tastebuds smart so badly that it closed my throat and I wasn't able to eat much more.

The act of eating exhausted me. I slumped alongside the deer, telling myself that I was just going to rest for a moment. But I fell fast asleep anyway. I woke with a start, convinced a lynx was looking me in the face only a few inches away, but it was only Cat. He turned, sticking his tail in my face, and gnawed at the buck's gaping belly. I sat up. Dazed, I looked around. Still alive, I thought.

I felt stronger and set to sawing off the deer's hind leg with my fish knife, not an easy job to accomplish with that little thing. But I got done most of what I wanted to and started back to camp, intent on getting there before nightfall. If darkness came on before I got there I was afraid I'd never find Henry again. I took the watch from my neck and found my bearings. After a good deal of crashing around in the underbrush, Cat and I came into the clearing just at dusk. Henry hadn't even moved.

I took the deer leg off my shoulder.

"Look here," I said. "I'll make you something to eat."

I started a fire and fried some meat on a stick.

"Here, eat this."

But he didn't want any.

"You stubborn son of a bitch. You've got to eat."

But he wouldn't.

I held the canteen to his lips. He wouldn't drink either.

I sat back against a tree and ate my portion, hoping he'd change his mind. I fed the fire and watched him, motionless against his tree. The shadows cast by the fire touched him all over his face and shirt front with a feverish curiosity and independent life of their own.

I fell asleep watching him.

In the morning I tried to get him to eat but again he wouldn't.

"Get you out of here," I told him. "You'll feel better right away."

We began the walk out. Despite the venison, I was still pretty weak. The dog seemed fine however. He trotted out front, his nose to the ground, as if he'd left the house only a half hour ago.

I had to stop often. Henry was just all air and birdbone. But it was all I could do to carry him for fifteen minutes at a time. At noon we stopped by a little brook where I filled the canteen.

Remember what I told you, whispered Henry.

I turned to look at him.

"You told me so damned many things. What am I supposed to remember now?"

You remember, he repeated.

I knew what he was talking about.

"I will," I said. "I'll remember this and everything else. You wait. Someday we'll laugh about this."

Remember, he said.

Hell, how was I supposed to forget?

I'd filled the pouch of Henry's fishing jacket with deer meat and I took some out and fried it for lunch. Again I tried to get him to eat and drink something but he wouldn't. I held the canteen to his lips. The water dribbled down his throat, wetting the front of his jacket.

"You're a stubborn old man," I said.

But he didn't even bother to answer.

I took a nap then.

When I woke I put him on my back again. We walked. We rested. We walked again. I had the sensation we were being dogged by shadows. I turned once at what I thought was the sound of twigs faintly crackling underfoot in the gloom of the trackless woods behind us. But the dog didn't seem to notice, so I let it go.

I turned and walked on. I staggered through the brush, ducked under the low branches, ground up endless hills, reeled over the dark, shaggy ridges. I'd lost all sense of time and lapsed into a dull senselessness till finally on one of countless needle-carpeted inclines my legs buckled, heaving us both heavily to the ground. I spit the dirt out of my mouth but lay unable to move, or even to roll Henry off my back.

When I woke it was dark. I shrugged Henry off and stood up. Immediately, I lost my balance, pitching down the hillside darkness, terrified that I was going to slam into a tree or a boulder and break my neck. Clawing frantically at anything in reach, I finally stopped my headlong slide. The dog, invisible in the dark, came and stuck his nose in my face, then went off again. At least, I think it was the dog.

That night I could not find Henry on the hillside. I crawled around on that slope in the pitch-dark, calling his name, but he wouldn't answer. I wore out at last and fell asleep. In the morning, I found him just a few yards away. I awoke shivering in a cold murky dawn and there he was.

I crawled over to him. He was lying on his back, looking at the trees overhead.

"Why don't you ever answer when I call? Didn't you hear me calling you all last night?"

I just shook my head at him.

His face was gray, his skin drumtight against his cheekbones and hollow temples. The long thin incision of his mouth had almost healed over perfectly, now that he had not picked at it with words for so long a time.

"Drink, damn you."

The water dribbled down his chin.

"What the hell's so special about those trees?"

He continued to gaze up at them but still wouldn't answer. I shook him gently.

"Come on."

But he still wouldn't answer me.

I built a fire and fried some meat. The meat sizzling in the fire was the only sound in the woods that morning.

Remember.

I will. You don't have to keep reminding me.

When I woke, I was surprised to see the meat had fallen into the fire and had charred to cinders. The fire itself was cold and gray.

I drank from the canteen.

"Henry?"

He was slumped against a tree, his hands twisted grotesquely in his lap.

"We got to get out of here," I said. "I don't know how much longer—"

With difficulty, I got Henry over my shoulder. This time I made it over the ridge.

For a long time afterward the walking was all downhill. I thought I knew where we were now. We came onto a path, the same one, I thought, that we ordinarily took into the woods when we set off for the lake.

"See? Look at this."

During our noon rest, I said, "We're almost there. You just hold on."

He smiled at the good news.

"Yes," I said. "We're not far from home now."

Careful, he said.

"I'm being careful. Haven't I been careful as hell?"

He'll be there.

"Sure he will," I said. "He won't have to come looking for me either. I'll kill that son of a bitch when I find him."

Careful.

"Let him be careful."

I finished the last of the meat.

Christ, I fell asleep again. It seemed I could no longer control or predict when sleep would take me. It came and went of its own accord now. Just as suddenly, I woke, snapped awake, as if in falling asleep I'd vanished on the air and now just as suddenly had reappeared again.

"Come on, old man. We got to get out of here."

I lifted Henry to my shoulder and we started again. I kept my feet on the path but I was numb to any sensation of locomotion. I leaned forward. The trees and the bushes slowly unwound past me. Once or twice I fell down. But these were not notable episodes. Numbly, I got up again and, clutching Henry to my shoulder, went on.

At four in the afternoon, we stepped out of the woods into a clearing above the old cemetery.

"Freeze, Dogshit!"

Dumbly, I turned in Summers' direction, not recognizing the sound of a voice for what it was.

The dog exploded at my feet. I watched him leap sideways into the air, his belly burst into bloody strings, his teeth bared as if readying to bite the pain in his guts. He fell in a sloppy mess against my shoes.

I looked in the direction of the noise going on forever. Summers big and fat, crouched beside a tombstone in my family's cemetery, leveling down on me with his pistol. I turned and ran back into the woods, clutching Henry to my back.

I ran, the old man weightless as a cape. I ran deep into the woods till my breath clawed painfully at my throat. And still I ran on. Till I ran into a tree and knocked myself cold.

I couldn't have been out for more than a second. When I came to, I told Henry, "I'm going to get that bastard now, Henry. We're through having trouble with him."

I crept Indian-quiet through the woods, slowly making my way back in the direction from which I'd come, not straight, but circling back till I came out on the other side of the cemetery. He was still crouching there behind one of the family tombstones. The shadow of the big obelisk fell across him like the ghost of a fallen tree. His gun in his hand, he was peeking out from behind the stone toward the woods. He was so intent on those woods. I suppose he thought I would just wait a little while and then walk right out into his gunsights the way I suppose he thought I'd row right back to camp after he'd shot Henry out of the boat.

I walked up behind him. I covered fifty yards in the tall grass. The fool never moved.

He turned at the last instant. Something made his skin creep, I guess, warning him at the final moment. He turned, his eyes widening with surprise and terror. I must have looked like the Windago, all bloody and scratches and pine pitch from head to foot, with a few dirty rags hanging off me.

He fired wildly. I don't know how many times. I don't think he had time to empty his gun. No, I know he didn't. I slashed him from the temple right through his eye and across his mouth and down into his throat.

He screamed like a woman, high and piercing and hysterical. It was such a shocking sound it made me hesitate. But when he tried to scramble from under the knife blade, I brought it down into the back of his fat neck. I put my knees into his back and hit him again with the knife, hacking at his mute and bloody, blubbery back like I was trying to chip away a giant block of ice.

I don't know how many times I hit him, but he was still for a long time before I quit.

I sat back, breathing hard.

Remember, said Henry, standing behind me.

I didn't even bother to turn. There was no need to.

I sat there panting, staring at the tattered bloodied gray mess of Summers' shirt.

I remember, I answered. How in hell would I ever forget?

They found me like that, sitting in the tall grass opposite Summers' body.

A little boy found me first. Like Summers, I didn't even hear him coming. Some little neighbor boy of Henry's come to play in the tall whispering grass at the old deserted cemetery. Suddenly he was there, standing beside me, looking down at Summers' body staining the grass, quietly sharing the experience.

"Hello," I said.

He turned without a word and walked deliberately away through the tall grass. I saw the top of his blond head disappear as he descended into the trees bordering the old washed-out cartroad leading back to town.

It was very peaceful, waiting there for them in the cool evening air. I pressed my head against the marble stone of one of my unknown relatives and shut my eyes. Very peaceful.

Finally a half dozen state police showed up, walking up on me almost as quietly as the child had.

They found Henry dead against a tree, back in the woods

where I'd left him. Found the dog too, his belly ripped to shreds, dead at the edge of the woods.

The newspapers say I stabbed Summers twenty-four times. But I don't know.

It was probably more times than that.

Twenty-two

My luck wasn't any good that year.

The slug they dug out of Henry was a thirty-eight, the same caliber as Dale's gun, which Summers had reported stolen from his office just a few days before all this happened. He himself carried a .357 magnum. That's what he used on the dog.

They never found Dale's pistol, which I figure Summers threw in the lake.

The coroner said Henry had been shot, beaten, maybe even strangled from the looks of the contusions on his neck, and finally drowned. The court took note of my violent temper. They served a paper on old Dale and he had to come in looking like a whipped puppy and tell everybody how I'd choked and beaten him, damn near killing him, and then how I'd run off with his thirty-eight pistol. Doreen was there too, wringing her hands, but I wouldn't even look at her.

The troopers filed in and testified one by one as to Sheriff Summers' outstanding record of service, and how he'd discovered me carrying a concealed weapon; and how I then resisted arrest and it had taken Summers and several others to subdue me. One even heard me say I'd kill Summers someday. *Did he actually threaten to kill Sheriff Summers? I'll git you for this, he said, your honor. I'll git you, those were his actual words, sir.* And they said how they found me in the grass next to Summers the day he was killed—brutally stabbed repeatedly, said the state's attorney—and the knife still in my hand. And how I had Henry's fifteen-hundred-dollar gold watch on me. And how he'd probably discovered it was missing and confronted me and that's when I'd beat, choked, shot, and drowned him. Only they never did explain why I carried him out of the woods.

I didn't stand a chance. I couldn't have stopped it any more than I could have held my breath through the dark parts of my life.

They wanted to take everything away. They even said you never made it out of the woods at all, Henry. They said I was just carrying a dead man around on my back all the time. Goddamned liars; you weren't dead. I don't care what other people say about it. I was there. I know what went on and what didn't; not those dinks. If you hadn't been alive, helping me, we'd never have gotten out of those woods at all.

The Judge came to see me right after they brought me down here. Why he bothered I don't know. I guess he wanted to make sure they had me under lock and key.

I told him, you sent Summers after us, didn't you?

Of course not, that's outrageous, he said.

You thought I was on to something, didn't you?

I haven't any idea what the hell you're talking about, he said.

Let me tell you something, Judge. I'd never have told anybody anything. Not even now. But not for you. No, not for you. But because it would hurt Kathleen too much.

He looked at me then as if he were seeing me for the first time.

Lawyers, he said. I'll get the best lawyers. We'll get you out of here somehow.

Save it, I said.

Listen to me, son. It's not too late. I'll go to the governor—

Get out, I said. Just stay away from me.

I heard he died a few years ago. I wonder if they buried him wrapped in his money.

I guess you probably came home for his funeral, didn't you, Kathleen?

I don't blame you for walking away. You always listened to your father; there was no reason not to listen to him that time. But I think you drew your own conclusions. You knew I was about to go into a free fall. There was no sense getting pulled off the ledge with me. You have good instincts, girl.

Where are you now?

Are you still in Amsterdam? Or have you moved on to some other foreign city?

Doreen keeps writing to me, pestering me on and off over the years. I don't know what she says or what she wants. I always tear the letters up unopened and throw them in the trash. A few years ago she came down here at Christmastime to see me, but I wouldn't do it. Like Henry, I hold a hell of a grudge.

She came at Christmas, the worst time of the year. Did you really think I'd see you, Doreen? When I wouldn't even answer your letters?

They said: Your mother is in the visitors' area, McCabe.

Not my mother, I said. She's been dead for years.

Well who is it then?

Got me, man. Some crazy lady.

In a sense, Doreen, you never went away after that. The thought of you was always rattling one of the cell doors in my brain.

Yesterday another one of your letters came. Worn down by
your long campaign, I opened it and held it far off from me,
afraid it might blow up in my face. It was very strange to see
your big childlike handwriting again against the blue page and
the little circles you use to dot your i's, rising over the words
like tiny moons.

You said you had important things to tell me and wanted to
see me. You said you'd changed your life and wanted to tell me
everything.

I've folded and unfolded the letter all day and read it half
a hundred times, but it doesn't tell me any more than that.

You used to say, Henry, that maybe I'd be a writer.

*Who knows, son. Maybe you'll be a writer yourself someday. God
knows, you got enough to write about.*

I said, bullshit, old man. I'm no writer. I haven't got time for
writing. I'd go crazy sitting around all day making peckertracks
all over pieces of paper.

But things change, don't they, Henry? Now I have all the
time there is, and nothing any better to do. So I read all the old
famous books, wet my pencil against my tongue, and bend again
to my notebook.

You will be happy to hear I passed my high school equiva-
lency test some time back. I am now more than half finished
with the course work for a college degree through the mail. Not
exactly Harvard. But I expect you're pleased even if it is only
going to be a post office degree. When I get out of here, I'll
see what I can do. I don't know if they take ex-cons at Harvard.
They might have a rule against it. We'll see. You'd like that,
wouldn't you? Might still surprise you, and actually do it. Who
knows?

Another thing I've been thinking about. When I get out of
here maybe I ought to go back and burn the house down. That

way nobody not a Weatherfield will ever live in it. We'll have to say that while I was in here time stopped, that people aren't really living in it now, they just think they are.

I expect Doreen sold all the furniture and the books, five cents on the dollar, fast as she could. Everything cast on a whirlwind of nickels and dimes and quarters. So the house without the books and pictures really is uninhabited, just possessed, not owned. Because it could never be owned by anybody not a Weatherfield, could it?

I hate the idea as much as you do. So it would be better just to burn it than let it stand violated in the middle of that village. But it's yours, isn't it, not mine to say what to do with. So you let me know if that's what you require. And I'll do it. But if you don't care anymore, tell me. Because I don't want to risk coming back here again if it's for nothing. So you think about it.

If I burned that house to the ground, Henry, then everything would be clean gone. Everything clean, reduced to gray ashes. Gone as if it never was. But all still alive, still standing, in this notebook I'm filling inch by inch, day by day, in the prison library. But even more real and enduring forever in its perfect place in time. Not lost, not any of it, but out of the reach of the hand of man forever.

But you think about it.

We have plenty of time. They're not going to let me out of here for a while.

I lie here in the middle of the night. Sometimes I think, Christ, I'm all alone. Then I remember, so is everybody else.

Insomnia, Henry. I remember how you dealt with the family disease. I heard you in your room nightly, cussing to yourself. Thrashing about till you were so straitjacketed by your sheets that you could hardly move.

I asked you what you had to think about so hard that you had to lie awake all night thinking it.

You said, "I have visitations."

"Visitations?"

"Yes," you said. "You don't live as long as I have and not have visitations. Your grandmother comes to me as a young woman with her hair pinned up and her mother's antique cameo brooch at the neck of her lace collar. She's so real, I reach out to touch her."

"And do you?"

"Of course not. But she's real all right. I think so hard or dream so powerfully, I don't know which. But I bring that young girl back to life in the dark. Sometimes I see that dead German boy in the hay in that stone barn. He's just a boy really. God, how could I have shot him, I wonder. He looks asleep. I want to shake him by the shoulder and say, come on son. Wake up. Go on your way, and no hard feelings. But it's too late. Too late for that. Hell, you ask me what I think about. I got lots to think about. I haven't got time for sleep anymore."

I have my visitations too. You don't have to be old to have visitations.

Sometimes at night I'm in the lake again. I'm lying on my back in the middle of the lake. I am scared to be in the water. But if I breathe slow and shallow, like a patient under anesthesia, I know I won't drown. Above me little silver fish dart and bob like Chinese kites in the wind. Far away is the surface of the lake, swaying and rocking like a gigantic mirror.

Suddenly it shatters.

A black star explodes out of a cloud of silver bubbles. It grows in size as it falls toward me. Then I see it isn't a star after all. It's an old man. His arms and legs flung wide give him his star shape.

Your eyes goggle, Henry. Your mouth gapes in surprise, but you don't say a word. Your hair is plastered in white spaghetti strings against your face. You look a sight, plummeting through the skylike immensity of the lake dressed in your funny fishing costume and rubber hip boots, still clutching that fly rod like a buggy whip.

As you pass me, your face lights up with a smile of recognition. The bubbles escape in a string of beads from the corners of your mustache. You act like this is perfectly normal. The fishhooks in your hat glint in the marine gloom as you pass with a wave of your hand. And you glide into the deeper reaches of the lake like the Big Dipper wheeling through the sky.

I've tried to remember everything and write it all down. I scribble everything down between the lines of my little grade-school composition book. It's here, all in a jumble. My whole life, everything you and I ever did together, everything about Kathleen and Doreen and Dale, even the lives and deaths of three dogs.

All the people here, all the ones I loved and hated, usually at one and the same time. Everything and everyone I ever lost. Maybe I've got it right, maybe I haven't. Maybe one night as you wheeled past I caught you in my web of words, I don't know.

I swing to the edge of my bunk and sit there, cold and sick-feeling in the dark.

It is winter again, but it always passes. I get up and go to the window. The moon is out tonight. Automatically, I look for the river. But at this time of year the river is always lost under a blanket of snow, just a frozen road without a track on it zigzagging among the trees. I think to myself: I'd like to know where that road or river goes that I've been staring at for the last seven years, what it sees on the way—the bridges, the houses, the trees, the dogs, and the people. One day, I promise myself, I'll follow it down to the ocean.

April 1967–September 1968
Maine State Prison
Thomaston, Maine